# MERCURY REVOLTS

## A NOVEL BY ROBERT KROESE

This is a work of fiction. Any resemblance to actual persons is purely coincidental.

Published by Westmarch Publishing
westmarchpub.com

Cover design based on Washington Crossing the Delaware by Emanuel Leutze. This painting is in the public domain. Mercury's wings were designed by Amiamy11 on DeviantArt.com: (http://amiamy111.deviantart.com/). Mercury's body was adapted from a photograph by Barry Kidd Photography. (http://www.barrykidd.com/) All photos used in the composite image are used with permission.

*For Xtoph.*

.....................................

*With thanks to: Joel Bezaire, Mandi Amaya, Colleen Diamond, Lars Hedbor and Mark Fitzgerald for their help in making this book more betterer.*

*Thanks also to those who supported the Kickstarter to get this book published, particularly TC Gemmell, Karen Minick, Elisa Lorello, Kristi Michels, Sean Simpson, Christopher Turner and Jeremy Kerr.*

# AUTHOR'S PREFACE

When I began writing *Mercury Falls* in 2007, I had no idea what I was doing. I'd tried to write a novel a few times previously but had never gotten very far. I liked coming up with the ideas, but my enthusiasm always began to flag after I got a few pages in. Having mapped out the plot in advance, I would get bored and my characters would rebel, making smartass remarks and generally not doing what they were supposed to be doing. I would be tempted to go off on tangents or deviate from my outline, but I knew you couldn't do that if you were writing a Serious Novel. So I kept trying, and kept failing.

Finally it occurred to me to give in to the temptation: to let the plot go where it wanted to go, and let the characters do what they wanted to do. Thus was born the irreverent Mercury and his somewhat chaotic adventures—as well as his narrator, the pompous and tangent-prone Ederatz. Originally I'd planned for *Mercury Falls* to have no plot, per se. I wanted it to be the kind of book where absolutely anything could happen. Ultimately I decided that readers wouldn't much care for a book that had no point whatsoever, so I did corral the action into a semi-coherent plot. The book became one of the first big indie successes on Amazon's Kindle platform, and shortly after I published it *Mercury Falls* was picked up by Amazon's publishing venture, Amazon Encore. I've since written two sequels, *Mercury Rises* and *Mercury Rests*, published by Amazon's sci-fi imprint, 47North.

I'd fully intended for *Mercury Rests* to be the final Mercury book. At the time I wrote *Mercury Falls*, I was thinking a lot about various theological issues, and *Mercury Falls* was a way of working through some of those ideas in a light-hearted manner. *Rises* and *Rests* diverged from theological matters, and *Rests* in particular dealt more with political themes. The religious dogma of Mercury Falls gave way to the crazed jingoism of *Mercury Rests*. I'd said what I needed to say, and the character had run his course.

Then, in the summer of 2013, I found myself trying to decide on my next project. I'd just finished a humorous sci-fi adventure, *Starship Grifters*, and a quantum physics noir thriller, *Schrödinger's Gat*. The Internet was awash with the news of egregious violations of privacy by the National Security Agency, and President Obama had just gone on *The Tonight Show* to proclaim, in a stunning example of Orwellian double-speak, that the United States government "has no domestic spying program." Journalists were being threatened with prison time for doing their jobs, and Bradley (now Chelsea) Manning had been sentenced to thirty-five years in prison for exposing war crimes—while the criminals themselves remained free. American drone strikes targeted civilians—and in some cases, American citizens—indiscriminately. The prison population of the United States, fueled primarily by the "war on drugs," continued to be the highest in the world, both in relative and in absolute terms, and 164 men, most of whom had never even been charged with a crime, languished in abysmal conditions in Guantanamo, as part of the ill-defined and apparently eternal War on Terror. Meanwhile, in an eerie bit of symmetry with *Mercury Falls*, the president seemed to be angling for war in Syria, for reasons no one seemed quite able to articulate. (In an even more bizarre parallel with the Mercury books, genetically modified corn that had been banned for human consumption was found running rampant in Saudi Arabia in August 2013.)

It seemed to me that in a very real way, the America that I had grown up in was disappearing before my eyes. Part of this was simply an awakening to the horrors of American history that are downplayed by the media and our schools, but much of it seemed like a genuine sea change that had occurred at some point. We had become a country that valued security over freedom, power over justice, and war over peace. I wanted to do something about it, but what could I do? I'm just a guy who writes silly books about angels.

So I once again considered writing a Serious Novel. It would be satirical, with elements of humor, but it would have some Serious Points to Make. As before, however, I found myself bored nearly to tears when I tried to write such a novel. It wasn't enough to tinge the prose with irony; to keep my interest the book needed to have a genuine sense of chaos and unpredictability.

At the same time, the ideas I came up with kept dovetailing strangely with the situation I had set up at the end of *Mercury Rests*. The basic premise was that some sort of alien beings had taken up residence in Washington, D.C. and were manipulating our government behind the scenes. *Catch-22* meets *They Live*, if you will. It bothered me that I'd already done something similar in *Mercury Rests*, but I also thought the idea deserved to be explored further.

Finally I gave up fighting and decided to write another Mercury book, which would pick up a few years after *Mercury Rests* left off. So this isn't a Serious Novel; any novel featuring an angel known for his wisecracks, short attention span and silver hair obviously isn't meant to be taken seriously. For all that, though, *Mercury Revolts* does touch on some serious matters. One matter, in particular, deserves some explanation.

If there's one moment in which the political climate of America changed, it was the morning of September 11, 2001, which saw the terrorist attacks on the Pentagon and the World Trade Center. In Mercury's world as in our own, these events served as a catalyst for a number of changes in government and society—a few of them good, many of them not so good. But despite the occasional eerie parallels, Mercury's world is not our own. The events of *Falls/Rises/Rests* take place over a span of about six weeks in 2012, and the events described in those books (notably the destruction of Anaheim and the implosion of a third of the Moon) have not occurred in our world. Given these discrepancies, I decided to take a little license with the events of September 11 as well.

It's widely known that a fourth plane, United Flight 93, was also hijacked, and was kept from hitting its target only by the courageous actions of a few passengers. We aren't sure what the intended target was; it may have been the U.S. Capitol. *Mercury*

*Revolts* asks the question: what if Flight 93 had hit its target? What if, in fact, the other planes were hijacked only to distract us from the actual purpose of the attack? And of course, in Mercury's world, the actual purpose is particularly diabolical and borderline ridiculous.

I'm well aware that the events of September 11 are fresh in the minds of many of my readers, and it's certainly not my intent to make light of the tragedy of that day. My sense of humor, for good or ill, has always been my means of coping with tragedy, and being able to laugh in a world filled with pain and stupidity is what the Mercury books have been about from the beginning. Sometimes humor also helps us to see truths that are otherwise too painful to accept.

Anyway, here it is, the fourth book in the Mercury series. Having learned my lesson with *Rises* and *Rests*, I've done my best to make this book accessible to those who haven't read any of the other books. Obviously there's a fair amount of background information in the prior books that would enhance your comprehension of this book, but as long as you're not one of those readers who insist on knowing exactly what's going on all the time, you should be fine starting with this one. I think of the first three books as a complete trilogy and *Mercury Revolts* as a separate, mostly standalone book. Whether it will be the first of another series I wouldn't presume to say.

# A NOTE ON ANGELS, DEMONS AND PERSONS

Occasionally a reader will note that I've referred to a particular character as an "angel," when in fact that character is a demon, or that I've called someone a "person" who is in fact an angel. I've done my best to explain this in the past, but just so there's no confusion:

Demons are fallen angels. They do not cease being angels when they fall. In fact, "fallen" is a rather arbitrary, bureaucratic category, and it's often not clear whether a particular angel is a demon or a regular (non-fallen) angel. I will usually refer to a fallen angel as a "demon" and a non-fallen angel as an "angel," although technically they are both angels.

The ranks of the angels are further divided into two distinct castes: cherubim (singular: *cherub*) and seraphim (singular: *seraph*). The vast majority of angels, particularly the lower level "worker bee" angels, are cherubim. The ruling class of angels, including the archangels and the Seraphic Senate, is comprised almost entirely of seraphim. The distinction between cherubim and seraphim is primarily sociological, not biological. In other words, you can't tell the difference between a cherub and a seraph just by looking at them.

I use the terms *person*, *persons*, and *people* to refer to both human beings and angels. Non-angelic persons are usually referred to as *human beings* or *mortals*.

To sum up the key points:

- All demons are angels. Only some angels are demons.
- All angels are persons. Only some persons are angels.

Here, maybe this will help:

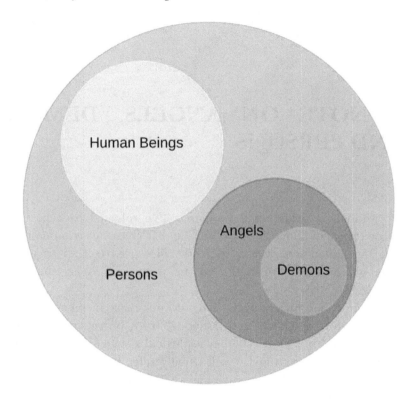

That's right, folks. This is the sort of novel that starts with a fucking Venn diagram. Buckle up, bitches.

# DRAMATIS PERSONAE

**Eddie Pratt (Ederatz):** A cherub who worked for the Mundane Observation Corps

**Mercury:** A cherub employed by Apocalypse Bureau

**Nisroc:** A dim-witted cherub now working for Chaos Faction

**Izbazel:** A fallen cherub (demon); former servant of Lucifer, now leader of Chaos Faction

**Suzy Cilbrith:** Software tester working on the Brimstone Project

**Gary Rosenfeld:** Former *Washington Post* journalist now writing for BitterAngels.net

**Lucifer (Rezon):** The devil

**Michelle (Michael):** Archangel; the general of Heaven's army

**Gabrielle (Gabriel):** Archangel; herald of Heaven

**Perp (Perpetiel):** A cherub who worked as a porter/escort at the planeport; friend of Mercury

**Tiamat:** Demoness; founder of Chaos Faction

**Travis Babcock:** Former President of the United States

**Danton Prowse:** Current President of the United States

**Uzziel:** Head of Apocalypse Bureau

**Gamaliel:** A fallen cherub (demon); servant of Tiamat

# PROLOGUE

To Your Holiness the High Council of the Seraphim,

Greetings from your humble servant, Ederatz,
Cherub First Class,
Order of the Mundane Observation Corps

"In the beginning, God created the Heavens and the Earth."

So that's the *when* sorted. No word yet on *how* or *why*. Now there's a question I'd like to have answered. *Why?*

Because he was bored, God created the Heavens and the Earth.

For his senior cosmology project, God created the Heavens and the Earth.

To fuck with Ederatz the Cherub, God created the Heavens and the Earth.

I was leaning toward door number three for a while, but it's been pretty quiet around here lately. In fact, it's been nearly four years since I was fucked with on a truly epic scale.

The whole apocalypse business turned out to be something of a bust;[1] Heaven couldn't get its act together, and Lucifer's plans to destroy the world didn't pan out either. If Mercury is to be believed, the End is still coming, but it's about ten thousand years off—and in any case Mercury said it's one of those "not with a bang but a whimper" deals. Of course, he also claimed that the world ends

---

[1] For a more detailed account of the Apocalypse, please refer to my earlier reports, pithily entitled *Mercury Falls*, *Mercury Rises* and *Mercury Rests*, respectively.

with a ping-pong match between Job and Cain, so it's hard to know how seriously to take him.

Given the fact that Mercury also blew up the planeport with a nuclear bomb, there's virtually no chance of this report ever getting to you. Travel and communications between the Mundane Plane and Heaven—as well as between all the other planes—has been disrupted, perhaps indefinitely. Angels in Heaven can't get here, and we poor saps stuck on the Mundane Plane can't get back to Heaven. On the plus side, travel to and from the Infernal Plane has been cut off as well. And I assume that Lucifer is still in Heaven's custody, so at least he won't be wreaking any more havoc here.

Anyway, here I sit, somewhere between the Beginning and the End, filling my days with beer and futile ruminations. I've given up on ever returning to Heaven; I assume most of my kind have come to accept their fate as well. Many other angels, both seraphim and cherubim, have been stranded on the Mundane Plane, but I've had minimal contact with them. Most of them have presumably been content to blend in with the human population, but of course the more ambitious seraphim were bound to cause some problems eventually.

And that's where this story begins.

# CHAPTER ONE

*Milhaus, Texas; August 2016*

The summoning wasn't going well.

Sean Simpson, who had been elected High Priest by dint of his encyclopedic knowledge of *Demonology for Imbeciles*, had accidentally drawn a hexagram instead of a pentagram, at which point the ceremony had devolved into an extended argument about whether a hexagram was an acceptable demonic gateway.

"What is your concern, exactly?" demanded Sean. "That the demon is going to be confused? Or offended, maybe? That he's going to show up and say, 'Whoa, hang on, that's a hexagram, I'm out.'"

"Don't be a douche, Sean," replied Brayden, an Unholy Acolyte. They were all Unholy Acolytes except Sean. "The book says the ceremony has to be conducted perfectly, or there's no telling what might happen." Brayden was the newest member of the group, and he was still a bit skittish about the idea of summoning a demon. He had suggested they start smaller and work their way up to a demon. "Maybe do a marmoset first," he had said, hopefully. "Or a ferret."

But the other Unholy Acolytes had overruled him. They didn't share Brayden's love of exotic furry animals, and in any case Sean was fairly certain that marmosets were mythical creatures.

All told, there were four members of the First Satanic Church of Milhaus, Texas: Sean, Brayden, Clay and Neva. The four of them had met in Mrs. Cheatwood's remedial Spanish class at Smith & Wesson Public High School and had bonded over a shared hatred of irregular verbs and Mrs. Cheatwood's in-class proselytizing, which was of dubious legality even by Texas standards. "Repeat after me," she would say. *"Vamos a la iglesia a orar por nuestros pecados." Let's all go to church to pray for our sins.*

"Screw that," said Sean defiantly one day, "I'm a Satanist."

This declaration had gotten Sean sent to the principal's office. The principal, a tired old phys-ed teacher, had insisted that Sean recant, but Sean sensed (correctly) that the longer he maintained this ruse, the fewer irregular verbs he would be subjected to. Eventually the ACLU got involved, and someone suggested that Sean would have a stronger case that his religious freedoms were being impinged upon if there were some solid evidence that he were a practicing Satanist. The next day he found a copy of *Demonology for Imbeciles* in his locker, and he had no trouble recruiting a few more aspiring Satanists whose struggles with conjugation left them feeling spiritually empty.

That was several weeks ago, and the ACLU had dropped its suit in exchange for assurances that Mrs. Cheatwood would curtail her proselytizing during school hours. The First Satanic Church of Milhaus, however, lived on. It never grew beyond its first four members, though, who met irregularly in Brayden's aunt's basement, and lately it had started to feel like they were just going through the motions. Enamored of his newfound authority and desperate to keep the group going, Sean had suggested that summoning a demon might spice things up. The idea wasn't as popular with the other members as Sean had hoped: Neva and Clay were convinced the summoning wouldn't work, and Brayden was terrified that it would.

"Seriously," said Brayden. "We need to be careful. If we do this and something goes wrong ..."

"What?" interjected Neva, through a menagerie of painful-looking piercings. "What's the worst case scenario, Brayden? We fail to summon a demon?" Neva was the only female of the group, and also the smartest of the four, which wasn't saying much. Her parents substituted permissiveness and cash for affection, which had resulted in Neva weighing nearly three hundred pounds, approximately six of which was in the form of hardware attached to her face.

Brayden shrugged. "I just think if we're going to do this, we should do it right."

"And by 'do it right,' you mean that we should try to summon a tamarind?"

Brayden's face flushed and he sank into the cushions of the lumpy old couch. Clay was to his left and Sean and Neva were sitting on easy chairs with badly worn and stained floral upholstery. Brayden's aunt's basement was like a furniture graveyard.

"Fine," said Sean, who had been dragging the edge of his sneaker around the pentagram in an effort to adjust the lines. "I fixed it, see?"

"What the hell is that?" asked Clay.

"Pentagram," said Sean defensively.

The group regarded the blurred lines dubiously.

"It looks like Bob Marley," said Neva.

"It does not!" Sean protested. Then, after a moment: "Who's Bob Marley?"

Neva sighed heavily. She already had her doubts about Sean's fitness as High Priest, and his ignorance of a revolutionary leader like Bob Marley[2] only cemented his incompetence in her mind.

"Whatever," said Clay, the most pragmatic of the group. "My mom wants me home by eleven, so if we're going to do this, we need to get started."

"OK," said Sean. "Let's do this." He rooted around his backpack, producing four black candles and a cigarette lighter. He lit each of the candles in turn and handed one to each of the three Unholy Acolytes, keeping one for himself. He directed them to take their places around the ersatz hexagram and opened *Demonology for Imbeciles* to the chapter on summonings.

*Demonology for Imbeciles* was a strange book, even by *...for Imbeciles* standards. After dominating the instructional book market in the 90s, the publisher of the *...for Imbeciles* books, I Don't Get It, Ltd., fell on hard times due to the rise of a plethora of free instructional websites written by and for imbeciles. Imbeciles wanting to build a

---

[2] Kaylee tended to confuse Bob Marley and Che Guevara.

gazebo or breed cuttlefish found all the information they needed online without having to pay $19.95 for *Building a Gazebo for Imbeciles* or *Breeding Cuttlefish for Imbeciles*. IDGI's response to this threat was to launch the *...for Cretins* line of books, aimed at people who were too stupid to get on the Internet. When titles such as *Watering Plants for Cretins*, *Four-Way Stops for Cretins*, and *Are My Clothes Inside Out Again? for Cretins* inexplicably foundered, IDGI spent $6 million on market research, which informed them that most of their target audience thought cretins were a kind of aquatic animal. The *...for Cretins* line was thus relaunched as the *...for Total F\*cking Dumbshits* line, but this effort failed as well because, as it turns out, even total f\*cking dumbshits have a little pride.

The end result of this series of failures was that IDGI began to skimp on the content of their books while simultaneously attempting to broaden their appeal. Thus *Quantum Physics for Imbeciles*, *Feng Shui for Imbeciles*, and *Urban Engineering for Imbeciles* shared the same cartoons, with minor variations in the captions. *Demonology for Imbeciles* was a rush job thrown together from various public domain sources of dubious credibility by an editor whose knowledge of the occult was gleaned entirely from Black Sabbath records and *I Dream of Jeannie*. As it happened, though, the editor had come across one of the few extant recipes for a bona fide demonic summoning in the semi-coherent ramblings of an eighteenth century inventor and occultist named Josiah Vandersloot, which Vandersloot had published under the awkward title *The Little Book What's About Demons*. Had Vandersloot's grasp of English syntax been on par with his knowledge of the dark arts, the publication of *The Little Book What's About Demons* might have ushered in a golden age of demonology, but unfortunately (or fortunately, depending on your perspective), most readers were unable to make any sense of his garbled prose. The IDGI editor cleaned up the verbiage as best he could, throwing in Rush lyrics when he got stuck.

The result was that although *Demonology for Imbeciles* was almost entirely rubbish, chapter fourteen included, purely by chance, a nearly flawless recipe for summoning a demon. The only thing missing was the name of the demon to be summoned. Demons guard their true names jealously, and it's virtually impossible to summon a demon without knowing his or her name.

Demonic names are represented by a complex sigil that is generally comprised of a geometric figure enclosed in a circle. It is commonly thought that the pentagram is a Satanic symbol, but in fact the use of a pentagram in Satanic ceremonies arises from a misreading of ancient texts in which a five-pointed star is used as a placeholder for the name of a particular demon. Trying to conduct a summoning by using a pentagram is the spiritual equivalent of asking the telephone operator to connect you to *Insert Name Here*.

By an odd coincidence, Sean's imperfect hex-*cum*-pentagram very closely resembled the sigil for a certain fallen angel who had been exiled on a distant plane as the result of the accidental detonation of a small nuclear device at an interplanar transport hub. And so it happened that shortly after Sean finished reciting the incantation on page 124 on *Demonology for Imbeciles*, a cloud of sulfurous smoke arose from the sigil, enveloping the terrified members of the First Satanic Church of Milhaus, who dove behind the furniture for cover. After a moment the smoke began to clear, revealing a lanky figure who immediately doubled over in a fit of uncontrollable coughing, apparently overwhelmed by the fumes. After some time it became clear that the man was trying to speak.

"...open... window..." the man gasped.

His initial fright having been supplanted with nausea, Sean eagerly complied, propping open one of the ground-level basement windows. Clay found a small electric fan which he turned on in an attempt to disperse some of the rotten egg smell.

"Ugh," said the man, waving his hand in front of his face. "You never get used to the smell." The four congregants stood gaping at the newcomer. They weren't sure what a demon looked like, but none of them had expected this. Other than being exceptionally tall and adorned with an absurd shock of silver hair, he looked like an ordinary human being. Male, good-looking—if a little lanky—apparently about twenty-five years old.

"Are you... a demon?" asked Brayden at last.

The tall man frowned. "Let's not get hung up on labels," he said, regarding the dilapidated furniture of the basement. "Speaking of which, what sort of operation are you running here?"

"We're Satanists," announced Sean, trying to sound confident.

"Ah, Satanists!" the man said, nodding. "Adherents of Lucifer. Of course you realize that Lucifer is in Heavenly custody, and therefore unable to continue his rebellion against the highers-up? And that even if he weren't, all transportation between the Mundane Plane and the Infernal Plane has been cut off, thanks to the some knucklehead detonating a nuke at the planeport?"

The assembled congregants of the First Satanic Church of Milhaus gaped, speechless.

"Of course, you must know something about interplanar travel," said the man, "seeing as how you summoned me."

Sean pointed wordlessly to the copy of *Demonology for Imbeciles*, which was resting on the back of a dilapidated easy chair. The man picked it up and thumbed through a few of the pages. "Ugh," he said. "Where do they get this crap? How in hell did you manage to… oh. Wow, they stole the whole summoning chapter from Vandersloot's *The Little Book What's About Demons*. Man, I thought we'd burned all of those." He frowned, staring at the corrupted pentagram on the floor. "But how'd you know my name?"

"Your name?" asked Neva.

"Well, you misspelled it," the man said, gesturing at the sigil, "but you got the phonetics right."

The four regarded the sigil. "That symbol is your name?" asked Sean.

The man nodded. "More or less."

"How do you pronounce it?" asked Sean.

"Oh, no," said the man. "I'm not saying it out loud. Bad enough you wrote it out like that." He dragged his foot across the sigil, obliterating it.

"But what do we call you then?" asked Neva.

"You aren't really going to need to call me anything," said the man, "because I'm not planning on hanging out with you morons." He walked passed Neva and began up the basement stairs. He stopped and turned, grinning. "But if you're wondering what name to give the malevolent entity you've unleashed on the world," he said, "you can call me Mercury."

# CHAPTER TWO

*Near Rapid City, South Dakota; August 2016*

"Are you sure this is a good idea?" asked Nisroc, pausing suddenly on the trail.

Izbazel stopped short behind him and thought about it for a moment, gazing at the massive granite faces towering over them. The fact was, Izbazel wasn't at all sure it was a good idea. In fact, if he were honest, he'd lay even odds that it was an absolutely terrible idea. But Izbazel wasn't particularly good at being honest with himself, and he was even worse at being honest with others. "Of course I'm sure," he said. "You'll see. This is going to be huge."

Nisroc sighed and continued trudging up the sloping path. Izbazel was immediately behind him, followed by Konrath and Scalzi. Each of them wore a heavy pack and carried two large duffel bags, and they were sweating in the heat of the South Dakota sun.

The four demons were all that was left of the once proud and globally feared organization known as Chaos Faction. After pulling off a string of several high-profile terrorist attacks around the world, Chaos Faction was betrayed to the federal agents by one of its own, a demon named Ramiel, and most of its members were arrested and never heard from again. Among those who were apprehended was Tiamat, the demoness who was the brains behind Chaos Faction, and her right-hand demon, Gamaliel.

The four demons who remained at large were decidedly second-string: they had only gotten away because Tiamat had insisted they be nowhere near the site of what turned out to be Chaos Faction's last major operation, knocking over Fort Knox.[3] That operation had failed, thanks to Ramiel, and now Izbazel found himself in charge of what was left of the organization, more-or-less by default. He and Nisroc were the only ones with any experience running covert operations, and Nisroc didn't have the temperament of a leader.

Given that the four of them were demons and therefore capable of manipulating interplanar energy fields, it would have been a simple matter for them to create chaos on a large scale—for example, by crashing the computers of the New York Stock Exchange with a freak magnetic pulse, or by replacing the face of Ben Franklin on ten million hundred dollar bills at the Federal Reserve with that of Rick Springfield. But the modus operandi of Chaos Faction had always been to use mundane technology, for reasons that Izbazel wasn't completely clear on. He thought it had something to do with not wanting to escalate the conflict with the powers of Order into a full-fledged war. Or maybe it was because Tiamat had wanted it to look like Chaos Faction was a large grass-roots operation expressing the frustrations of millions of disenfranchised people and not merely a band of rogue demons wreaking mischief. The subtleties of Tiamat's decision-making processes were beyond Izbazel's somewhat pedestrian mind.

Whatever the explanation, Izbazel intended to stay within the operational guidelines Tiamat had established. Eventually he hoped to figure out where Tiamat and the other demons were being held and break them out—but not before he had established himself as Tiamat's obvious choice for second-in-command. Ideally he'd find a way to rescue Tiamat while leaving that asshole Gamaliel to rot in prison.

For now, though, he needed to focus on the mission at hand. So far, Chaos Faction had encountered no resistance in its latest mission—only confused glances and giggling from tourists who couldn't imagine why anyone would need an oversized backpack and two duffel bags full of supplies to hike the half-mile circuit of the Presidential Trail. Izbazel now saw that their luck had come to

---

[3] Not a figure of speech. They literally planned to knock over the building. Tiamat had a weakness for puns.

an end, though: a park ranger was walking down the trail toward them, and he didn't look happy.

Izbazel pushed Nisroc aside, taking the lead. Picking up his pace, he pretended not to see the ranger in the hopes that if he didn't stop, the ranger wouldn't bother to ask about the packs.

"Hold on there, guys," said the ranger, a hippie-looking blond guy with his hair in a ponytail. "What's in the packs?"

"We have the right to travel unmolested by fascist thugs," snapped Izbazel, while the other three simultaneously shouted, "Just water!" In the heat of the moment, Izbazel had forgotten their agreed-upon response.

"Water, huh?" said the ranger, ignoring Izbazel's outburst. "Mind if I take a look?"

"You don't need to look in our packs," said Izbazel, with a slight wave of his hand.

The ranger stared at Izbazel. "I don't need to look in your packs," he said.

Izbazel smiled and started to walk past the ranger.

"But I'm going to," the ranger added, placing his hand on Izbazel's shoulder.

Before Izbazel could react, something flew over his shoulder from behind, smacking the ranger in the forehead. The ranger's eyes went wide, and then his pupils rolled back in his head and he fell to the ground. The golf ball-sized rock that had struck him skittered into the underbrush.

Izbazel whirled to face Nisroc. "What the hell was *that?*"

Nisroc held his hands up. "It looked like you needed some help."

"You think I couldn't have hit him with a rock if I had wanted to?" growled Izbazel. "You thought to yourself, 'Man, Izzy's in real trouble here. What he needs is someone capable of throwing a rock at a forest ranger's head from five feet away. It's a good thing I'm here, because that's right at the top of my impressive list of talents.' Is that it?"

Nisroc's brow furrowed. "I'm sorry," he said. "I don't think I understand the question?"

"Forget it," Izbazel snapped. "Let's get out of here before he comes to."

Izbazel pressed on, leading the three demons up the trail. Soon they had looped around to the rocky plateau on the back of Mount Rushmore.

"Alright," said Izbazel. "For this next part, we need to cut across country so we can get to the faces."

"Which way?" asked Scalzi, peering into the distance.

"That way," said Izbazel, pointing to his left.

"Can't be," said Scalzi.

"Why not?" asked Izbazel.

"We should be able to see the backs of their heads."

"The backs…" started Izbazel. "You realize that it's just the faces carved into the rock, right? Not the whole head?"

Scalzi frowned. "That's a bit misleading then, isn't it?"

"How is it misleading?" asked Izbazel.

"Well, when you see George Washington's face, you say, 'Look, it's George Washington.' You don't say, 'Look, it's George Washington's face, behind which is probably a big pile of loose gravel and shrubbery.'"

"It's not… look, just shut up, OK? No more talking. That goes for you too, Konrath. Konrath!"

Konrath, who had stopped to pick daisies a few paces behind the rest of the group, suddenly jerked to attention. "Yessir, Izzy," he said. "No talking."

"Good," said Izbazel. "Now, we're going to cut across here and climb down the faces, just like *North by Northwest*. Got it?"

The three demons nodded.

Izbazel left the path and started to cross the rocky field toward the front of the mountain. He had gotten about ten paces when he realized no one was following him. He turned to see the other three demons walking the opposite direction.

"What in blazes are you guys doing?" he yelled.

The three stopped and exchanged confused glances.

"You said north by northwest," said Nisroc at last.

"The movie!" growled Izbazel. "Cary Grant and Eva Marie Saint scale the faces of Mount Rushmore to get away from Martin Landau."

"Oh!" cried Nisroc. "Why?"

"Why what?"

"Why were they trying to get away from Martin Landau? Seems like a nice enough fellow." The other two demons nodded in agreement.

"Forget I said anything about *North by Northwest*!" snapped Izbazel. "Just be quiet and follow me."

The demons shrugged, muttered to each other, and fell in line behind Izbazel. It wasn't long before they had reached the top of the gigantic sculpture. They lined up on the edge of a lock of Jefferson's hair, overlooking the vast slope of the Founder's forehead.

"How long did this take to make?" Konrath asked.

"Millions of years," answered Scalzi confidently. "Erosion."

"You idiot," spat Izbazel. "They carved it out of the rock with explosives, just like the Grand Canyon. Tie the end of this rope around that rock over there."

Scalzi and Konrath took the end of the rope and tied it to the boulder Izbazel had indicated.

"OK," said Izbazel. "Nisroc, you're going to climb down the rope and swing over to Washington."

"Why me?" asked Nisroc.

"You said you had experience with explosives."

Nisroc frowned. "You asked me if I had ever blown a nose."

"You must have misunderstood. Anyway, there's nothing to it. Just shove the explosives up Washington's left nostril. I'll activate the detonator from here."

"Why Washington?" asked Nisroc. "What's wrong with Jefferson?"

"There's nothing *wrong* with Jefferson. But George Washington is the alpha male of the group.

"He's the what?" asked Konrath.

"The alpha male. The leader. Father of his country, all that."

Nisroc rubbed his chin. "I kinda think Roosevelt could take him."

"Sure," agreed Izbazel. "It's generally agreed that Teddy Roosevelt was the manliest of all the presidents. If they were all in a bar fight, Teddy would come out on top. Lincoln would make a good show of it, but he's too lanky and slow. And Jefferson—well, let's be honest here, a delicate guy like Jefferson isn't going to last long against dudes like Washington or Roosevelt. But as manly as

Roosevelt was, Washington was the original American badass. Stood up to the greatest military of the time. Cracked walnuts in his bare hands. Valley Forge, cherry tree, all that. First in war, first in peace, first in the hearts of his countrymen. So he's the one whose nose we need to blow."

The demons nodded, having been persuaded of the wisdom of Izbazel's plan.

Once he was satisfied the rope was securely tied, Izbazel tied the other end around Nisroc's waist. The rest of the rope lay coiled on the ground near the boulder. Izbazel had Konrath and Scalzi hold the rope, instructing them to slowly let it out as Nisroc made his way down the slope. "Once you're in place," he said to Nisroc, "I'll pull the rope up and then lower the explosives down and swing them over to you."

Nisroc nodded uncertainly, taking the rope in his hands. He began to slowly back down the sheer rock face. "I don't think I like this very much," he said.

Izbazel shrugged. "At least you can see where you're going." he said. "Imagine climbing down Washington's big dome. With Jefferson, it's a straight shot from his widow's peak to the tip of his nose. Now get moving."

Nisroc grumbled but continued down the granite slope. Soon he had crossed Jefferson's brow and was making his way down his long, straight nose. When he got to the tip, he stopped, flattening himself against the rock. Down below, he could hear tourists shouting.

"Don't stop!" cried Izbazel. "They've seen you. We don't have much time. We'll lower you another thirty feet or so, and then you need to swing over to Washington."

"I don't think I'll be able to reach!" yelled Nisroc. "Can't I just fly?"

"No!" shouted Izbazel. "No miracles."

Nisroc grumbled to himself but allowed them to lower him so that he dangled thirty feet under Jefferson's nose. He could hear shouting far below.

"Now what?" he yelled.

"Swing over to Washington's shoulder!" shouted Izbazel.

Nisroc remained hanging from the nose, the rope digging painfully into his midsection. Izbazel had tied it with a slipknot, and every time Nisroc moved, it tightened a little more. He thought he knew what a balloon animal felt like. He worked one of his hands into the loop of the rope to try to widen it, but only succeeded in getting his hand hopelessly stuck.

"I can't move!" he gasped. His vision was starting to blur at the edges. "I don't feel right!"

"Ugh," said Izbazel in disgust. "All right, we're going to have to swing him. Konrath, climb down the nose and see if you can get him going."

Konrath clambered down the nearly vertical rock face. When he reached the edge, he lay down, with his left hand clutching the rope and his head hanging over the edge. He reached down with his right arm and began to pull sideways on the rope. Soon Nisroc had begun a slow, back and forth swing.

"I don't think I can do this," groaned Nisroc, whose face had turned a bright shade of purple.

"Keep quiet and swing!" Konrath yelled at Nisroc, who didn't have much choice in the matter.

Soon Nisroc was swinging in great arcs back and forth, like a gnat buzzing across Jefferson's chin. He was on the verge of losing consciousness.

"Almost there!" shouted Konrath.

"Hyeergh," Nisroc replied. The arc was now bringing him within a few yards of Washington's shoulder, but there was no way he was going to be able to grab hold of the rock and halt his motion. His fingers had gone numb and he could barely move his one free arm. As he swung over the shoulder, he managed to grab hold of enough interplanar energy to weaken the rope around his waist. It snapped and he fell to the rock. He rolled uncontrollably for several yards, finally managing to get enough control over his appendages to stop before he tumbled off the edge of Washington's shoulder.

"No miracles!" shouted Izbazel disapprovingly from atop Jefferson's scalp.

Down below, a huge crowd of spectators had gathered, and were watching the exploits of Chaos Faction with great interest. A large black Humvee pulled up and men in heavy tactical gear jumped out. They began working their way up the trail to Lincoln's left.

"Hurry!" yelled Izbazel. "Get the rope back up!"

They pulled the rope up and Izbazel threaded it through the handles of the duffel bags and the loops at the top of the backpacks. He tied the end of the rope to itself, making a loop, and he and Scalzi began to slide the several hundred pounds of explosives down Jefferson's forehead. Konrath helped the package over the brink of the nose and they lowered it another thirty feet so they could swing it to Nisroc.

Nisroc, for his part, was sitting with his back against Washington's lapel, trying not to vomit.

The load of explosives was considerably heavier than Nisroc, and Konrath had a hard time getting any momentum going. The bags were lazily swinging back and forth in an arc of about three feet.

"Hurry!" yelled Izbazel, who was watching over his shoulder for the arrival of the cops.

"I can't get it going!" Konrath shouted back.

"Try harder!" yelled Izbazel. "The cops are here!" It was true: the SWAT team had reached the plateau and were cutting across the field right toward them. It was pretty rough going, particularly for guys in combat gear, but it wouldn't take them more than two minutes to close the distance. Izbazel fingered the radio detonator nervously.

Konrath had managed to get the load of explosives to swing a bit farther, but he was having trouble keeping the trajectory straight, and the pendulum was still several yards out of Nisroc's reach. The cops were almost on them.

Now none of the four assembled demons was particularly bright, but they did each possess some basic mental faculties and a fairly robust sense of self-preservation. And so it occurred to each of them, simultaneously but independently, that what they needed right now was a miracle. Nisroc, Scalzi and Konrath were convinced that Izbazel wouldn't go along with the idea, and Izbazel didn't want to admit his plan wasn't working out. So what happened is that each demon simultaneously harnessed a bit of interplanar energy and gave the pendulum just enough of a push to get it to Washington's shoulder. These four small pushes combined to form one big push, causing the load of explosives to jerk violently toward Washington's head. Before Konrath could let go, he was jerked off his feet. He slid off Jefferson's nose, plummeting to the rocks below. The explosives smacked against Washington's wig and then fell directly on Nisroc, knocking him flat. The combined mass of Nisroc and the bags then began to slide down Washington's shoulder. Nisroc, dazed, was unable to do anything but marvel at the sensation of granite sliding under his backside.

The SWAT team was now within fifty yards of Izbazel, and they were yelling at Izbazel to get on the ground and drop the detonator. Izbazel, realizing that his carefully thought out plan had gone awry, did what leaders generally do under such circumstances: he panicked. Izbazel pushed the button on the detonator.

A deafening explosion sounded below, accompanied by a shock wave that knocked Izbazel and Scalzi against Jefferson's hairline. Dazed, the two demons stumbled, lost their balance, and fell forward onto the great statesman's brow. They rolled head over heels down the forehead, slowed momentarily when they reached the gentler slope of the left eyebrow, and then pitched into the open air, plummeting to join Konrath and what was left of Nisroc.


Up above, the SWAT team had reached Jefferson's coif. At the head of the group was a stocky young sergeant named Daniel McCann, who was as well-known in Rapid City, South Dakota for his impressive marksmanship as for his ridiculous handlebar moustache. Daniel stepped to the edge of Jefferson's hair and peered into the gravelly hillside that led away from the monument. At the bottom of the hill lay the body of one of the terrorists, and two others were rolling down the slope toward him, their limbs flailing crazily. Finally they came to rest as well, and the three lay motionless on the rocky valley floor. Behind a wooden fence a hundred yards or so away, tourists gawked and gasped at the horrifying scene.

Then something unexpected happened.

The first of the terrorists to fall slowly sat up and began rubbing his head. The other two were soon moving as well, and after a moment the three of them were on their feet, rubbing bruises and dusting themselves off as if they had just fallen off a hayride. One of the terrorists walked a few feet away and picked up something that Daniel at first took to be a rock about the size of a human head. When the man held it in front of his face and began talking to it, Daniel realized it was, in fact, a human head.

"Well," said Daniel, observing the strange scene unfolding below, "that's not normal."

Another man came up from behind and stood next to him. "No," he replied. "It isn't."

The other man was taller than Daniel, close to six foot two, and had the build of a heavyweight boxer. His skin was a dark chestnut brown and his short-cropped hair was black flecked with gray. Rather than the loose-fitting combat gear of the SWAT team, he wore a precisely tailored dark gray pinstriped suit and aviator-style sunglasses. He wore no badge or nametag, but he didn't need to. Those who didn't know his name called him *sir*. Those who did called him Zion Johnson. Or sometimes Mr. Johnson. Or occasionally sir. Nobody on the mountain knew who Zion Johnson was exactly, or who he worked for, but they all knew he was in charge.

Daniel brought his radio to his mouth. "Hey, Jim," he said. "You got these guys?"

After a moment a voice crackled over the radio. "Say the word and we'll take 'em out."

Daniel glanced at Zion Johnson, who tilted his head half a degree to the left.

"Stand down," said Daniel.

"Seriously?" said the voice over the radio. "We're going to let these assholes go?"

"Out of my hands," said Daniel.

Daniel and Zion Johnson watched as the three figures fled the scene. One of the men had the fourth's head under his arm.

"I hope you know what you're doing," said Daniel to Zion Johnson.

"This is just a distraction," said Zion Johnson. "Chaos Faction is up to something much bigger."

Daniel frowned. "The intel I have says there are only four members of Chaos Faction unaccounted for. And we just let them go."

Zion Johnson shook his head. "We didn't let them go. I've got eyes on them."

"Oh yeah?" said Daniel. "Funny how your 'eyes' didn't keep them from almost giving George Washington some unnecessary rhinoplasty."

"It was a calculated risk," said Zion Johnson. "Chaos Faction is more dangerous than you think."

Down below one of the men lost his footing and stumbled into the man carrying his compatriot's head. The head slipped from under his arm and tumbled into a ravine below, causing the two men to erupt into loud recriminations while the third man clambered down to retrieve what was left of the fourth.

Daniel McCann cleared his throat.

"You'll see," said Zion Johnson.

"Uh huh," replied Daniel.

Zion Johnson turned to leave.

"Your work is done here, huh, Johnson?" said Daniel. "Back to Washington for you?"

Zion Johnson stopped and looked back at Daniel. "That's *Mister* Johnson, Sergeant."

"Back to Washington, *Mister* Johnson?"

Zion Johnson sighed. "Let me introduce you to a phrase that's going to come in very handy over the next few days, when the press starts asking questions about what happened here today."

"Oh yeah?" said Daniel. "What's that?"

"No comment," said Zion Johnson, and walked away.

# CHAPTER THREE

*Milhaus, Texas; August 2016*

Mercury walked out onto the street, blinking in the bright Texas sunlight. It seemed like a long time since he had seen the sun. How long had he been away from the Mundane Plane? Days? Years?

He stopped a young man on the street and asked him what the date was.

"August nine," said the man.

"The year!" cried Mercury, gripping the man's lapel. "What year is it?"

"Twenty-sixteen!" yelped the man, tearing himself away from Mercury's grip. He ran off down the street.

"OK, thanks!" yelled Mercury after him.

2016, he thought. He'd been gone for almost four years. He wondered how much had changed in that time. He hadn't seen any flying cars or teleportation pods yet, but this looked like kind of a backwater town. There was some kind of crowd gathered up ahead; he hoped they were handing out Soylent Green. Mercury could go for some Soylent Green, and maybe a Guinness.

But as he approached, his hopes faded. The people in the crowd were chanting something, and many of them were holding signs and waving them at passing cars. Some of the messages had strange, cryptic phrases on them, like

RFID IS NOT OK!

and

KEEP YOUR CHIPS OUT OF MY BODY

and

WE DON'T TRUST MENTALDYNE

There was a red circle with a line through it superimposed on "MENTALDYNE", so whatever MENTALDYNE was, it was hard to say whether the protester was against MENTALDYNE or against *not* MENTALDYNE, making him pro-MENTALDYNE.

Others had Bible verses. Revelation 13:16 seemed to be particularly popular:

IT ALSO FORCED ALL PEOPLE, GREAT AND SMALL, RICH AND POOR, FREE AND SLAVE, TO RECEIVE A MARK ON THEIR RIGHT HANDS OR ON THEIR FOREHEADS, SO THAT THEY COULD NOT BUY OR SELL UNLESS THEY HAD THE MARK, WHICH IS THE NAME OF THE BEAST OR THE NUMBER OF ITS NAME. THAT NUMBER IS 666.

"Oh, man," groaned Mercury. "Not this again." Mercury had been through so many Apocalypse scares that he had lost count of them. As he approached the rear of the crowd, he strained to understand what they were chanting. "Hey," he said, tapping an elderly woman on the shoulder. "What are you guys saying?"

"RFID is not OK!" the woman shouted in his face.

"Gotcha," replied Mercury. The woman turned back to face the street. After a moment Mercury tapped her on the shoulder again. "What's RFID?" he asked.

The woman turned around again, now a bit irritated. "Radio… something. Don't you watch the news?"

"I'm a bit behind on current events," said Mercury. "You're against radios?"

"Not radios," the woman spat. "The chips, you know. Mentaldyne."

"What's a Mentaldyne?"

"They're the company that makes the chips."

"Right," said Mercury. "The chips. Oh, I think I get it. These chips, they're made of people, right?"

The woman stared aghast at him. "What? No! They put them *in* people. There's this whole secret government program. They're already putting them in prisoners and mental patients. They're going to make us all get them."

"Oh, *chips!*" Mercury cried. "Like tracking devices. But, um, what does the Mark of the Beast stuff have to do with anything?"

"Wow, you really don't know anything, do you?" the woman said, shaking her head. "It's all in here." She handed Mercury a tract. On the front was a cartoon of a man, woman and child bowing before a hideous horned creature, who seemed to be touching the child on the forehead.

"What's this?" Mercury asked, pointing at the picture. "Why is Mr. Gruesome Pants violating Timmy's personal space?"

"It's the End Times!" the woman shouted in exasperation. "Just read it. It's all in there. The government making us get chips implanted, the great winepress of God's wrath... Just read it."

"OK," said Mercury. "But just so you know, it isn't actually the End Times. Trust me. I've been through all this. The whole Apocalypse thing, it was a bust. The more I think about it, the more I'm convinced that Apocalypse Bureau completely misread the prophecies. Between you and me, I'm pretty sure all that stuff in Revelation was meant to be metaphorical."

"Metaphorical!" the woman cried angrily. "The Bible means exactly what it says!"

"Except for the part where the Mark of the Beast is actually an RFID chip," replied Mercury.

"Huh?"

"Well, that's a metaphor, right? It's not literally a mark; it's a computer chip. If the Bible was meant to be taken one hundred percent literally, it would just say, 'The government is going to force everybody to get a computer chip implanted,' not 'the beast will force them to receive a mark.'"

The woman stared at Mercury, momentarily dumfounded. "What are you, some kind of atheist?" she finally demanded.

"Not at all," said Mercury. "I just think God has a twisted sense of humor. Anyway, good luck stopping the Apocalypse."

The woman continued to glare at Mercury as he continued down the street. Man, Mercury thought. Not only are there no flying cars, but people haven't learned a damn thing. They're still obsessing over the End Times, just like they were four years ago. And four hundred years ago. Granted, there was some reason to think the world was ending four years ago—a third of the Moon had imploded, after all. That was some scary stuff. Mercury knew first hand just how scary, since he was the one who had imploded it. Only he and a few others knew that it had almost been Earth that had imploded instead.

Where did people get this crap about RFID chips being the Mark of the Beast? He seriously doubted whether Lucifer had the technological savvy to pull something like that off, even before he was incarcerated. The idea of him masterminding such a scheme like that now was ridiculous. If there was any truth to the claim that the government was putting RFID chips in people, it was probably some completely sensible program to keep tabs on criminals or something. People always got all worked up about the silliest things.

Less than half an hour on the Mundane plane and he'd already encountered a crazy mob. Was there something about him that caused this kind of crap to happen? Hadn't he been through enough of that sort of idiocy? Why couldn't those faux-Satanist knuckleheads have just left him alone? Mercury found himself nostalgic for his early days on this plane, back when everything seemed new and hiding two hundred sweaty Greeks inside a giant wooden horse seemed like a good idea. These days everything was just so... predictable.

He despaired of finding a cure for his malaise, but he knew one sure-fire way to forget about the problem for a little while, and that was to get stinking drunk.

# CHAPTER FOUR

*Washington, D.C.; August 2016*

Zion Johnson waited in the antechamber of the Oval Office. He sat upright on a couch, looking straight ahead, his mind clear. Zion Johnson didn't get nervous. "Superior attitude, superior state of mind," Zion Johnson mouthed silently. This was his mantra. Zion Johnson had never studied Zen or Eastern philosophy, but he had watched every Steven Seagal movie ever made, many of them a dozen times. His favorite was *Hard to Kill*.

Twenty minutes later, he was summoned into the Oval Office. The president was seated behind his desk. He smiled as Zion Johnson entered.

Zion Johnson took a step into the room and stopped. Something wasn't right. He had specifically been told that the president would be meeting with him alone, and yet there was someone else in the room. Zion Johnson resisted the urge to draw his gun—which wasn't in its holster anyway; you couldn't take a loaded gun into the Oval Office. He turned toward the interloper, sitting unmoving, unassuming, almost invisible, in a chair to his left.

It was a young girl, maybe thirteen years old.

Zion Johnson looked at her, looked at the president, and looked back at the girl. Zion Johnson was rarely at a loss for words, but he simply couldn't process this data. She might have been the president's daughter, but Zion Johnson knew the president had no children. And what would his daughter be doing at a top secret briefing? Also, the little girl was black. Her skin wasn't as dark as Zion Johnson's, but she was clearly of African descent. Flawless chestnut brown skin with long, curly black hair. She regarded Zion Johnson with what appeared to be detached bemusement.

Zion's heart sank as it occurred to him that the 'new phase' of his assignment to keep tabs on Chaos Faction was in fact an entirely unrelated and highly undesirable assignment. Presumably the president wanted him to babysit this girl, probably the daughter of some paranoid diplomat, worried that his daughter was going to be abducted or get mixed up with the wrong element during the family's stay in D.C. Twenty-eight years of government service, and Zion Johnson had ended up as Denzel Washington in *Man on Fire*. "Superior attitude, superior state of mind," Zion Johnson recited to himself, willing himself back into Seagal territory.

"Mr. President," said Zion Johnson at last. "We seem to have a visitor."

President Danton Prowse smiled that effete Connecticut smile that would have cost him the election had he been running against anyone but Travis Babcock, the dim but affable Republican who had spent the last few months of his term mired in scandal. President Babcock had, for some reason that had never been fully explained, authorized a secret program to build a so-called "suitcase nuke"—a ten-kiloton nuclear bomb small enough to fit in a backpack. Congress had been kept in the dark about the program; only Babcock, the scientists and technicians involved in the project, and a handful of advisors knew about it. When details about the program appeared in a *Washington Post* story, most of those involved pleaded ignorance about the program's purpose and lack of proper authorization, and Babcock was left to twist in the wind, defending a program that seemed indefensible.

Babcock had been a popular president up to that point, and the Democratic challenger Danton Prowse had been running a somewhat perfunctory campaign against him. Prowse had only gotten the nomination because none of the top-tier Democrats wanted the humiliation of being defeated by a grinning buffoon like Travis Babcock. But when the Wormwood scandal broke—that's what the secret program was called, Wormwood—suddenly Babcock's popularity plummeted and Danton Prowse was the frontrunner. Even with the inconvenient revelations about

Wormwood, Babcock probably would have come out on top, except for one very troubling fact: he couldn't explain where the bomb had gone. If Project Wormwood had one redeeming quality, it was that it had been successful: the technicians had managed to create a single ten kiloton nuclear bomb roughly the size of an Oxford dictionary. But no one seemed to know what had happened to it.

As it turns out, the American public will put up with a president who undertakes a morally dubious and illegal program, but only if it gets results. Constitutional experts disagreed on whether Babcock had the authority to run a secret nuclear weapons program in defiance of Congress and various international arms treaties, but everyone agreed that misplacing the bomb was unforgiveable. Was it tucked away in a corner of some government warehouse, its nuclear core gradually decaying? Had it been stolen by some terrorist group? Disposed of somewhere in the depths of the Pacific? There were plenty of theories, but no one—not even Travis Babcock himself—seemed to know for sure. Babcock insisted that he had only recently learned about Wormwood and planned to tell Congress about it (after the election, of course), but only the blindest of Republican hacks believed that.

Babcock, although he was no Rhodes Scholar, was at least smart enough to keep the truth to himself: that the bomb had been sent through a portal to the interdimensional hub known as the planeport, where it had detonated, destroying the planeport and cutting Earth off from every other plane of existence. That hadn't been the goal, of course. The goal had been to blow up Heaven itself.[4]

Three months after Wormwood came to light, Prowse was elected President of the United States, and no one was more surprised by this than Danton Prowse. A two-term senator from Hartford, Connecticut, Prowse combined the animal magnetism of Michael Dukakis with the unbridled energy of John Kerry. Zion Johnson hadn't voted for him and didn't particularly like him, which put him in the company of forty-nine and eighty-seven

---

[4] All in all, it was one of Travis Babcock's worse ideas, and that was saying something.

percent of the American people as a whole, respectively. For his part, Zion Johnson preferred a Commander-in-Chief who exuded more of an air of authority. Travis Babcock may have been an idiot, but at least he always seemed sure of himself. Danton Prowse always seemed to be thinking things through as he spoke, emphasizing each word that came out of his mouth in turn, eventually arriving at his point the way he had arrived at the Presidency: with a demeanor that suggested he wasn't sure where he was or how he had gotten there, but he was happy enough to be there, all things considered.

This was the first time Zion Johnson had met Danton Prowse in person (although they had spoken several times on the phone), and if anything the man was less impressive in real life than on television. He was tall but reedy and slightly hunched over, with a sort of grayish cast to his face, as if death had decided to claim him but then gotten distracted. Zion Johnson tried not to let his disappointment—both in the president himself and in the presence of the little girl who was undoubtedly to be Zion Johnson's charge—show, but it took a great deal of effort. *Superior attitude, superior state of mind.*

"This is Michelle," said the president, indicating the girl. "She's an advisor of sorts."

The girl nodded toward Danton Prowse and smiled almost imperceptibly.

"An advisor," repeated Zion Johnson, trying to make sense of the meaning of word in this context. Politicians never just came out and said what they meant.

"Please, sit down, Mr. Johnson," said Prowse. "You're making me nervous."

Zion Johnson glanced again at the girl, who continued to observe him impassively, shrugged, and took a seat across from the president.

"We were disappointed with the events in South Dakota," Prowse said.

Here it comes, thought Zion Johnson. "Mr. President," said Zion Johnson. "I'll do whatever is required of me in service of my country. But I have to tell you right now that personal security is not my specialty."

Prowse seemed confused. "Personal security?"

"I assume," replied Zion Johnson, "that you want me to babysit our young guest here."

At this, Prowse burst into laughter. The girl—Michelle, if that really was her name—smirked a little and rolled her eyes. Her reaction made the hair stand up on the back of Zion Johnson's neck. It wasn't the dramatic exasperation of a teenage girl; it was the knowing smile of someone who was in on a joke that she despaired of anyone else ever getting.

"Michelle is not your concern," the president said. "As I mentioned, she is an advisor. I know she looks too young to be able to advise me on anything but the latest Justin Bieber song, but looks can be deceiving."

Zion Johnson smiled inwardly. Danton Prowse had a reputation of being "out of touch," and he'd just confirmed it. Even Zion Johnson knew Justin Bieber hadn't had a hit since his meltdown in 2014.

"Zion, I need you to focus," said Prowse. "I've got a job that needs doing. It's extremely dangerous, not technically legal, and needs to be done for the good of the country."

"I'm listening," said Zion Johnson.

Danton Prowse leaned back in his chair. "I assume you're familiar with the Wormwood project?"

"Of course," replied Zion Johnson. "Illegal project started by the Babcock administration to build a suitcase nuke. It cost him the election. It's the reason you're president."

Prowse smiled painedly. "Hmm, that and my winning personality," he said.

Zion Johnson said nothing.

"That was a joke," added Prowse.

"I know," replied Zion Johnson coolly. "Why did you ask me about Wormwood?"

Prowse glanced at Michelle, who was still quietly observing the two of them. "As you know, Wormwood was an embarrassment for this country. Not just for Travis Babcock, for the whole country. To lose track of such a powerful weapon… it doesn't look good."

"It doesn't look particularly good for the executive branch to have gone completely rogue with a secret weapons program either," said Zion Johnson.

"No, no, of course not," replied Prowse hurriedly. "The whole thing, it was a big clusterfuck, the way it was handled. But you know, we've had these sorts of Constitutional squabbles before. Iran-Contra, the Teapot Dome scandal... it's all part of the give-and-take of a healthy democracy. Losing a nuclear weapon, though... that's just embarrassing. It damages our image overseas. I know you understand the importance of projecting a strong image to our enemies, Zion."

Zion Johnson nodded, agreeing in principle, but not following where the conversation was going.

"I had a few meetings with Babcock during the transition period," Prowse went on. "We agreed that it was of utmost importance that the bomb be located. And he made it very clear to me that was very unlikely to happen, unless... extraordinary steps were taken."

"I don't follow you, sir," said Zion Johnson.

"Babcock assured me that if we were to cooperate and keep any nosy congressmen from poking around, and that if we put enough money into it, a bomb could be located. Do you follow me now, Zion?"

"You're saying that the bomb that was lost..."

"...now is found," finished Prowse. "Technically it's not exactly the same bomb, but there's no way anyone could know that."

"How the hell did you manage to build another bomb?" Zion Johnson asked. "Wormwood was shut down. The facility was cleared out. There were inspections and congressional hearings. It was all over the news for two years!"

"We had some help," said Prowse, glancing at Michelle. "We have... allies who are very good at hiding things, and very good at convincing people not to dig too deeply."

Zion Johnson frowned. "But, Mr. President, if your concern was loss of face with other countries, why haven't you produced the bomb? Why haven't you gone public with it?"

Prowse sighed. "The problem is, even with help from our friends, the Wormwood bomb took nearly three years to replicate. By that time, the damage had been done. At this point, everybody just assumes the bomb is hidden away in some top secret facility. After all, if it had been stolen by terrorists, they would have used it by now. It would almost be more embarrassing for us to come out and say, 'Hey, look what we found!'"

Zion Johnson shook his head. "Just so I understand you correctly, your response to your predecessor's career-ending scandal was to recreate the exact conditions that led to that scandal?"

"I suppose that's one way to look at it," said Prowse. "The difference is that we're not going to get caught. And even if we do, how upset can people really get at this point? If a Republican president can run a secret nuclear weapons program behind Congress' back, then it's only fair that my party gets a shot at it."

Zion Johnson shrugged and nodded. It made sense in a completely amoral, Machiavellian way—which is the way Zion Johnson tended to look at things anyway. It was why he kept getting put in charge of illegal top secret programs.

"So what is my involvement in all this?" Zion Johnson asked. "What do you want me to do?"

"Well, as you know," Prowse said. "There's been a lot of pushback lately regarding some of our more aggressive anti-terrorism policies. A lot of bleeding heart types making noise about civil liberties and whatnot. And I get it, I do. I mean, I campaigned on a lot of that stuff. Transparency, civil liberties, it's all good stuff in theory. But it's getting to the point where it's getting difficult for me to do my job, which is to keep the American people safe."

"I understand," said Zion Johnson.

"The problem is, people have forgotten how great the threat to our way of life is. We prevent these attacks—like that attempted poison gas attack in the New York subway last week, but it doesn't really penetrate. People don't understand how close we are, all the time, to the brink of chaos. I see the intelligence reports, and let me tell you, it's some scary shit. I mean, what if Wormwood had been stolen by terrorists? Can you imagine?"

"I can," said Zion Johnson, carefully.

"Do you know what the original purpose of Wormwood was? They were trying to determine how small a nuclear bomb could be made, so that we'd know what to look for. I guess it turned out that the simplest way to figure that out was to actually build the bomb. Of course, nobody else has a hundred billion dollars in secret funds to spend on building a miniature nuke, but still, it's scary to think how easy it would be to detonate something like that in a medium-sized American city."

Zion Johnson regarded the president coldly. "How easy would it be?"

"For someone with your skills and contacts," replied Prowse, "it would be a cakewalk."

Zion Johnson stared at the president, trying to parse his words. "Sir, are you suggesting...?"

"Such a bomb must never be detonated in a heavily populated area," said Prowse. He turned to Michelle, who nodded slightly. "What I'm envisioning is a scenario in which Homeland Security narrowly saves an entire city from destruction, and the bomb detonates safely somewhere nearby. Far enough away not to cause any serious damage, but close enough to put the fear of God into the citizens."

Ah, thought Zion Johnson. This was more like it. When he had been mysteriously instructed to 'step back' his efforts to wipe out Chaos Faction, he suspected something like this was in the works. It was about time somebody in the Oval Office had the balls to do what was necessary to protect America from its enemies. He never expected that person to be Danton Prowse, though—and as he glanced over at the young girl sitting quietly to his left, it occurred to him that maybe it wasn't.

"What city do you think the terrorists would pick?" he asked. "Baltimore?"

"Too big. Too close to Washington, D.C."

Zion Johnson nodded. Medium-sized city, far from Washington, he thought. "Modesto, California?"

"Too obvious. Travis Babcock's hometown. And have you ever been there? A nuke would improve the place."

"Also, California's not a swing state," said Zion Johnson.

Prowse smiled. "I like the way you think," he said. "I was thinking Grand Rapids, Michigan."

"A conservative stronghold in a Democrat-leaning state," said Zion Johnson.

"Exactly."

Zion Johnson frowned, turning to look at Michelle. She met his gaze impassively. It was clear he wasn't going to get a straight answer about who this little girl really was. Maybe he would never know. But Zion Johnson, having worked with agents from Mossad and the Saudi Arabian intelligence service, was used to dealing with shadowy figures. If the president didn't want to tell him who she was, he didn't have to. Danton Prowse didn't answer to Zion Johnson. All Zion Johnson needed to know was that this mission served America's interests.

He turned back to Danton Prowse. "Mr. President," he said, "is this some sort of test?"

"What do you mean?"

"I mean, are you pretending to propose a false flag terrorist attack just to see how I'll react?"

"Why would I do that?"

"I'm not sure. Either you're testing my conscience or my loyalty."

The president leaned forward and studied Zion Johnson's face. "Do you *have* a conscience, Zion?"

Zion Johnson thought for a moment. "A conscience is a weakness of the will, sir."

"You didn't answer the question."

"My will is strong, sir," said Zion Johnson.

"Good," said Prowse. He turned toward Michelle. "What do you think?"

The girl eyed Zion Johnson for a moment, then said, "I think he will do."

Prowse nodded and turned back to Zion Johnson. "So, Zion, are you in?"

"I'm in."

"Excellent," replied Prowse. "Oh, one more question. "Aren't you a Republican?"

"I am," said Zion Johnson. "But my country comes first."

# CHAPTER FIVE

*Brimstone Research Facility, Milpitas, California; August 2016*

It was the coffee pot that finally did Suzy Cilbrith in. Later she would claim it was simply an attack of conscience, but in reality it was the abject refusal of any of the male engineers to start a new pot of coffee that really made her lose her shit. It was bad enough that these Lawrence Livermore rejects couldn't get the calculus right on a damage assessment for a medium-sized American city, but it was simply unacceptable that they would take the last cup from the pot and not make a new one. It was a matter of basic human decency.

In the back of her insufficiently caffeinated brain, various moral and ethical qualms had been trying for some time to get some traction, but it was the coffee issue that finally brought things to a head. Suzy began to wonder what sort of monsters she was working with, who would deliberately empty the coffee pot and not make a new one. Occasionally she would confront one of the engineers, holding a pot that was empty save for a quarter inch of foul brown liquid swirling about the bottom, like a prosecutor dangling a revolver in front of a suspect, but the guilty party would just sit and stare at her, like *she* was the crazy one.

After the third such unproductive confrontation, she started to get philosophical about the problem. How was it possible for them to be so completely unaware of their own crime, even when presented with incontrovertible evidence? This line of thought led her to wonder whether she possessed similar blind spots about her own foibles. She spent her lunch breaks for several weeks cataloging her own day-to-day behavior, but was unable to pinpoint any particular activity that could be considered a true offense against her fellow engineers. She arrived on time, did what was expected of her, was cordial and professional (if not particularly warm) in her exchanges with co-workers, and respectful of her superiors. But then maybe her own biases had skewed her selection of criteria for acceptable behavior. She considered asking one of her co-workers to assess her criteria, but (for obvious reasons) she didn't trust their judgment. And perhaps such a request itself could be considered a violation of some workplace norm. How could she know? It was an ethical quandary.

Eventually she became so obsessed with this philosophical conundrum that it began to affect her work. She started to make mistakes in her calculations and miss deadlines. She justified these lapses by reasoning that determining whether she was committing any horrible ethical breaches in her interactions with her co-workers was at least as important as doing her actual job. This line of reasoning led her to reflect on the value of her job, which led her to the realization that she was working on an illegal program to produce an insanely dangerous weapon whose only conceivable purpose was to kill thousands of innocent civilians. Not only that, but the ultimate rationale for building the bomb was old-fashioned political ass-covering: the government had to produce a bomb so that it could claim that the bomb produced by the previous illegal nuclear weapons program hadn't been misplaced. The people she was working for weren't just evil; they were complete fucking assholes.

And that's how Suzy Cilbrith found her ethical blind spot.

She wasn't sure how her job had morphed from low-level quality assurance engineer into accomplice to mass murder (or at least mass deception). Her job had originally been to help assess the damage that would be caused by a Wormwood-style bomb to an American city. Specifically, she ran tests on the software that simulated a ten kiloton blast to make sure the software was working properly. The data from the simulations would be given to

Homeland Security, who would theoretically use it to train first responders, like firefighters, police and paramedics. The program—called Brimstone—was created by Congress after the Wormwood scandal, to make sure first responders were as prepared as possible in case the missing bomb were ever used in an American city. Congress was so concerned about the possibility of the Wormwood bomb being used on American soil that it approved a budget for Brimstone that was ten times that of the Wormwood project. All the scientists and engineers who had been fired from the Wormwood project were rehired for Brimstone, and many more were added. Suzy had been in college during Wormwood, but she was swept up in the Brimstone hiring spree, given top secret clearance, and put to work testing software.

All of this was kept secret, of course. Congress never explicitly authorized Brimstone; the funding was hidden in a vague bill aimed at "nuclear non-proliferation." It wouldn't do to let the public know that the government was terrified one of its own bombs would be used against it. The truly ironic part of all this was that the senior personnel on the Brimstone project (who were also the senior personnel on the Wormwood project) knew very well that Brimstone was completely unnecessary, because the bomb hadn't been stolen; it had been commandeered by agents working for President Babcock. They didn't know what Babcock had done with the bomb, but they knew it was unlikely to turn up anywhere in the United States. So these bomb-makers, who had been given a pointless task by bureaucrats who were in no position to judge whether the task were being properly carried out, went back to the President, who was in hot water over a lost bomb, and asked him whether their efforts might be better spent "finding" the missing bomb. Babcock met with the president-elect, Danton Prowse, and they agreed (with some prodding from a certain angelic advisor) that "finding" the bomb would indeed be Good for the Country. And just like that, the program designed to deal with the fallout of the Wormwood bomb became a program to build another Wormwood bomb.

None of the lower-level engineers—like Suzy—knew about any of this, of course. Suzy's first hint came when she tried to explain to the Homeland Security liaison how data in her simulation report could be of use to paramedics, and was met with a blank stare. He tried to cover it up, but it was clear to Suzy that the man had never actually talked to any first responders. Which was absurd, unless her superiors were misleading her about the whole purpose of Brimstone. She tried dealing with the problem the way she normally did: by getting a pedicure and changing her hair color—purple, this time—but this cure-all failed to soothe her conscience. Three months and twenty-eight empty coffee pots later, she finally snapped.

Suzy downloaded every incriminating document she could find about the program (there were a surprising number of them, now that she actually looked) to a thumb drive, slipped the drive into her pocket, and walked out the door.

It had been an impulse decision; she hadn't thought through what she was going to do. But she knew that she didn't want to be part of what Brimstone had become, and she suspected that she wouldn't be allowed to just walk out on her job. If she had been thinking clearly, she would have put in her notice and quit in a more acceptable fashion, but she couldn't imagine spending two more weeks in that facility. She was already ridden with anxiety; two more weeks would surely push her over the edge. Copying the files had been more an act of reflexive self-preservation than an outright act of defiance; she wanted to be sure she had some leverage in case her superiors tried to keep her from quitting or blackball with other potential employers.

But sitting home alone in her apartment the day after she walked out, she began to feel even more agitated than she had at work. She had the feeling that at any moment, somebody from Homeland Security was going to break down her door, ransack her apartment, and throw her in prison. She tried to imagine where they would look for the thumb drive, and then tried to imagine places where they wouldn't look. First she hid it in a potted plant, then inside one of the couch cushions, then taped it onto one of the blades of her bedroom ceiling fan. But all of these seemed like obvious places to look for contraband. Finally she hit on the idea of microwaving a tub of margarine just long enough for it to get soft, and then pushing the thumb drive (wrapped in cellophane) into the viscous goo. She smoothed out the surface of the margarine, put the cover on, and put it back in the refrigerator. If somebody knew of the existence of the thumb drive, they would undoubtedly still find it eventually, but she highly doubted anyone would dig through her margarine on a purely speculative basis.

With the thumb drive ensconced in its buttery home, Suzy should have felt some relief, but she didn't. She felt at loose ends, and not just because she had quit her job and had no way of making next month's rent. She felt like she had started something that needed to be finished.

She sat down at her computer and did an Internet search for "Wormwood scandal." She was familiar with the basics of the scandal, of course, but she'd been working part time and taking a full load of upper level computer science classes at Cal Poly when the scandal broke, so she hadn't had the time (or the interest, truth be told) to look into it very thoroughly. At the time she had no idea she would soon be working on the project that would succeed Wormwood.

The story was originally broken by a reporter named Gary Rosenfeld, who had been working for the *Washington Post* at the time. Rosenfeld's reporting was based largely on information gleaned from an unnamed source who had managed to get a hold of a lot of details about the Wormwood project. It didn't sound to Suzy like the source actually worked for Wormwood, but rather was a third party who had somehow found out about it—perhaps a foreign intelligence agent. Rosenfeld's initial reporting was borne out by admissions by the Babcock administration and an official investigation, but as the months wore on, Rosenfeld's articles and op-eds became more bizarre and speculative. In his final piece for the Post, he claimed that the U.S. government had been infiltrated by beings from another dimension, and that President Babcock had sent the bomb through an inter-dimensional portal in a pre-emptive attack on these beings' home dimension. That was a bit much to swallow, even for readers of the *Washington Post*, and Rosenfeld was canned.

Further research revealed that Rosenfeld was still at it: he was now writing for a fringe website known as BitterAngels.net. A quick perusal of the site indicated that Rosenfeld hadn't backed down from his bizarre claims, and had actually gotten even more outlandish. Now working out of San Francisco, Rosenfeld claimed that the "beings from another dimension" were in fact angels. Suzy had to read several of his articles to be sure that Rosenfeld wasn't using the term as a figure of speech; he really did mean that the U.S. government had been infiltrated by supernatural beings who had originally come down to Earth from Heaven. Many of these angels were technically demons, as they were in rebellion against Heaven. In any case, supposedly the gateway to Heaven had been cut off (by the detonation of the Wormwood bomb!), and now the angels/demons were running amok on Earth, causing all sorts of problems. Other than the fact that it featured angels instead of some more prosaic class of villain, most of it read like standard conspiracy theory drivel. In fact, if you replaced all the instances of "angel" with "Jew," the site could pass for anti-Semitic propaganda.

Suzy pondered her options. The more she thought about it, the more she realized she *had* to tell someone. Quitting in protest was all well and good, but it's not like the loss of a single software tester was really going to throw a wrench into the Brimstone bomb-works. If she was serious about her objections to the program, she needed to do more than quit. And while she feared retribution from those running the program, it occurred to her that she would be much easier to get rid of if she hadn't yet gone public about Brimstone. If she disappeared now, she'd be just another young woman gone missing. If she disappeared after releasing damning information about a secret government program, it would look very suspicious.

Was she being paranoid? Maybe. But she reminded herself that she was dealing with a government that had reacted to a scandal about an illegal weapons program by creating a bigger, more illegal weapons program. The Wormwood bomb—which was still missing—was capable of killing tens of thousands of people in a split second. And now the government was well on its way toward building another one just like it. Was it paranoid to think the people who created it would "disappear" one lowly software tester to keep it secret? She thought not.

But who should she release the information *to?* Her first thought had been Gary Rosenfeld, but if he had degenerated into some third-rate conspiracy theory hack, what was the point? On the other hand, at least Rosenfeld would probably take her seriously. She wasn't sure how damning the information on the thumb drive was. What if she went to a respectable news outlet and they rejected her? Then what? What if the Brimstone people found out she'd been approaching journalists? That would be the worst possible scenario: she'd get disappeared and nobody would ever know why.

Maybe the best bet was to go to Rosenfeld first and let him go through the contents of the thumb drive. Then at least somebody would have the information, so she wouldn't have to worry about being abducted by secret agents while waiting for a callback from the *Post*. If there were any bombshells (so to speak) on the thumb drive, the more respectable media organizations could always pick it up later. She was pretty sure that happened sometimes.

She found an address for the BitterAngels.net office in San Francisco and plugged it into her phone. It was less than an hour from Milpitas, so if the drive ended up being pointless, at least it wasn't long. She grabbed the tub of margarine from the refrigerator, got in her Toyota Tercel, and made her way to the address. It turned out to be a somewhat dilapidated tenement building in a rather seedy area. She left the Tercel on the street, unlocked. Anyone who wanted her shitty old stereo could take it without breaking a window, at least. She debated how to transport the thumb drive, finally deciding to keep it in the margarine tub, but not put the tub in her purse. She assumed that if she were mugged, the mugger would opt for the mystery prize inside her purse (a dollar forty-seven in change, Chapstick, eyeliner, and several used Kleenexes) over a guaranteed score of fifteen ounces of congealed vegetable oil.

But she made it to the building unscathed, and walked the three flights of stairs to the apartment in question. Taking a deep breath, she knocked on the door. After a moment of furious scurrying about inside the apartment, the knob turned and the door shot open a crack. An unassuming man with a three-day beard and tufts of brown hair sticking out from his scalp at various angles peered out at her. He didn't look much like the pictures of Gary Rosenfeld she had seen online.

"How much?" the man asked anxiously.

"Huh?" replied Suzy.

"Come on, come on," said the man. "For the butter. How much?"

"I don't... it's margarine," Suzy managed to bluster after a moment.

The man made a sort of retching sound and slammed the door. Suzy stood in the hallway staring at the plastic tub in her hand. After a moment, she raised her hand to knock again.

The door flew open and a fist shot out.

"I'm not..." she started again.

"Take it or leave it," said the man's voice from inside, wagging his fist at her. She held out her palm and the man dropped a fistful of change into it. It was mostly nickels.

"I'm not selling the margarine," she said. "I—"

"Free samples?" said the man.

"What?"

"Are you giving out free samples then?"

"I wasn't planning to..."

"Oh, I see!" shouted the man in sudden consternation. "Going around the neighborhood waving margarine in front of people's faces and then not even giving out samples. You're a margarine tease, that's what you are."

"It's just that..."

"Margarine tease!" the man screamed. "Margarine tease!"

Down the hall a door opened a crack and an old woman yelled back, "What's all the racket down there?"

"Margarine tease!" shrieked the man again.

"All right, all right, you can have as much as you want!" said Suzy. "Just quiet down!"

"Gimme my change back."

She handed him back the nickels and the door slammed again.

"Keep it down!" shouted the woman down the hall.

Suzy was just about to raise her hand to knock again when the door flew open once more. The fist shot out again, this time holding a butter knife. "Sample!" cried the man.

Suzy sighed and removed the lid. "I'm really not here to give out margarine samples," she said, as the man dug into the stuff with the knife. He pulled the knife back inside.

"Oh?" said the man, "then why did you bring it?"

"Well," replied Suzy, uncertainly, "there's something in it."

There was a spitting sound, followed by chunks of something that looked like half chewed bread flying through the crack in the door.

"Gyeeychhhh," groaned the man. "What do you mean? What's in it?"

"Are you giving away margarine samples down there?" shouted the woman down the hall.

"Yes, but it's got something in it!" shouted the man.

"What? Like jam?" asked the woman.

"Is it jam?" asked the man.

"No, it's… I'd rather not say. I'm looking for Gary—"

"It's not jam!" shouted the man.

"Is it sprinkles?" shouted the woman.

"Is it— "

"Please!" cried Suzy. "Stop yelling! I'm not here to give out samples!"

"Margarine tease!" shouted the woman.

"Margarine tease!" shouted the man.

"Margarine tease!" shouted the woman.

Soon they were chanting in unison. Halfway down the hall another door opened and a small Filipino woman stepped out in the hall. She seemed momentarily confused, but shortly was overcome by the spirit of the occasion. "Mar-jar-een-tees! Mar-jar-een-tees!" she shouted, and began to clap her hands. Two other residents opened their doors and joined in as well.

Suzy began to think she had made a terrible mistake. She put the lid on the tub, slipped it into her purse, and began to trudge back down the hall toward the stairs, the deafening chant ringing in her ears. As she opened the door to the stairwell, the chant broke off, turning into boos. By the time she made it to the first landing, it was quiet again, the building's occupants apparently having found something else to entertain them.

A hand fell on Suzy's shoulder. She screamed and tore herself away, bounding down the stairs in sheer panic. Tripping on torn carpet, she fell headlong down the steps, and for a brief moment she was convinced that she was going to die in a rundown tenement in Georgetown, her neck broken and her purse full of margarine.

But then something strange happened. Just as her head was about to hit the edge of a step, she just... stopped. For a second she hung there, almost completely upside down, her legs splayed in the air, staring at the stained carpet on the steps. Then gradually her body began to right itself, rotating until she floated a foot or so above the second floor landing. The feeling was odd—not like she was being suspended in a harness, but like gravity itself had been warped around her. Whatever mysterious force had gripped her, it slowly and gently lowered her to the landing.

Then she fainted.

# CHAPTER SIX

*Near Fernley, Nevada; August 2016*

Zion Johnson glanced at the clock on the truck's dash. It read *2:58*. In two minutes, with any luck, the truck would be hijacked by gun-toting terrorists. He'd posted information about the truck's payload and its designated route to an Internet chat room that he knew was frequented by members of Chaos Faction. His initial post, which was as explicit as he could be without attracting the attention of half a dozen different law enforcement agencies, was met with puzzlement by the terrorists. Zion Johnson could hardly believe they were having trouble parsing the meaning of his post; he'd been so explicit that shortly after posting he'd made preemptive calls to the FBI, CIA, NSA, and three other intelligence agencies to reassure them that his message was part of a Secret Service sting operation. The exchange went like this:

> **InsideDope1776:** recd tip on brimstone pkg heading east tmrw nite
> **Nisroc001:** hi insdiedope welcome back wats brimstone
> **InsideDope1776:** google
> **Nisroc001:** brimstone = google??
> **InsideDope1776:** no, google it
> **Nisroc001:** "Brimstone is an alternative name for sulfur." ???

**InsideDope1776:** google brimstone project
**Nisroc001:** wat is pkg
**InsideDope1776:** package
**Nisroc001:** wat is package
**InsideDope1776:** results of brimstone/wormwood project
**Nisroc001:** wat is wormwood
**InsideDope1776:** google wormwood
**Nisroc001:** "Wormwood is a shrubby perennial plant" ???
**InsideDope1776:** google WORMWOOD PROJECT
**Nisroc001:** oh! nuclear bomb!
**Nisroc001:** O.o
**InsideDope1776:** ...
**Nisroc001:** we r busy tmrw nite
**InsideDope1776:** srsly?
**Nisroc001:** no jk ☺ we can hijak bomb
**InsideDope1776:** advise verbal discretion ☹
**Nisroc001:** sorry we can hijack bomb
**InsideDope1776:** advise STOP SAYING B*MB
**Nisroc001:** sorry we can hijack nuclear device
**InsideDope1776:** jfc
**Nisroc001:** wat is jfc?

It took nearly forty-five minutes for Zion Johnson to communicate the critical details: that a truck transporting a small nuclear bomb would be passing Fernley, Nevada at 3am the next evening, traveling east. The at large members of Chaos Faction were to descend upon the truck just after it had passed Fernley and steal the bomb. As Zion Johnson watched the Fernley exit recede in his rearview mirror, he found himself hoping that the members of Chaos Faction weren't all as stupid as the one he had chatted with online the previous day.

As it turned out, they weren't, but only by a slim margin. The one called Izbazel landed with a loud thump on the truck's hood, making Zion Johnson glad he'd taken his blood pressure medication that morning. "Sorry we're late!" yelled Izbazel. "We stopped by Reno and Nisroc was on a bit of a lucky–"

BAM! BAM! BAM! BAM! BAM! BAM!

Izbazel's speech was cut short as he was riddled with bullets. The man sitting next to Zion Johnson, whose job was to protect the package in the back of the truck, had pulled his firearm and managed to get eight rounds into Izbazel's midsection before Izbazel fell backward onto the road and was promptly run over by the truck.

"We're under attack!" yelled the man next to Zion Johnson to the six men in the truck behind him, who were guarding the bomb. He slid the partially spent magazine out of his gun, grabbed another, and turned to Zion Johnson. "Did that guy apologize for being late before I shot him?"

Zion Johnson sighed. This was not how it was supposed to go down. He pulled the wheel to the right, driving off the road, and slammed on the brakes, bringing the truck to a halt in a cloud of dust. "Yeah, he did," said Zion Johnson. "And I know it doesn't help, but I'm sorry too, Dave." With that, Zion Johnson shot Dave three times in the head.

"What the hell was that?" yelled one of the men in the back.

"Everything's under control," said Zion Johnson, grabbing Dave's gun. "Stand down."

"Sir?" said one of the men in the back. Then: "Hey, back away from the truck!"

The sound of automatic weapon fire and incomprehensible shouts came from the back of the truck. After a few seconds, all was silent.

A figure dropped to the ground in the headlights of the truck and walked around to the driver's side door: Izbazel. He was covered in blood.

"Could have told me they were going to shoot at us," Izbazel said.

"You're stealing a nuclear bomb!" yelled Zion Johnson. "You didn't expect it to be guarded?" He got out of the truck and walked around to the back. Three unarmed men were standing at the rear of the truck. The back was open, and inside was a grisly scene. It appeared that the men had opened fire on each other, leaving no one alive. In the middle of the six corpses was an unmarked steel crate.

"You guys are bastards," said Zion Johnson.

"They were shooting at us," said one of the men. "I just redirected the bullets a little." It was hard to tell in the dim light, but Zion Johnson thought it was the one called Nisroc.

"Yeah, I see that," said Zion Johnson. He shook his head. He had hoped this could be done without bloodshed, but Chaos Faction obviously wasn't capable of that sort of finesse.

Izbazel walked up next to him. "Alright, what now?"

"First," said Zion Johnson, "get those guys out of the truck."

The three men hopped into the truck and began tossing the corpses onto the ground. Zion Johnson wanted to tell them to show a little respect, but it would be more convincing if it looked like the bodies had been carelessly thrown on the dirt. If all went as planned, there wouldn't be any investigation; the official story was going to be that the Wormwood bomb had been stolen years earlier, on Travis Babcock's watch. But Zion Johnson believed in being thorough, and that meant covering his tracks.

When the corpses had all been removed from the truck, Zion Johnson handed Dave's gun to Izbazel. "OK," he said. "Now shoot me in the leg."

"Really?" asked Izbazel.

"Yeah," said Zion Johnson. "And be quick about it. I see headlights up ahead. Try not to hit the—"

BAM!

Zion Johnson fell to the ground, clutching his leg. He had been about to say "artery," but now he was wishing he had said "kneecap."

"Jesus Christ, that hurts," he groaned.

"You want me to fix it?" asked the one called Nisroc. "I can just—"

"No!" growled Zion Johnson. "Just go! Take the bomb and go!"

Nisroc shrugged. Izbazel tossed the gun on the ground near Zion Johnson and then got into the driver's seat of the truck. Nisroc got in the passenger seat and the other two climbed into the back. The truck pulled away, leaving Zion Johnson lying in the dirt on the side of the highway.

"Superior attitude, superior state of mind," said Zion Johnson, and then passed out.

# CHAPTER SEVEN

*Milhaus, Texas; August 2016*

Mercury sat hunched over at the bar, nursing a Guinness and shaking his head. "Just when I thought I was out," he muttered, "they pull me back in."

"*Godfather*," grunted a beefy trucker sitting next to him.

Mercury turned to look at the man, who smiled sheepishly back at him. Mercury slowly leaned over, looking the man in the eye, and said, in a low, gravelly tone, "We've known each other many years, but this is the first time you ever came to me for counsel or for help. I can't remember the last time that you invited me to your house for a cup of coffee, even though my wife is godmother to your only child. But let's be frank here. You never wanted my friendship. And you were afraid to be in my debt."

The trucker's eyes widened and he leaned away from Mercury. "Wha...?" he started.

"I understand," Mercury continued, gesturing wildly with his right hand while leaning on the bar with his left. "You found paradise in America, you had a good trade, you made a good living. The police protected you and there were courts of law. You didn't need a friend like me. But, now you come to me, and you say: 'Don Corleone, give me justice.' But you don't ask with respect. You don't offer friendship. You don't even think to call me Godfather. Instead, you come into my house on the day my daughter is to be married, and you ask me to do murder for money."

"Oh, I get it," said the trucker. "That's pretty good. You're doing the—"

Mercury shook his head ruefully, wagging his hand at the man. "*Bonasera, Bonasera.* What have I ever done to make you treat me so disrespectfully? If you'd come to me in friendship, then this scum that wounded your daughter would be suffering this very day. And if by chance an honest man like yourself should make enemies, then they would become my enemies. And then they would fear you."

The man got up, downed the rest of his beer, and backed away.

"Someday!" Mercury called after the man, "And thatdaymaynevercome!" He paused for effect. "I'll call upon you to do a service for me. But until that day, accept this justice as a gift! On! My daughter's wedding day!" He let out a loud belch, and the patrons scattered about the bar laughed nervously, as if they weren't certain whether this was the end of the performance or the beginning of something far worse.

"Seen that movie three hundred times," said Mercury to the bartender.

"Congratulations," said the bartender, a dour old man. "Sounds like you've led a full fucking life."

"You don't know the half of it," said Mercury. "The half of it." He paused, mouthing the words to himself. "Is that right? It doesn't sound right. The half of it. Thehalfofit. Thehaffuvit."

"Jesus Christ, will you shut up?" growled a man further down the bar. "I'm trying to watch this." His eyes were on the TV screen overhead, which was displaying a news report.

A haggard, bearded man's face filled the screen. "…spent most of his years in a remote cabin in Idaho…" the newscaster was saying.

"What's this show about?" Mercury murmured to himself. Then louder, to the man down the bar, "Hey, what's this show about anyhow?"

"It's the news, you idiot," the man replied. "They're talking about Chris Finlan."

"Who?" asked Mercury.

"Shit, man, where have you been for the past six months?" asked the bartender incredulously.

Mercury shrugged. "Out of town?" he offered.

"Off your ass, more like," grumbled the man down the bar.

"Chris Finlan," said the bartender. "The guy that sent all those letter bombs. They tracked him down to some cabin in Idaho. Crazy motherfucker."

Mercury studied the leathery, hirsute image on the screen. "Crazy motherfucker," he repeated.

The bartender handed a beer to the man down the bar. "Do you think he was nuts before he moved to that cabin," the bartender asked, "or do you think being alone up there all the time drove him crazy?"

"One of them chicken/egg things," said the man.

"Hm," grunted the bartender.

"So," Mercury said thoughtfully, "this guy was all alone in a cabin, hundreds of miles from civilization?"

"Yep," said the bartender. "Can you imagine?"

"Yeah," said Mercury, nodding. "What did he do the whole time?"

"I guess he was working on some kind of book. He called it a mephisto."

Mercury frowned. "Why'd he name it after that asshole?"

"Huh?" replied the man.

"He means 'manifesto,'" said the bartender.

"Oh," said Mercury relieved. "That's good. Mephisto still owes me a hundred bucks on a bet we made about the lyrics of Pearl Jam's 'Yellow Ledbetter.' He said it was 'I don't know why I waited for a boxer or a bag,' but *I* said..." He trailed off, realizing nobody was listening to him. "So what was the manifesto about?"

"Who knows?" said the man. "Global warming or Communism or some shit. Sounds like he was pissed off about just about everything. He's a nutcase."

"Yeah," Mercury said, with a nervous laugh. "Sounds like it. So he just hung out in his cabin all day, writing crazy shit and making bombs?"

"I guess so," said the man.

"I suppose he probably read a lot," said Mercury. "You know, like all of those Charlie Nyx books."

"The kids' books?" the bartender asked, confused.

"Young adult fantasy," corrected Mercury. "Lots of grownups read them. Not just crazy people. Do you think he had beer? He must have, right? You don't go hang out in a cabin for six months

63

without beer. And Rice Krispies. No reason you couldn't just order an assload of Rice Krispies. Maybe get them delivered right to the cabin."

The two men were now staring dumbly at Mercury.

"Son," the bartender said, "what in blazes are you talking about?"

"I'm just... you know, theorizing," said Mercury. "Like those FBI profilers. Trying to get into the mind of a madman."

"Uh huh," said the bartender.

On the screen, the bearded man was being led away from the cabin in handcuffs.

"So that cabin," Mercury went on. "I suppose it's on the market now?"

The bartender stared at Mercury. "You want to buy that lunatic's cabin?"

"Sure, why not?" asked Mercury.

"How the hell are you going to do that?"

Mercury grinned. "I'm going to make him an offer he can't refuse."

# CHAPTER EIGHT

*Near Elko, Nevada; August 2016*

Izbazel drove until a little after dawn, finally parking the truck in an empty stretch of asphalt behind a gas station near Elko, Nevada.

"Why are we stopping?" asked Nisroc.

"Let's take a look at what's in the crate," said Izbazel.

They got out of the cab and went around to the back of the truck. Izbazel opened the door to find Konrath and Scalzi sitting hunched over the crate, playing cards.

"Out of the way," said Izbazel, climbing into the truck. Scalzi scooped up the cards and the two demons backed away.

Izbazel waved his hand over the crate and the latch popped open. He swung the hinged lid open and whistled as he looked inside.

"What?" asked Konrath. "What is it?"

"Another crate," said Izbazel. He reached in and pulled out a smaller crate, setting it down next to the first one. He opened the second crate and whistled again.

"Another crate?" asked Scalzi.

"No," said Izbazel. "One of these." He picked up a roughly rectangular object wrapped in brown plastic.

"What's that?" asked Konrath.

"Cute little nuclear bomb," said Izbazel.

"Awww," said Konrath and Scalzi in unison.

"What are those numbers?" asked Nisroc. Someone had written on the side of the bomb, in permanent marker:

*LAT: 42·94 LON: -85·06*

"What's LAT mean?" asked Konrath.
"What's LON mean?" asked Scalzi.
"Is there anything else in the crate?" asked Nisroc.
Izbazel looked. In fact, there was something else in the crate: a manila envelope. Izbazel opened the envelope and pulled out a thick sheet of folded paper. He unfolded it. It appeared to be some sort of schematic. On the lower left corner was printed:

### VANDEN HEUVEL BLDG—FLOOR 35

"Looks like some kind of map," said Konrath.
"For the Vanden Heuvel Building, wherever that is," said Scalzi.
"Anything else in the envelope?" asked Nisroc.
Izbazel looked inside the envelope, finding a sheet of paper on which was typed:

### BLUE PRINTS ARE FOR DIVERSION ONLY.
### LEAVE IN GRAND RAPIDS, MI
### WHERE POLICE CAN FIND.

### DETONATE BOMB AT SPECIFIED
### COORDINATES ONLY.

### PRESS RED BUTTON TO ARM.
### BOMB WILL DETONATE 30
### MINUTES AFTER ARMING.

### DESTROY AFTER READING.

"Is there anything else in the envelope?" asked Nisroc. "Something blue?"
Izbazel looked in the envelope. "Nope," he said. "Just the note and this map thingy."

"What's that?" Scalzi asked, pointing at a red X in the center of the map.

Izbazel shrugged. "Treasure?" he offered.

"Maybe that's where we're supposed to set off the bomb," suggested Nisroc.

"That's it!" exclaimed Izbazel. "We're supposed to bring the bomb to the thirty-fifth floor of the Vanden Heuvel Building, in Grand Rapids. The X is where we're supposed to detonate it. Good thinking, Nisroc!"

Nisroc smiled. It was nice to be recognized for good thinking. It didn't happen to Nisroc very often. But something still bothered him. "What about the blue prints?" he asked. "Why aren't they in the envelope?"

"What difference does it make?" asked Izbazel. "It says right here the blue prints are a diversion. From what I know about diversions, we're better off without them."

"But it says to leave them in Grand Rapids where the police can find them."

"I think it means the bomb," offered Scalzi. "We're supposed to leave the bomb where the police can find it."

"That doesn't make any sense," said Konrath. "Why would he want the police to find the bomb?"

"Beats me," said Izbazel. "Why did he ask me to shoot him in the knee?"

None of them knew the answer to that one.

"We'll just leave the bomb at the spot marked with the X," said Izbazel. "If the police find it, it's none of our business."

They all agreed this was a sound plan.

"What does 'destroy after reading' mean?" asked Nisroc.

"I think it means the numbers on the bomb," said Izbazel.

"What do the numbers mean?"

"Beats me," said Izbazel. "But we read them, so I guess we'd better destroy them."

"How?" said Nisroc. "That's permanent marker. He should have put some nail polish remover in the envelope."

There was general agreement that it would have been a good idea for Zion Johnson to provide them with nail polish remover if he was serious about them destroying the indecipherable markings on the bomb. Fortunately, Nisroc came up with yet another brilliant idea: wiping down a nuclear bomb with gasoline. It took a fair amount to completely obliterate the markings, but they knew that Zion Johnson would want them to be thorough.

Once the bomb was completely clean and drenched with highly flammable liquid, they put it back in the stolen army vehicle and got back on the road, headed for Grand Rapids, Michigan. Things were going well for Chaos Faction for a change.

# CHAPTER NINE

*San Francisco; August 2016*

Suzy regained consciousness on a couch that she gradually realized was inside the apartment of the strange man who had demanded to sample her margarine. The place was a mess, littered with newspapers, magazines and fast food containers. A few feet from the couch sat a small balding man who looked to be about forty. After a moment, Suzy recognized him as Gary Rosenfeld, the former *Washington Post* reporter. He sat at a small desk, tapping away at a laptop, apparently oblivious to her.

Suddenly remembering the hidden thumb drive, Suzy sat up and looked around feverishly for her purse. She needn't have worried: it was at the foot of the couch, with the margarine tub still inside. As she removed the lid to inspect the contents, the man she had met earlier walked into the room.

"Oh, hi," he said cheerily. "Do you want some bread with that?"

She ignored the man, turning toward Rosenfeld, who hadn't taken his eyes off his laptop screen. "Excuse me," she said. "Are you Gary Rosenfeld? The reporter?"

Rosenfeld didn't stir.

"Don't bother," said the other man. "He's in the zone. Can't hear you. I'm Eddie, by the way. Sorry about earlier. Sometimes I get a little crazy being cooped up here all day. Did you say you wanted bread?"

"I don't want bread," Suzy said. "I came here because of this."
She reached into the margarine and dug around until she found the
thumb drive.

Eddie regarded her with a look of horror as she held up the
device covered in yellowy goo. "Why would you *do* that?" he asked.

"Figured nobody would look in the margarine tub."

Eddie shuddered. "What's on it?"

Suzy began unwrapping the cellophane. "Information on
Project Brimstone. It's the—"

She jumped as the thumb drive disappeared from her fingers.
Rosenfeld had grabbed it from her and was greedily inserting it into
the side of his laptop.

"You said the magic word," said Eddie.

"Apparently," said Suzy, watching Rosenfeld tapping his fingers
impatiently on the desk as he waited for the files to come up. "So
what's your deal? Do you guys run the website together?"

Eddie sat down next to her. "BitterAngels dot net? Yeah. Well,
it's mostly Gary. I write a little, but mostly I just help out."

"What happened in the stairwell? Was that an example of you
'helping out?'"

Eddie shrugged. "You could say that."

"Seriously, how did you do that?"

"Levitation," Eddie said. "Minor miracle. All angels can do it.
Watch." He held out his hand and the margarine container floated
up from the coffee table where Suzy had set it.

"How are you doing that?" she asked. Her tone wasn't so much
awed as accusatory, as if Eddie were pulling something over on her.

"Manipulation of interplanar energy," he answered.

"Bullshit."

Eddie smiled. "Watch."

The lid popped off the container and a glob of margarine
emerged from the tub, slowly forming itself into a vaguely
humanoid shape. Eventually she realized that it was the likeness of a
young child, standing on some sort of pedestal. As Suzy watched,
the figure sprouted wings—and then another, much smaller
appendage. As she stared, open-mouthed, the appendage began to
emit an arc of yellowish effluent into the tub.

"Ew," Suzy said, aghast at the image.

"It's a cherub," said Eddie.

"It's revolting," said Suzy.

Eddie frowned. "I thought it was pretty good. He's a friend of mine. His name is Perpetiel."

"Keep your friend out of my margarine."

Eddie shrugged and the figure melted back into the tub.

"What is this crap?" asked Rosenfeld suddenly, tabbing through the contents of the thumb drive. "There's nothing new here."

"What?" said Suzy, who instantly forgot about the miraculous work of margarine sculpting she had just witnessed. "That's top secret stuff! I know it doesn't spell it out in so many words, but it's pretty obvious that they've resurrected Wormwood. The program intended as damage control for Wormwood became a program to build another bomb! Brimstone is just Wormwood Two!"

Rosenfeld shook his head. "Tell me something I don't know. Let me guess, the whole thing is run by angels who have infiltrated the government and are using their miraculous powers to keep everybody in the dark."

Suzy looked from Rosenfeld to Eddie to the margarine tub and back to Rosenfeld again. "Um, no?" she ventured.

"Ah," said Rosenfeld, with a knowing smile. "So you're still in the dark yourself. You've glimpsed the machine, but you haven't figured out who's running it yet."

"I read some of the stuff on your site," said Suzy. "So I know all about your 'angel' theory..."

"You just witnessed the spontaneous formation of a peeing cherub statue from a tub of margarine," Rosenfeld interrupted. "How do you explain that?"

"I also saved her life in the stairwell," said Eddie proudly.

"I'm still processing that," said Suzy. "I'll grant you that something unusual is going on here."

Rosenfeld laughed. "Unusual, right. Here's the deal: a while back, probably around 2002, Lucifer started assigning demons to infiltrate the U.S. government in Washington..."

"Whoa," said Suzy. "Lucifer? Like, the Devil?"

"Correct. Satan himself. You've read the Bible?"

"I saw the movie."

"All right, well I'm going to assume you're familiar with the basic mythology. Lucifer rebelled against God and took a bunch of angels with him. Those angels became demons. Really, it's just a bureaucratic distinction; it's not like they grow horns and bat wings or anything. Demons are just angels who aren't doing their assigned job. OK?"

"OK…"

"So Lucifer has been wreaking havoc on the Mundane Plane— that is, on Earth—for thousands of years. Some time in the past ten or fifteen years, he started assigning agents to infiltrate the U.S. government."

"Agents," repeated Suzy. "You mean demons."

"Correct. Fallen angels. Lucifer's agents kept a low profile for the most part; at first he was more interested in collecting information than actively influencing policy. But then he found out about Wormwood, and hatched a plan to get Babcock to use the bomb against Heaven."

"He did *what?*"

"It's complicated. The point is, the bomb blew up in the hub that connects Earth to all the other planes. So all the angels and demons on Earth are now stuck here, probably forever. Lucifer was apprehended by Heavenly authorities, so now there was this whole intelligence apparatus inside the U.S. government that had no one running it. A headless monster, if you will."

"So who's running Brimstone, if the monster has no head?"

"Somebody stepped in to fill the gap," said Rosenfeld. "Another angel."

"Like, a bad angel?"

Rosenfeld sighed and looked at Eddie.

"She didn't start off bad," Eddie said. "In fact, I always kind of liked her. I think she probably had good intentions when she took over for Lucifer…"

"She?" asked Suzy. "The angel is a woman?"

"Her customary appearance is that of a little girl," said Rosenfeld. "Her name is Michelle."

"Michelle?" said Suzy. "That doesn't really sound like an angel name."

"You probably know her by the male version of her name, Michael."

"Michael? You mean…"

"Right, the archangel," said Rosenfeld. "General of God's own army."

Suzy thought for a moment. "Are you sure you aren't just imagining all of this?"

"Are you sure you didn't just imagine a cherub peeing in your margarine?"

"No," Suzy said. "Actually I'm not. It occurs to me that maybe I hit my head in the stairwell and I'm hallucinating all of this."

Rosenfeld nodded. "One way to find out."

"What's that?"

"Fall down the stairs again. This time Eddie won't catch you."

She looked at Eddie, who smiled and held up his hands innocently.

"OK," said Suzy. "I'm going to provisionally accept that you aren't completely full of shit. But your story doesn't hold together. If Lucifer has been around for thousands of years, why did he just start infiltrating the U.S. government a few years ago? Wouldn't he have done his best to get agents in every major government, starting centuries ago?"

"He did," said Eddie. "How do you think the Holocaust happened? You don't get millions of people to close their eyes to something like that without some demonic influence."

"To answer your question, though," Rosenfeld said, "we don't know why he didn't infiltrate the U.S. on a large scale before now. He did have quite a bit of influence over some policies—we think that he had something to do with dropping the bomb on Nagasaki, and probably the internment camps during World War II, for example. But there was never any major effort to get demons into positions of importance in Washington before now. The few agents that Lucifer did have in the capital were all corrupted humans, which leads us to think that there may have been some kind of shield around Washington that prevented demons from entering. But whatever was keeping the demons out, it's gone now. The place is completely overrun."

"But this Michelle, the archangel, she's in charge now, right? So that's good?"

Rosenfeld sighed. "From what Eddie tells me, Michelle has mostly been on the right side throughout history. But now her biggest enemy, Lucifer, is out of the picture, and she's cut off from Heaven, so she has no one to point her in the right direction. Eddie's theory is that she's trying to create Heaven on Earth."

"And... that's a bad thing?"

"Michelle is all about control," Eddie said. "You can't create paradise if you give people freedom to screw it up. So she's going to keep looking for ways to increase her control—over the United States, and over the world as a whole. So far she's been pretty subtle about it, but she'll use fear if she needs to."

"What does that mean?"

"It means," replied Rosenfeld, "that her turning Brimstone into Wormwood Two is a very worrisome development."

"Well, we agree on that much," said Suzy. "Is there any way to stop Brimstone before they finish the bomb?"

Rosenfeld chuckled. "Not without going back in time," he said.

"Wait, what?" said Suzy. "Are you saying...?"

"They've done it. According to my sources, the bomb already exists. God knows what they're planning on doing with it. Hey, what's this?" Rosenfeld was looking at something on his screen.

"What?" asked Suzy. "I didn't have time to look through it very closely."

"It's a PowerPoint presentation that seems to have been saved in the wrong directory. The rest of the stuff in there is all technical crap, but this is higher level strategic stuff. Some kind of briefing for the higher-ups."

"Anything interesting on it?" asked Suzy.

"Hmm," replied Rosenfeld. "Mostly buzzwords and bullshit. But hey, check this out. The slide labeled 'Areas of Concern.'"

Suzy and Eddie peered over his shoulder.

There was only a single bullet point on the slide. It read

## • Mercury—Milhaus, TX?

"What's Mercury?" asked Suzy.

"Mercury isn't a what," said Eddie. "It's a who. But I thought he was gone, exiled on another plane."

"Well, somebody thinks he's in Milhaus, Texas," observed Suzy.

"But if that's true..." started Eddie.

"What?" asked Rosenfeld, who was apparently as much in the dark on this one as Suzy.

74

"Then we may have a chance to stop Michelle before things get out of hand."

"How?" asked Suzy.

"Well," said Eddie. "It isn't completely true that nobody knows why Lucifer didn't infiltrate Washington before this century."

"What are you talking about, Eddie?" demanded Rosenfeld. "What haven't you told me?"

Eddie shrugged sheepishly. "I never mentioned it before because I never thought we'd see him again… but I'm pretty sure Mercury knows how the demons were kept out of D.C."

# CHAPTER TEN

*The English Moor; Spring, 1773*

Angels and demons have fought with each other for control over the course of history since Lucifer first made an unauthorized appearance in the Garden of Eden. This struggle is rarely overt; it occurs almost entirely behind the scenes, unnoticed and unrecorded, save for the tireless efforts of the Mundane Observation Corps. In some cases the machinations of Heaven or Hell are so subtle that it's difficult even for a seasoned member of the MOC to determine who is working for whom, or what exactly they are trying to accomplish. Double agents and subterfuge abound, on both sides. The byzantine nature of the Heavenly bureaucracy also complicates matters; occasionally an MOC agent has found two different branches of Heaven to be working at cross purposes, such as when Apocalypse Bureau had assigned several agents to stoke the fires of the Crusades at the very moment Morality & Scruples were doing everything they could to get everybody in Christendom to just calm the hell down and think things over.

Sometimes one side or the other will achieve what appears to be a decisive victory only for the pendulum of history to swing dramatically the opposite direction. Heaven fought long and hard to bring about the ascendancy of Rome, for example, only to have the Republic devolve into a corrupt, despotic regime. Lucifer, working to corrupt Rome from within and urging the barbarian tribes on the borders to attack, eventually got his wish when the great city itself was sacked and the Empire dissolved. But Lucifer was powerless to stop the spread of Christianity and the diffusion of new ideas and technology throughout Western Europe that eventually led to the Renaissance and the Reformation. Good follows evil and evil follows good, and it isn't always clear which is which—even to the angels and demons who fighting for one side or the other.

Such was the case in the British colonies in North America toward the end of the eighteenth century. It was generally agreed in both Heaven and Hell that the acquisition and settlement of the American territories had been a positive development for the British Commonwealth. Heaven thus tended to assign its agents with the purpose of assisting the colonists in their efforts to subdue the new land and thereby increase Britain's hold on the continent. Lucifer, being opposed to positive developments on principle, did everything he could to wreak chaos with the situation. He wanted to see the nascent settlements devolve into chaos and cannibalism, and to make Britain regret ever staking a claim in the New World. Or, at the very least, he wanted to see France or Spain take the lead in the new continent. The French and Spanish were still in love with the idea of a centralized, autocratic authority. They loved their Popes and their Kings—and Lucifer loved them too, because they were so much easier to manipulate than those damned British assemblies and parliaments. Sure, occasionally you'd get stuck with an incorruptible pontiff like Gregory or a strong-willed and well-intentioned king like Frederick II of Prussia, but for the most part autocrats were pretty easy to control. The main advantage for Lucifer, of course, was that he had to corrupt one man instead of a hundred. Ever since the advent of parliamentary government in England, he'd had half his field agents running back and forth across the English countryside to whisper in the ear of some minister or other. It was exhausting.

So when Lucifer saw the possibility of sowing a rift between the colonists and the mother country, he took full advantage. Initially a full-scale revolution seemed unlikely; Lucifer hoped only to incite King George III into strong-arming parliament to pass some particularly onerous laws affecting the colonies. He would then encourage the colonists to overreact, preferably by rioting and maybe lynching a few British soldiers. The Brits would react by clamping down even harder on the rights of the colonists. And as an added bonus, once a precedent had been established for denying rights to certain subjects of the British Crown, the same principles could be applied elsewhere—even within England itself, and Britain would be well on its way back to an autocratic form of government.

Lucifer expected to encounter resistance to his plan from Heaven, but after working on the king and parliament for a few years he was surprised at how smoothly it was going. Guys like Edmund Burke tried to talk some sense into parliament, but Lucifer had George III in his pocket, and there were still enough sycophants to the throne that it was no great feat for the more intemperate minds to shout down the voices of reason. The Brits went along with every bad idea Lucifer whispered into George's ear, culminating with the Tea Act in 1773.

The only difficulty Lucifer had in his plan was his failure up to this point to incite the colonists to do anything particularly rash. Other than a mild riot in 1768 and the so-called Boston Massacre in 1770, his agents had been unable to foment any large-scale violence whatsoever. The Boston Massacre was a particular disappointment: months of groundwork had resulted in the killing of a grand total of six colonists, followed by the orderly arrest and trial of the implicated soldiers. Lucifer began to wonder whether there was something congenitally wrong with the colonists that left them so ill-disposed toward violence. They weren't cowards; he knew that. They'd shown no qualms about letting King George know exactly what they thought of his unreasonable demands. But if Lucifer was going to get the crown to crush the colonists with an iron fist, he needed the Americans to lash out in anger. He'd had several of his agents assigned to trying to stir up the rabble in Boston, but nothing had come of it. Finally, having decided that the matter required a more subtle touch, he summoned an old acquaintance who had no shortage of experience in plotting coups, revolutions, and other sorts of mayhem. The two met on a moonless night on the English moor in the spring of 1773.

"You're late, Tiamat," grumbled Lucifer. They had agreed to meet at the stroke of midnight.

"Humblest apologies, dear," replied Tiamat. "I've been dreadfully busy suppressing Jesuits in Portugal."

"Hmph," replied Lucifer. Tiamat's new thing was religious persecution. Lucifer had given up on persecution as a means to bloodshed and chaos when Constantine converted in 312 AD. As Christianity was a religion based on love, peace, and respect for the conscience of the individual, Lucifer had presumed that the dominance of Christianity would mean the end of orthodoxy enforced at swordpoint. As usual, though, Lucifer had underestimated humanity's capacity for irony. Tiamat, who had long been jockeying to get in on the religious persecution game, had taken over where Lucifer left off, inciting the emperor to outlaw various heresies and gleefully overseeing the execution of Pelagians, Antinomialists, Donatists and anyone else not willing to toe the line on any of the various complex and obscure Church doctrines that had been settled on. Lucifer still wasn't sure what Tiamat's endgame was; he suspected that partly she was just resentful of organized religion ever since the Babylonians picked that pinhead Marduk over her as their patron deity. As with most haters of religion, her hatred was more about herself than any particular creed.

"In any case, I'm here now, love," said Tiamat, in the highly affected aristocratic accent she adopted whenever she was in Britain. "How might I be of service to your lordship?"

"You can drop the 'love' nonsense," said Lucifer. "I'm well aware that you hate me, and be assured the feeling is mutual. And it would be ever so wonderful if you'd stop trying to sound like you're at high tea at the palace."

"Fine," said Tiamat, dropping the accent. "What do you want, Luce? I'm busy."

"I need your help," replied Lucifer. He'd practiced the words, but he still had a terrible time getting them out.

"Wow, that must have just about killed you," said Tiamat. "Must be important. Are the seeds of rebellion you've been sowing not bearing fruit?"

"A bit of a mixed bag," said Lucifer. "I've got King George and parliament passing repressive laws left and right. And from what my agents in America tell me, the colonists are just about fed up. The only problem is, I can't get them to react. Ordinarily I'd expect angry mobs burning King George in effigy and the like, but these Americans are impossible to get riled up. You know me, I'm all about violence and mayhem. If I don't see peasants with pitchforks, I start to worry."

"So you want me to stir up some trouble in the colonies?"

"Not necessarily," replied Lucifer. "I was hoping you could make some calls, figure out if Heaven's running some kind of psy ops campaign."

Tiamat chuckled. "What, an angel on Sam Adams' shoulder, that sort of thing? You have demons in Boston, don't you? Wouldn't they have noticed something like that?"

"I would have thought so, yes," replied Lucifer. "But maybe it's something subtler than that. Something my agents are missing. I'd just like to know what I'm dealing with."

"I can look into it," said Tiamat. "I've still got quite a few well-placed angels feeding me information. What are you going to do for me?"

"Well, what do you want?"

Tiamat smiled. "France."

Lucifer coughed. "What? The country?"

"No, the laundry detergent. Yes, the country. I want you and your demons out of France."

"What are you planning?"

"None of your business."

Lucifer thought for a moment. He, Tiamat, and several other demons had been fighting for dominion over Western Europe ever since the fall of Rome. Tiamat had substantial influence in most of the Catholic countries, but Lucifer had free rein in Britain, Germany and the lowland countries. He only had enough agents in France to keep Tiamat in check.

"For how long?" he asked.

"Fifty years," said Tiamat.

"Thirty," said Lucifer. "And I want your spies out of Britain for the same period of time. Don't insult my intelligence by acting like you don't know what I'm talking about."

Tiamat smiled. "Deal," she said.

"Hang on," said Lucifer. "You haven't said what you're going to deliver to earn your prize."

"What's your goal?" asked Tiamat. "What do you really want out of this?"

"The usual," replied Lucifer. "Mayhem and destruction."

Tiamat sighed. "You know what drives me nuts about you, Lucifer?"

"My impeccable fashion sense?"

"Your complete lack of imagination. It's all riots and lynchings and massacres with you. You don't see the big picture."

Lucifer didn't argue the matter. When Tiamat wanted to expound on something, it was usually best just to let her. And if he was honest with himself, she did have a point: Tiamat had always been better at seeing the big picture than he. The whole religious persecution thing was only one example. But Tiamat's focus on the big picture was also her downfall: her tendency to overlook details had more than once brought one of her grand schemes crashing down. It was how Lucifer had been able to maintain the edge in their rivalry over the past 4,000 years.

"So I ask you again," Tiamat went on, "What do you really want out of this mess in the colonies? What's your endgame?"

Lucifer tried to think like Tiamat, focusing not on petty crimes and minor massacres, but on the big picture.

"War," he said.

Tiamat smiled. "Better," she said. "I'll give you a war."

"When?" asked Lucifer. "I don't want to have to wait a century for this thing to boil over."

"Within two years of today," said Tiamat. "There'll be a pitched battle between the Americans and the British."

"Two years?" said Lucifer dubiously. "You realize I've been working on this for close to a decade. These people do nothing but talk. The British pass an outrageous law and the Americans tear it up and send an angry letter to the king. That's all they've done for five years now. It's like trying to start a fire underwater."

"Give me two years," said Tiamat. "You'll have your war."

Lucifer shrugged. "Then you'll have France, my dear."

# CHAPTER ELEVEN

*San Francisco; August 2016*

"So this Mercury," Suzy said. "Is he an angel or a demon?"

"Ehhh…" Eddie replied.

"What does that mean?"

"Well, you remember when the Moon got imploded?"

"Doesn't ring any bells."

"Seriously?"

"Of course I remember when the Moon got imploded. How would I not remember something like that? A third of the Moon just disappeared, and nobody knows why."

"Yeah," said Eddie. "That was Mercury."

"Um, no. It was the Moon."

"No, I mean Mercury was the one who imploded the Moon."

"Whoa," said Suzy. "So a bad guy then?"

"He was actually trying to keep Earth from getting imploded."

"So a good guy."

"Ehhh…"

"You're not being very helpful."

Eddie sighed. "Mercury is basically a good guy. He's gotten into some trouble in the past though, because he doesn't always follow orders."

"But that's good, right?" Suzy asked. "He follows his conscience instead."

"Ehhh…"

"Stop doing that!" Suzy snapped.

"Mercury tends to do his own thing," Eddie said. "But I think he could be convinced of the seriousness of the problem. He's a good guy to have on your side, if you can keep him focused."

"So how do we find him?"

"Well, he's easy enough to spot," said Eddie. "He's about six foot four and he has silver hair. Also, he tends to stand out for other reasons."

"Like?"

"He's... well, he's just... Mercury."

"Milhaus, Texas has a population of 2,014," said Rosenfeld, looking it up online. "Shouldn't be too difficult to find an unusually tall guy with silver hair in a town that size."

"Unless the feds have already found him," added Suzy. "What's the date on that PowerPoint?"

Rosenfeld peered at the screen. "File was created August ninth."

"Shit, that's two days ago," Suzy groaned.

"Hang on," said Rosenfeld. "The date on the title slide is August twelve."

"So that's the date the presentation will be made," said Suzy. "With any luck, nobody's even seen this yet!"

"Nobody except whoever made the presentation. And whoever they got the intel from."

"Is there a name on the presentation?"

"Not that I can see."

"It was probably put together by some low-level paper-pusher," said Suzy. "Look at the rest of this crap. It's all standard project management jargon about low-hanging fruit and core competencies. This is probably just a standard weekly project status update."

"They buried a serious threat to their entire program on the sixteenth slide of a PowerPoint presentation?" asked Rosenfeld skeptically.

"You have to understand how these guys work," said Suzy. "This isn't a military intelligence operation. These guys are mostly software geeks and engineers. So when they see a potential problem, they make a note of it and it goes on a PowerPoint presentation for some manager to deal with eventually. Somebody at the FBI or some other agency probably spotted Mercury—if he stands out as much as Eddie says, he's undoubtedly on some terrorist watch list—and they reported it to their higher ups. Somehow that information eventually filtered over to somebody inside Brimstone, and they put it on the PowerPoint for next week's meeting."

"So it might have been days or weeks ago that Mercury was spotted in Milhaus," said Rosenfeld. "There's no telling where he might be now."

"Well, if this is the only guy who knows how to put a stop to Brimstone, we've got to take our chances."

"Whoa, I didn't say that," said Eddie. "I said I thought he might know how the demons were kept out of D.C. I don't know whether he'll be able to help with Brimstone, or whether he'll even want to. Besides, Gary and I have a lot of work to do here."

"What kind of work could be more important than preventing the government from creating an illegal nuclear bomb whose only purpose would be to commit a major terrorist attack?" Suzy demanded.

"Look, we're not activists," said Rosenfeld. "We're journalists. We just gather information and post it online. We don't have an agenda."

"Of course you have an agenda!" exclaimed Suzy. "What's the point of any of this if you don't have an agenda? What's the point of exposing that the U.S. government is overrun with demons if nobody does anything about it?"

"You seem to have gotten over your skepticism," Eddie noted.

"Frankly," said Suzy, "I don't know what to believe. A few days ago I suddenly realized that I was working on a secret program to build a nuclear weapon, so apparently it's time for me to reassess some things. I'm not entirely convinced that you guys aren't a little loony, but you seem to have a better grasp of what's going on than most people I've talked to lately. So if you tell me there's a guy in Milhaus, Texas, who might be able to help put a stop to Brimstone, I say we go to Milhaus, Texas."

"We can't just leave," Rosenfeld protested. "We've got a website to run. There are thousands of people depending on us for information."

"Yeah, more people hiding in their apartments not doing anything about the secret coup that's somehow taken place under all of our noses. You know they have the Internet in Texas, right? You can update the site from there."

Eddie and Rosenfeld fell silent. It was clear that neither of them had any interest in leaving the apartment, much less traveling to Texas.

"Fine," Suzy snapped. "I'll go myself. I'll find this Mercury guy and we'll put a stop to this." She had hoped she might be able to shame them into going, but neither of them took the bait.

Rosenfeld handed her a BitterAngels.net business card. "Email me if you find him," he said. The card showed two angels, complete with halos, standing back-to-back, their arms crossed and frowns on their faces.

"Whatever," said Suzy, pocketing the card. "I need to use your bathroom."

Eddie pointed to a room down a short hall and she stomped off.

She was washing her hands when she heard a loud crash from the other side of the door, followed by the commotion of several men bursting into the apartment and shouts of "On the floor!"

Suzy ran for the one small window in the bathroom, and struggled to get it open. It wasn't locked, but it appeared to have been painted shut. She pulled as hard as she could, but it wouldn't budge.

Another crash sounded behind her, and she realized someone had kicked in the door to the bathroom.

"Hands up!" yelled a gruff voice. "On your knees!"

Suzy sighed and held up her hands. But as she did so, she noticed something odd: the paint had cracked all along the edge of the window, and the window was slowly sliding up.

"Hey!" yelled the man behind her. "Don't..." He trailed off. "What the hell?"

Suzy risked a glance behind her, and immediately saw the cause of the man's consternation. The man was wearing full combat gear and pointing an assault rifle at her, but the barrel had begun to droop, slowly going limp before his eyes.

"You're getting older," Suzy said. "Nothing to be ashamed of." And with that, she launched her upper torso through the open window. Vertigo overwhelmed her as she took in the view of the street below. She was only on the second floor, so a fall was unlikely to kill her, but it was also unlikely to be painless. And if she broke a leg, she'd never get away from these gun-toting goons. There was a small ledge outside the window, though, and from there she thought she could jump to the fire escape.

She managed to climb the rest of the way out the window and get herself perched on the ledge. Just as she was about to jump, though, a hand reached through the window and grabbed her ankle. She lost her balance and fell, bracing herself for impact with the street below.

But the hand held on. After a moment, another hand gripped her ankle, and then a head appeared. It was the same guy who had busted in the bathroom door.

"Hey, it's Mister Projectile Dysfunction," Suzy said, hanging upside down. "You're pretty strong. Steroids?"

"Ha ha," said the man. "I'm going to pull you up now. Don't fight me, or—" He broke off as the sound of gunfire erupted inside. "Shit!" he exclaimed, and began to pull her in through the window.

But Suzy, who was convinced that if she were apprehended now, she'd never see daylight again, did fight. She kicked and screamed and twisted, trying not to think about what would happen if she actually managed to get away. Down below, a garbage truck was making its rounds, and Suzy had seen enough action movies to know this was just the break she needed. If she could time her fall with the passing of the garbage truck, she'd only fall about five feet. Still farther than she'd ideally like to fall, especially considering that she'd be doing the falling head first, but she'd probably avoid serious injury.

As the truck approached, she fought with even more ferocity, and finally the man apparently had enough. He let go and she fell toward the truck below.

And missed it by six inches. She'd either miscalculated the truck's speed, or the man had let go a half-second too late. Either way, she was about to kiss pavement.

But she didn't.

For the second time in one day, she stopped falling in mid-air, eight inches from the ground.

And then she started falling again.

And stopped when she hit the ground.

"Son of a bitch!" she yowled, curling into the fetal position and holding her head. Falling from a height of eight inches was surprisingly painful. She wasn't bleeding, but she was going to have a nasty bump on the top of her head.

"Sorry about that!" called a voice from the window. It was Eddie. "I got distracted. Oh, shit." He disappeared back inside.

There was another burst of automatic weapon fire, followed by someone groaning in pain.

"Cripes, that hurts," moaned Eddie, sticking his head out the window again. "Hang on, I'll be right down."

By the time Suzy had gotten to her feet, Eddie had appeared at the door of the apartment building. He was carrying a Spider-Man backpack, which seemed a little weird to Suzy. Not nearly as weird as the six bloody bullet holes torn in Eddie's shirt though.

"Oh my God," she cried, rushing to him. "You've been shot!"

"Only six times," he said. "It's—ow—not so bad. I'll be fine in a few minutes."

"You're in shock," she said, putting her arm around him to steady him, as if he were about to fall over at any second. "We've got to get you to a hospital."

"I'm *fine*," Eddie insisted. "Look." He pulled up his shirt to reveal bullet holes that had already begun to close up.

"How... how is that possible?" she asked.

"Immortality, accelerated healing," muttered Eddie. "Benefits of being an angel. Too bad Rosenfeld wasn't so lucky."

"Rosenfeld!" cried Suzy. "Where is he?"

"Boy, that's the real question, isn't it?" said Eddie. "Beats me."

"What? Isn't he upstairs?"

"His body is, but Rosenfeld isn't home anymore. Poor bastard. I never should have dragged him into this."

"He's dead?" she gasped.

"Afraid so. My fault, too. I should have killed all those guys as soon as they walked in the door. This is what I get for trying to minimize violence."

"So did you kill them?"

"No, they're unconscious. Killing them actually would have been easier. Stop their hearts, just like that." He snapped his fingers. "Anyway, we should get going. Where's your car?"

"My car? Where are we going?"

"I thought you said Texas."

"Oh. Right now?"

"Well, there will probably be about fifty more federal agents here in about two minutes. Probably three or four demons too, now that they know who they're dealing with. So unless you want to be around for that, I'd suggest we leave now."

"Gotcha," said Suzy. "This way."

# CHAPTER TWELVE

*Boston; November 17, 1773*

Mercury trudged up the narrow wooden steps to the meeting room he'd been told was above the tavern. Stopping at the top of the stairs, he knocked three times, paused, knocked again, paused a little longer, then knocked six more times.

The door opened and a young blond man peered out at him.

"Who are you?" the man asked.

"My name," said Mercury, "is Lord Quinton Squigglebottom, Earl of Northwest Halfordshire."

"I see," said the man. "And why do you knock in such an odd manner?"

Mercury shrugged. "I figured you guys had some kind of secret knock. Did I get it right?"

"Who is it?" called a voice from inside the room. "If it's not Tobias with more beer, send him away."

Mercury surreptitiously slipped his hand behind his back and then revealed it again, holding a pitcher of dark brown liquid.

"How did you..." gasped the man.

Mercury grinned and slid past the man into the room. The room was small and windowless, with just enough room for a table and a dozen chairs, in which sat a dozen men of greatly varying appearance, dress, and social station. Some were well-dressed and apparently affluent; a few looked like they had just gotten off work at the docks.

"Greetings, Sons of Liberty!" cried Mercury. "I am Lord Quinton Squigglebottom, Earl of Northwest Halfordshire. I have been moved by reports of the oppressive treatment of your people by the British government and have journeyed long across the sea to come to your aid." He began refilling the men's mugs. Several of the men grunted in appreciation.

"Northwest Halfordshire, you say," said one of the better dressed men. "Where is that, exactly?"

"It's in the north," said Mercury. "Between East Blandwich and South Doorchester Croft. Ing. Ham."

"Uh huh," the man replied.

"Anyway," Mercury went on, "After hearing of your plight, I've decided to commit the considerable resources of my estate to your cause. Starting by paying for your beer."

The well-dressed man, whom Mercury took to be the leader of the group, seemed unconvinced, but he motioned for Mercury to take a seat. "My name is Samuel Adams," he said. He motioned toward a dapper-looking gentlemen to his right. "This is John Hancock, whom you no doubt know by reputation." He continued around the table: "Henry Bass, Thomas Chase, Everett Drake, Adam Johnson, Benjamin Edes, Patrick Henry, James Otis, Paul Revere, Benedict Arnold."

Mercury nodded at the men in turn. "Lord Quinton Squigglebottom at your service, gentlemen. Please, call me Quinton. But I've interrupted your discussion."

Samuel Adams nodded and gestured toward John Hancock.

"I was just saying," said Hancock, "that we've received word that the King seems intent on enforcing the Tea Act—"

"Oh!" cried Mercury suddenly. Hancock frowned, and all eyes turned to Mercury.

"It's nothing," said Mercury. "Please, go on."

"As I was saying," Hancock went on, "if His Majesty insists on forcing the issue by sending ships laden with..."

Mercury had his hand clamped over his mouth, and he was bouncing up and down in his chair like a three-year-old with a secret.

"What is it, Lord Squigglebottom?" demanded Hancock.

"Quinton, please," said Mercury. "It's nothing, really. Well, not nothing. I didn't want to interrupt your high-minded discussion of democratic ideals with mere facts."

"To what facts are you referring," said Paul Revere. "Speak plainly, sir!"

"Oh, just the three ships on their way to Boston right now, stacked to the jibs with British tea."

Outraged groans and gasps escaped several men at the table.

"How do you know of this?" Hancock asked.

"They were loading the tea as my ship disembarked from Portsmouth. I'd expect them in a fortnight, at the latest."

"Outrageous!" cried Patrick Henry. Several of the men murmured agreement. An animated discussion ensued about the proper response to the ship's arrival, and quickly turned into a contest of who could suggest the most extreme action in the matter. At first it was suggested that the tea be unloaded and left in a padlocked warehouse to rot. Then someone suggested throwing the tea overboard and burning the ships. Finally, Mercury suggested that the Sons of Liberty should dress up as Indians, burn the ships, and slaughter the crews. This had the effect of both solidifying Mercury's status as a patriot and horrifying the rest of the assembly.

"That seems... a bit extreme," said Samuel Adams. Hancock, Revere, and several others nodded in agreement. Patrick Henry shrugged, as if he'd been willing to go along with it but wasn't going to argue the point. Benedict Arnold remained silent. The man who had first suggested burning the ships, Everett Drake, was trying to get the floor back, but Adams wouldn't yield.

"I think the most reasonable course of action is to leave the ships and crews alone, but to dump the tea into the water. That makes our point without resorting to unnecessary violence. After all, it isn't the fault of the East India Company or its crews that the King is illegally taxing the tea."

"Hear, hear!" cried Hancock and Revere.

Mercury seemed a bit put out. "Can we still dress like Indians?" he asked hopefully.

"I'm not sure I see the point of that," replied Adams.

"Indians are bad ass," answered Mercury.

"Pardon me?" asked Adams, puzzled.

"I just thought it would be neat," mumbled Mercury quietly.

"It would be a good idea to conceal our identities," noted Revere. "Perhaps Quinton is on to something."

"Really?" asked Mercury, a bit surprised to hear one of his ideas taken seriously.

"I agree that we should wear disguises," said Revere. "But I don't quite grasp the Indian angle. I was thinking we would wear sheets, with pillowcases for hoods."

"That's... not a good look," said Mercury.

"I like the Indian idea," said Hancock. "And it's easy. Strip down to your pants, rub on some warpaint, grab a hatchet, and start whooping it up with war cries."

Mercury winced. "Well, you're not going to win any sensitivity awards, but yeah."

"Plus," said Thomas Chase, "we can use the hatchets to break open the crates."

"Good point," said Adams. "OK, then it's agreed. When the ship arrives, we board it dressed as Indians and throw the tea into the water."

The men murmured agreement and then, having finished the pitcher of beer Mercury had miraculously produced, adjourned for the evening. Several of the Sons of Liberty proclaimed how happy they were to have such a prestigious and wealthy nobleman on their side, and Mercury, in return, expressed how lucky they were to have him. They said their goodbyes and Mercury walked off alone down the darkened cobblestone streets of Boston.

"Quite a performance in there, Lord Squigglebottom," said a woman's voice from the shadows.

Mercury shrank back. "Hawk your wares elsewhere, foul harlot!" he cried, "Unless you have change for a sixpence."

The woman stepped out of the shadows, smirking wickedly at him.

"Oh," said Mercury. "It's you."

"I thought you'd be happy to see me," said the woman, affecting profound disappointment. "It's been so long."

"What do you want, Tiamat?" asked Mercury. "I'm working."

"I know you are," said Tiamat. "The question is, who are you working *for*? You've got Lucifer's agents completely befuddled."

"Yeah, well, that's not exactly difficult. Lucifer isn't known for the intellectual caliber of his minions. Like that Everett Drake, or whatever his name really is."

Tiamat smiled. "How long did it take you to pick him out?"

"I had my suspicions as soon as I walked in the room. He's got that shifty, stupid look that characterizes so many of Lucifer's agents. Like somebody who thinks he's clever for figuring out a joke ten minutes after everybody else has stopped laughing. I knew for sure when he suggested burning the ships. Such an obvious Lucifer play. The guy has no sense for the big picture."

"Exactly what I was just saying," Tiamat said with a chuckle. "Unlike you."

Mercury shrugged. "I just go with the flow."

"You follow your instincts," said Tiamat. "Everett Drake—his real name is Ramiel, by the way—comes up with a bad idea, and instead of arguing against it, you trump him with an absolutely terrible idea. Suddenly the rabble-rousers are split between two bad ideas, and the more sensible members realize they need to reassert control. So instead of burning the ships, the Sons of Liberty agree to just quietly toss the tea overboard. Understated but effective."

"Hmm," Mercury said. "So what's your interest here? I thought you were busy eviscerating Huguenots."

"I'm taking a break," said Tiamat. "Doing a favor for Lucifer."

"I thought you hated that guy."

"I do. I suppose I should say that Lucifer *thinks* I'm doing him a favor. He's frustrated that his agents haven't been able to provoke more mindless violence in the colonies. So I told him I could start a war between Britain and America in less than two years."

"What does war have to do with mindless violence?" Mercury asked. "War takes deliberate planning and organization. There's no natural progression from mob violence to war."

Tiamat sighed. "See, this is why I like you, Mercury. You get me. Lucifer doesn't see any arbitrary, random violence going on, so he worries that war is never going to break out. He hasn't grasped the fact that the bloodiest wars happen after resentments have simmered quietly for years."

"You really think war is going to happen within two years?"

"It better. My plan to conquer France is riding on it."

"Your what?"

"Never mind. Private business between me and Lucifer. Isn't war what you want? I thought that's why you're here."

Mercury sighed. "You know how Heaven is. I can't get any straight answers. My assignment was to 'stir up patriotic sentiment' in the colonies. I don't exactly know what that means. In any case, there's plenty of patriotic sentiment already. Mostly I'm just trying to keep these guys from doing anything incredibly stupid."

"Well, you seem to be doing a fine job, from what I can tell," said Tiamat.

"So you aren't going to interfere?"

"Of course not," replied Tiamat. "I don't care if the so-called Sons of Liberty have a little tea party. I just came here to confirm what I already suspected: war is going to break out, and it's going to happen whether Sam Adams' little band act like bloodthirsty brigands or the paragons of civilization."

"Well, I guess that's what Heaven wants too, so for once everybody's in agreement."

"Except you."

Mercury shrugged. "I'm not a big fan of war, but the matter seems to be out of my hands. So I'll just keep stirring up patriotic sentiment."

"Have fun with that," said Tiamat. "Well, I'd better go. Those Huguenots aren't going to eviscerate themselves."

With that, Tiamat disappeared into the night. Mercury shook his head and continued on down the street. Having no need of sleep, he planned to fly to New Hampshire overnight and do some reconnaissance to gauge the level of support in that area for declaring independence from British rule. First, though, he had to get out of Boston. It wouldn't do for some nosy shopkeeper to see him taking flight.

As he neared the end of the cobblestone street, he heard what sounded like a footfall behind him. He spun around, peering down the dark street, but saw nothing but the dark outlines of rooftops against the night sky. Even with his preternaturally acute angelic vision, he saw no sign of anyone.

"Tiamat?" he asked, uncertainly. But there was no answer. He doubted it was Tiamat anyway; she wasn't known for slinking around—and certainly not after making one of her dramatic exits.

After a moment, Mercury shrugged and continued walking. Whoever it was, they were unlikely to be a threat to Mercury. Even if one of the locals did see him leaving the ground, he'd be dismissed as a lunatic by his peers if he said anything about it. Mercury walked a ways onto the muddy ground beyond the cobblestones, took another look around, and leaped into the air.

As he arced to the south, he took a glance behind him again. He couldn't be sure, but he thought he saw a lone figure leaning out from behind a building, watching him.

# CHAPTER THIRTEEN

*Somewhere in Idaho; August 2016*

Suzy held her breath as the Tercel struggled up the steep, winding mountain road. The inside of the car was silent except for the whine of the motor and the barely audible strains of Duran Duran's "Rio" squawking from the radio. Neither she nor Eddie had said a word for at least a hundred miles, neither of them wanting to put voice to the worry that was going through both of their heads.

"What if it's not him?" Suzy asked at last.

Eddie sighed. "What if it *is* him?" he replied. After walking around Milhaus, Texas for a couple of hours, they found a bartender who recognized Mercury by Eddie's description. The bartender said the man had expressed a disconcerting amount of interest in the remote cabin previously occupied by crazed bomber Chris Finlan.

Suzy's brow furrowed and she looked over at Eddie in the passenger's seat. "What does that mean?"

"It means don't borrow trouble from the future. Or be careful what you wish for. Something like that. Anyway, let's just concentrate on getting this rust bucket to the cabin."

"I thought you could perform miracles," Suzy said. "Or do they only work on domestic autos?"

"I don't know anything about cars," Eddie said defensively. "I can use interplanar energy to push a car up a hill, but it's not like I can miraculously fix your carburetor."

"You think something is wrong with my carburetor?" asked Suzy, suddenly worried.

"I have no idea!" exclaimed Eddie, irritably. "I wouldn't know a carburetor from Carmen Sandiego. And frankly I'd have better luck finding the latter."

"Usually it's not too hard," she said. "If you pay attention to the clues."

"Slow down," said Eddie. "The turn should be just ahead. There."

Suzy braked and turned down the dirt track. "Are you sure this is it? It doesn't even look like a driveway."

"What are you expecting, a remote mountain cabin with an expressway up to the front door? This is it."

They drove another three miles down the track, mostly in first gear. The ground was uneven and peppered with rocks and potholes. After nearly an hour of punishing conditions, the Tercel groaned to a halt in a small clearing. On a small ridge overlooking them was a tiny, crude wooden structure that looked vaguely like a chicken coop.

"That can't be it," Suzy said.

"I think that's it," replied Eddie.

"Chris Finlan *lived* in that thing? No wonder he went crazy."

"He was crazy before he moved in."

"He'd have to be."

They left the car and made their way up a steep path leading toward the cabin. Two minutes later they were standing in front of it.

"We're here," said Eddie.

"I thought it was farther away," replied Suzy.

The cabin was even smaller than it seemed at first sight, and in worse repair. Suzy doubted any self-respecting chicken would voluntarily live there.

"So what now?" asked Suzy.

"What do you mean?"

"I mean, is there some kind of special angel greeting?"

"Yeah, it's called knocking."

They walked up to the door, which seemed to be basically a sheet of plywood on hinges. Suzy knocked three times. They waited.

"Maybe he's sleeping," said Suzy.

"Angels don't sleep."

"Maybe he's out for a walk."

"Angels don't walk."

"Maybe there's some kind of secret knock," said a voice from behind them. "Try knocking three times, waiting, knocking again, waiting a little longer, and then knocking six more times."

"Mercury!" cried Eddie, turning around to face the lanky angel. Suzy turned and backed away a step. Eddie was right: this guy would be hard to miss.

"Hey there, guy!" said Mercury enthusiastically. "And you!" he exclaimed, turning to Suzy. "How *are* you?"

"You have no idea who I am, do you?" asked Eddie, a bit dejectedly.

"Of course I do!" cried Mercury. "You're... that... guy... that I met that time... in that place. And how could I forget your adorable purple-headed friend!"

"We've never met," said Suzy coldly.

"Exactly," said Mercury, "You're unforgettable, so obviously we've never met."

"I'm Ederatz the cherub," said Eddie. "I used to work for the Mundane Observation Corps before... well, before you blew up the planeport with a nuclear bomb, trapping me here forever."

"Right, right," said Mercury. "And we met at the..."

"In Los Angeles. Remember? I was the one who told you about the bomb."

"Of course! The bomb that blew up the planeport. Man, how do you sleep at night?"

"We're here because Eddie thought you could help us," said Suzy, who was getting irritated at Mercury's antics.

"Sure, sure," said Mercury. "Come on in."

He pulled on the block of wood that passed for a handle on the plywood door, eventually managing to wrench the badly warped door open, and gestured for them to enter. Eddie ducked under the low doorway and Suzy followed. Mercury had to get almost on his knees to get inside.

The cabin was so small that once inside, Mercury could simultaneously touch all four walls, the floor and the ceiling. In fact, he didn't have much choice in the matter. He arched over Suzy and

Eddie like a curious pterodactyl. There was no furniture in the cabin except for a lumpy mattress that covered half of the floor.

"It's rustic," said Mercury, by way of apologizing for the tight quarters.

"It's cramped," said Suzy, wrinkling her nose. "And it smells like pot and urine."

"Not urine," said Mercury. "Ammonia. The previous owner was a little eccentric." He leaned over and put his face close to a discoloration on the carpet. "And he seems to have spilled some... well, no, that's pretty clearly urine."

Suzy threw the door open and stomped outside. She could hardly believe she had driven halfway across the country to find this buffoon. *This* was the guy that Eddie thought could help them shut down Brimstone? She pondered getting in her car and leaving the two nut cases to catch up while she figured out what the hell she was going to do with whatever was left of her life. Or would Eddie miraculously cause her car to break down as she drove away? Even a mechanical dimwit like Eddie could give a car a flat tire. What was the range of his miraculous power, she wondered—if that was what it was. And could this Mercury character perform "miracles" as well? If so, why hadn't he done something about that *smell?*

"How about if we talk outside?" said Mercury, emerging from the cabin. Eddie followed behind him.

"We're leaving, Eddie," said Suzy.

"What?" asked Eddie. "Why?"

"This guy can't get a urine stain out of his carpet," said Suzy. "What makes you think he's going to be able to help us with our demon infestation?"

A hurt expression appeared on Mercury's face. "It's not that I can't get the urine stain out. It's just that I've been busy."

"Busy doing *what?*" asked Suzy.

"I'm writing a manifesto," announced Mercury proudly. "Hey, Eddie, aren't you some kind of writer?"

"I've dabbled a little with—" Eddie started.

"Hang on, you're going to love this." Mercury ducked into the cabin and then reappeared with a sheaf of paper. "Now keep in mind that I'm not a professional writer like you, so this may be a little rough." Mercury cleared his throat and began reading. "Mercury's Manifesto," he began. "By Mercury."

"I would like to talk to you today about some political issues that I think are important. First, I want to talk a little about a woman's right to choose. I strongly support a woman's right to choose. It should go without saying that I also support a man's right to choose. To my way of thinking, they should take turns. For example, first the man might choose a nice restaurant for them to go to. Then the woman could choose a top to go with her beige capri pants without asking the man whether he likes the blue one or the green one better. Then the man might choose to have cheesecake for dessert, and the woman might choose to get her own cheesecake rather than eat all of the man's.

"Next, I would like to talk about flag burning. A lot of people say flag burning isn't a serious issue, because hardly any actual flag burning takes place. These people are missing the point. The point is that without a law forbidding flag burning, anyone could hypothetically burn a flag whenever he or she sees fit. And that's what I have a problem with: the hypothetical flag burning. I believe that we should not only outlaw burning flags; we should also outlaw the hypothetical burning of flags. Let's say, for example, that you were to burn a flag in your backyard. Under a typical anti-flag burning law, you would go to jail. But under my enhanced anti-flag burning law, you and I would *both* go to jail: You for burning the flag, and me for suggesting a hypothetical situation in which you burned the flag. And there we would sit, in our respective jail cells—mine real, yours hypothetical—reflecting on our respective real and imaginary crimes.

"I also have some opinions on the War on Terror. I am strongly in favor of the War on Terror. In fact, I think the War on Terror should be drastically expanded to include all other unpleasant states of mind, such as boredom and 'the heebie jeebies.' I don't think we should stop fighting until we are all happy all of the time. But we must stop before we hit Complacency, because the war will be on that too.

"Finally, what is the deal with the climate controls in cars today? I mean, can they make these things any more complicated? It's like somebody decided—"

"STOP!" shouted Suzy. "That is the worst manifesto anyone has ever written, and I'm including *The Communist Manifesto*, which led to the deaths of ten million people in Stalinist Russia. Ugh. For someone who's supposedly thousands of years old, you sure act like a hyperactive middle-schooler."

Mercury smiled and turned to Eddie. "I like her. She really gets me."

"Let's go, Eddie," growled Suzy.

"No, wait," said Eddie. "Look, I know he's kind of a lot to handle, but I really do think he can help us."

"Help you with what?" asked Mercury. "It's not urine stains in the carpet, is it?"

"You know Wormwood?" said Eddie. "The program that created the bomb you detonated at in the planeport?"

"Um, sure," said Mercury.

"Well, they've re-launched it. It's called Brimstone now."

"So?" Mercury replied. "The U.S. government has like eighty bajillion nukes. What's one more?"

"Those nukes are tightly controlled by the military. And they're not exactly easy to steal. You saw the Wormwood nuke. You could fit it in a backpack. The only real reason to build a weapon like that in the first place is to stage a false flag terror attack. And it's outside the military chain of command, so it could easily go missing... just like the last one did. And this isn't theoretical. We have intelligence indicating the second bomb has already been built."

"Yeah, yeah," said Mercury. "False flags, rogue nukes, secret programs... typical political bullshit. Not interested."

"Hang on, you haven't heard the worst of it," said Eddie. "It turns out the whole government is lousy with demons. They were the ones behind Wormwood, and now Brimstone. The whole thing was probably Lucifer's idea. And you know who's running the show now that Lucifer is out of the picture?"

"Karl Rove?"

"Michelle."

"*The* Michelle?"

"Yep."

"Well," said Mercury. "That's... um, good, then, right?"

"You tell me." said Eddie. "Would you trust Michelle with control over the U.S. government, now that she has no one in Heaven giving her orders?"

"Hmm." Mercury said. "I'll grant you that Michelle can be a little... overzealous at times."

"A little? Am I the only one who remembers the Crusades?"

"Hey," said Mercury. "Back up a minute. How can the government be overrun with demons? They can't get into Washington. What, are they telecommuting from Virginia?"

Eddie shook his head. "That's the problem. Whatever barrier there used to be to angels and demons getting into Washington, D.C., it seems to have fallen. The place is crawling with them. We came to you because I remembered that you were around when the barrier went up. I thought maybe you could help us figure out what happened and fix it."

"What difference, at this point, does it make?" Mercury asked. "The demons are there now, and the bomb already exists. Even if we were somehow able to chase the demons out of D.C., the damage has been done. You think this country is going to be better off with *humans* running it?"

"Alright," said Suzy, putting her hands on her hips. "Now you're just pissing me off. We did just fine running this country until you guys came along with your secret programs and plots and schemes. If you don't want to help put things right, that's fine, but don't act like we're better off because your kind is in charge now. From where I'm sitting, it looks like you guys have royally fucked us all. What is that?"

This last was in reference to a faint whistling sound that could be heard in the distance. It was quickly growing louder.

"Get down!" cried Mercury, tackling both of them.

The cabin exploded with a deafening blast and a great orange fireball. A sound like prolonged thunder followed and then subsided into a dopplerized whine as the jagged silver shape of a small jet airplane shot overhead, not a hundred yards up.

"Into the woods!" yelled Mercury, grabbing them by their arms and hoisting them to their feet. The three of them ran for cover as the jet arced back toward them.

# CHAPTER FOURTEEN

Mercury sighed as he knocked on the door to Uzziel's office. As if his weekly status reports weren't bad enough, he was required to show up in Heaven once a month for a face-to-face meeting with the director of Apocalypse Bureau. This required flying halfway around the world, from Boston to Megiddo, Palestine, taking the interplanar portal to the planeport, and then taking another portal from the planeport to Heaven. The trip usually took about ten hours, depending on the weather, and it was almost always completely pointless. Uzziel was a typical bureaucratic paper-pusher: he rarely had any real guidance to give, and Mercury was convinced that he insisted on these meetings primarily to remind Mercury of his authority. Mercury, who didn't like being reminded of anyone's authority, tended to look at the meetings as an opportunity to make Uzziel rethink just how badly he really needed to see Mercury.

"Come in!" Uzziel barked, and Mercury opened the door.

"Ah, Mercury," beamed Uzziel. "How go things in the colonies?"

"The colonies," said Mercury, "are brimming over with patriotic fervor. Parades, fireworks... it's like the fourth of July over there."

"Huh?" replied Uzziel. "What's happening on the fourth of July?"

"Don't you remember the supernova that started on July four, 1054? The whole sky was lit up."

"Hmm, yes," said Uzziel. "That was quite something. So it's going well?"

"More or less," replied Mercury. "There have been some complications, though."

"Oh?"

"Yeah, Tiamat showed up yesterday."

"Tiamat! What does that crazy bitch want?"

"I did some investigating, and it looks like she's working for Lucifer. I know, I know, I didn't believe it either at first. They've got some kind of deal worked out. Anyway, Lucifer does *not* want the colonists to revolt, and he's got Tiamat doing everything she can to dampen the patriotic fervor I've striven so hard to cultivate. Striven? Strived? I've strived to cultivate. Striven. The patriotic fervor I've been working so hard on. STROVE! That's it."

"Are you going to need help? I can probably free up a couple of agents..."

"No, no, you know me," said Mercury. "I can handle it. But I'm going to be working a lot of overtime dealing with this whole Tiamat situation. Going to need some extra time off when this assignment is done to decompress."

"Sure," said Uzziel. "Just make sure this war happens."

"War?" asked Mercury. "You never said anything about war."

"Didn't I? Well, technically we're anti-war, of course. But the higher-ups are very big on popular sovereignty right now. You know, democracy, the will of the people, all that. They've seen how much more work it is for Lucifer to corrupt the British parliament than to manipulate a king, and they've decided to go all out in favor of democracy. And the more democracies, the better. So if we can get the Americans to make a clean break with Britain, it's win-win. For that matter, if it goes badly enough for the Brits, they might start to rethink their imperialistic policies in other areas of the globe. Anyway, that's the thinking upstairs. No need to trouble yourself with all that. Just keep stoking the fires of American patriotism."

"You know me," said Mercury. "Jingo is my middle name."

"Your middle name is what?"

"Jingo. J-I-N-G-O."

Uzziel glared at him. "I can see where this is going, and if you think I'm going to play along…"

"J-I-N-G-O, J-I-N-G-O, and Jingo is my name-o!" Mercury sang.

"Very nice," Uzzile said coldly. "You're dismissed."

Mercury got up and went to the door. "Don't forget about my extra vacation time," he said. "I'm working my ass off down there."

"Uh-huh," replied Uzziel. "I'm making a note of it right now."

"You're not writing anything down."

"It's a mental note. Please go."

Mercury opened his mouth to object, thought better of it, and left the room. It was better not to push too hard when Uzziel got in one of these moods. It seemed like he was taking this whole democracy thing pretty seriously. Mercury didn't really get it; to him democracy just seemed like the same old thing with a bigger group of idiots running the show. But who was he to argue with Heaven?

Mercury left the Apocalypse Bureau building and took the portal to the planeport. While he was walking down the planeport concourse to the portal that would take him back to the Mundane Plane, he spotted a familiar face. It was a face of an infant, and it was attached to the body of an infant, which sprouted birdlike wings from its torso. The odd-looking creature fluttered down the concourse toward him.

"Perp!" cried Mercury. "Good to see you."

"Good to see you too, Merc. Still stirring up patriotic fervor? You should clean and re-tighten a thatched roof once a year." Perp's other major idiosyncrasy—besides appearing to be a winged infant—was his compulsive need to give out impertinent and unsolicited advice. Mercury had always liked Perp, so he did his best to humor the strange little cherub.

"Once a year," said Mercury. "Got it. Hey, what do you know about democracy?"

"Terrible idea," said Perp. "A line of salt on a windowsill will deter ants."

"Why do you say that?" Mercury asked. "Not the ant thing."

"You can't put common people in charge. What do they know about anything? That's why God created noblemen. Use vertical strokes when washing windows outside and horizontal for inside windows. That way you can tell which side has the streaks."

"You really think noblemen are a better class of people than commoners? They all seem about the same to me."

"I don't know about *better*," said Perp. "But they're more suited to ruling. Commoners don't know what's best for them. Nobles see the big picture. You can clean brass with a paste made of corn meal and white vinegar."

"I suppose," said Mercury. "I mean, they wouldn't be in charge if they weren't better at governing, right?"

"Exactly," said Perp. "Cream rises to the top. Good talking to you, Merc." And with that, Perp buzzed off down the hall.

"Yeah, you too," said Mercury. "Hey, wait. Was that last thing one of your tips, or…?"

But Perp was already out of earshot. Perp was an Interplanar Transport Facilitator, and as such he was always busy carrying luggage or escorting some VIP from one end of the planeport to another. By virtue of his job, he heard a lot of gossip, so he was Mercury's go-to guy for the breaking news. It was hard to say how much he really understood about abstract concepts like the divine right of kings or popular sovereignty, though. Probably he was just repeating what he had heard from some bigwig, the way he repeated his tips without really thinking about them. He supposed that corn meal and vinegar probably made a decent brass polish, but he wasn't convinced Perp's political philosophy was as sound.

Mercury sighed and made his way to the portal that would take him back to the Mundane Plane.

# CHAPTER FIFTEEN

*Somewhere in Idaho; August 2016*

The F-15 wasn't alone. It was followed by another, which roared overhead even lower than the first, strafing the ground with its machineguns. Having taken cover as best they could in the trees, Mercury, Eddie and Suzy huddled together on the ground. There wasn't much point in trying to outrun a pair of fighter jets.

The first plane arced right and the second arced left. Either jet had enough firepower to kill them all a thousand times over, so Suzy desperately hoped that Mercury wasn't as big of an idiot as he seemed.

"Eddie, defense!" Mercury yelled over the roar of the jets.

"Got it," said Eddie.

"Don't move, don't do anything, understand?" Mercury said. "Just keep purple-head safe."

"I'm on it," said Eddie. "Go!"

"Go?" squeaked Suzy. "Where the hell is he…"

But Mercury had already shot into the air, and was soaring directly toward the jet on the right.

"You guys can *fly*?" asked Suzy, awed.

"We're angels," said Eddie. "Of course we can fly."

The jet continued to roar toward them; Mercury looked like he was going to intercept it in about five seconds.

"What's he going to do when he gets there?" Suzy asked, getting to her feet.

The jet's machine guns fired again, and Mercury rolled to the right to evade the trails of fire and metal tearing through the sky.

"I have no idea," said Eddie. "Stay close. I need to make a protective bubble around us, and the bigger I have to make it, the weaker it is."

Suzy remained standing, transfixed by the sight of the tall man soaring through the sky toward the jet, his silvery hair glinting in the sunlight. This Mercury guy might have the mental capacity of a hyperactive teenage boy, but he had balls of steel. He remained on a collision course with the jet, and she felt the muscles tighten in her shoulders as she realized he wasn't going to be able to get out of the way. The jet was going to hit him.

Had that been his plan? Take out the jet by flying directly into it? If so, then Mercury's bravery was outweighed by his stupidity. Even if he managed to take out one jet that way, what about the other? How was Eddie supposed to handle the other F-15 if he was guarding her? For a moment, she considered taking off at a run to free up Eddie to take on the other plane, but in the split second before Mercury collided with the plane, he suddenly pitched sharply, sliding along the F-15's underside. Suzy exhaled and slumped down next to Eddie on the ground. The plane that Mercury narrowly missed continued on its course toward them, with the second plane close behind.

"What was the point of that?" Suzy asked. "Is he just playing chicken with fighter jets for fun?"

"Well, it wouldn't be the first time, from what I've heard," said Eddie. "But I don't think so. Look!"

The pilot had ejected from the plane. His chute deployed and he began to drift lazily to the ground, while the plane kept going. It roared overhead and disappeared behind the trees.

Suzy peered after the plane. "Did he—" she started.

"Keep your head down!" snapped Eddie. "Here comes the other one."

Plumes of dust erupted as the ground in front of them was pelted with bullets. She clamped her eyes shut and clutched tightly to Eddie as the gunfire bore down on them. Suzy had never prayed before, and she had never given much thought to the existence of miracles, but she was praying for one now.

And then the bullets were hitting the ground on the other side of them. Suzy could hardly believe they hadn't been hit.

"You OK?" asked Eddie.

"I think so," Suzy replied. "How…"

"I bent space around us a few inches," said Eddie. "I can bend time too, but it takes too long."

Suzy felt something warm and wet on her thigh. She pulled away from Eddie, thinking she had lost control of her bladder in her terror, but then she saw a dark spot spreading rapidly across Eddie's shirt.

"You're hit!" she cried.

"Yeah," he said glumly, as if he'd just scratched off a losing lottery ticket. "Bending space… it's tricky."

"Can you fix it?"

"Yes, but not… while I'm shielding us from… those bullets."

Suzy bit her lip, watching the blood spread across Eddie's midsection. If angel biology was anything like human biology, he was going to lose consciousness in a matter of seconds. The jet had passed over and was now arcing back toward them. Mercury remained poised directly overhead, contorting his limbs in various strange configurations.

"Um," said Suzy, forgetting for a moment about Eddie's condition. "What is he doing?"

"Stretching, I think," said Eddie quietly, staring placidly up at the sky. "It's important to be… limber when you're going… head-to-head with an F-15."

The jet was now bearing down on Mercury, a blaze of automatic weapon fire tearing through the air toward him. This time, though, Mercury didn't remain in place. He shot upward into the clouds, disappearing from view. After a moment, the jet altered its course, dipping lower toward the ground. Its guns were now trained on Eddie and Suzy.

"Where did he go?" asked Suzy urgently.

But Eddie was beyond responding. His eyelids were fluttering, and his eyes had begun rolling back in his head.

"DEFENSE!" shouted Suzy, slapping Eddie on the cheek.

Eddie jerked awake, blinking in the sunlight.

Gunfire tore up the ground, showering Eddie and Suzy with dirt and gravel, but once again Suzy was miraculously spared. The jet shot into the distance.

Suzy regarded Eddie. His eyes were closed, and his head slumped to his chest. Blood was everywhere. Her understanding was that angels were immortal, so presumably he would somehow recover from this, but he wasn't going to be much help in the near future. She was torn between her desire to help Eddie in any way she could and her instinct to get as far away from him as possible. Finally deciding that Eddie was beyond her help and that tactically it made more sense for them to split up, she got to her feet and started running. Maybe she could draw the F-15's fire long enough for Eddie to recover. She'd probably get herself killed in the process, but there was no helping that.

The plane was arcing back around once again, and she realized with mixed emotions that her plan was working: she'd successfully drawn the pilot away from Eddie; the plane was bearing down on her directly. She was running as fast as she could, but she might as well have been sitting still as far as the F-15 was concerned. Still, she wasn't going down without a fight.

Then she tripped on a root and fell sprawling to the ground. Dazed and panting, she rolled onto her back and watched as the jagged silvery shape of the plane grew steadily larger. At any moment those guns would open up, and she'd be done for.

But as she watched, something shot down from the clouds past the plane, clipping its right wing and sending it into a spin. As it passed overhead, the spin slowed but the plane developed a bad wobble.

Suzy jumped as something crashed through the foliage behind her, and she whipped around in time to see Mercury land on his back with a thud.

"Oooowww," He groaned. He turned his head to look at Suzy. "Hey, how's it going?" he asked.

"Um, OK," she replied.

"Where's Eddie?"

"Back that way. He got shot."

"But you're OK?"

"I think so."

"Cool."

The plane pitched upward, trying to gain some altitude, but the wobble was growing worse. Black smoke was pouring from its tail. It was pretty clear the plane was going to crash, but the pilot hadn't ejected.

"Ugh," said Mercury, getting slowly to his feet. "Be right back."

He shot into the sky again, heading after the F-15. Soon they both disappeared behind the trees.

After some time, Suzy became aware of a figure shambling toward her through the woods.

"Eddie!" she cried. "You're alive!"

"Yeah," he said, with his hand clamped over his belly. "I don't seem to have much choice in the matter. Where's Mercury?"

"He's..."

But just then, Mercury appeared overhead, with a flight-suited figure slumped over his shoulder. He touched down and lay the man out on the ground.

"Is he alright?" Suzy asked.

"Yeah, just unconscious. Took a knock when I winged him." Mercury unstrapped the man's helmet and face mask. "Earth to Maverick," Mercury said, slapping the man lightly on the cheek. The pilot groaned and opened his eyes.

"You OK?" asked Mercury.

"Mmmm," groaned the man.

"Are you sure?" asked Mercury.

"Yeah," said the pilot. "I'm fine. Head hurts, but I'm fine."

"OK, good," said Mercury, and slapped the man hard across the face. "That's for firing on civilians, you ass-brained fucktard." Mercury got to his feet. "Alright," he said to Eddie and Suzy, "we should probably go before they send in the big guns."

# CHAPTER SIXTEEN

*Vermont; May 1775*

If the political situation in Revolutionary America was complicated by the intriguing of angels and demons, it was even more so by the bickering and rivalries going on in the colonies themselves. Lucifer, short-sighted as always, had done his best to inflame local prejudices, not realizing that this interference would make it difficult to unite the colonies in an all-out war against the British.

Take, for example, the New England militia known as the Green Mountain Boys, which was founded by a farmer/philosopher/land speculator named Ethan Allen. When they weren't at their day jobs, the Green Mountain Boys spent their time harassing and occasionally beating up land surveyors from New York. This was due to the British Crown granting New York authority over land that locals considered part of New Hampshire (now Vermont). New York's governor insisted that the Vermonters pay for land that they had already purchased from New Hampshire, and the Vermonters were understandably resistant.

It was only when news of the British firing on Americans at Lexington and Concord that the Green Mountain Boys realized they had a bigger problem than the New Yorkers. And even then, Ethan Allen took some convincing.

"Don't you see?" asked Mercury, sitting on Ethan Allen's front porch. "It's the British who are the problem here. Get rid of the

British and you can settle your quarrel with New York on your own terms."

"I've got a few dozen men, all volunteers." said Allen. "Stout men, who could undo a Redcoat's buttons from 300 yards, but still, a small group. You want me to take on the British Empire with a few dozen men?"

"Not the whole empire," said Mercury. "I was thinking Ticonderoga."

"A fort in New York," said Allen, grinning. "I like the way you think, Mr. Mercier." Mercury had dropped the Lord Squigglebottom act in favor of posing as a Frenchman who had come to America to support the independence movement and seek adventure. He didn't bother with affecting an accent; he figured he looked odd enough to pass for French in these parts without going overboard. He'd made some vague statements indicating that he had powerful friends back in France who would be sympathetic to the American cause.

"It makes good strategic sense," said Mercury. "If you hold Ticonderoga, you cut off communications between the northern and southern units of the British army. Also, it would be a good staging ground for an invasion of Quebec." These were talking points he'd received from Uzziel, who presumably got them from somebody in Michelle's organization. These days the Heavenly Army seemed to spend most of its time keeping track of troop movements in Europe and America; there was a lot going on. Mercury didn't pay much attention to it; he just hoped he wasn't spouting utter nonsense to Ethan Allen. "Just think," he went on, "if you attack the fort now, the Brits will be taken completely by surprise. Ethan Allen would be forever known as the first great hero of the American Revolution." This part Mercury had come up with on his own.

Allen threw his head back and laughed. "Very good, Mr. Mercier. All right, let's storm Ticonderoga. It'll take a couple of days to get the guys ready. Maybe you can send word to your friends in France."

"Certainly," replied Mercury. "They'll be very excited to hear of your plans."

The two shook hands and Mercury left on another reconnaissance mission. He spent the next two days mostly in

North Carolina and Virginia. Although war had not been declared, the scent of gunpowder was in the air after Lexington and Concord. Everywhere Mercury went, the inevitability of war seemed to be sinking in. The atmosphere was infused with a sort of melancholy excitement, like the lull before a storm. Everybody—Lucifer, Tiamat, and the powers-that-be in Heaven—were going to get what they wanted. That was good news, Mercury supposed, although he wasn't particularly excited about having to go through another war. Having been around almost since the beginning of human civilization, he'd seen more than enough wars. The good news was that once war officially broke out, this assignment would be over and he could finally take some time off. He had nearly eighty years of vacation time saved up, and he planned to take it as soon as he could away from this backwater continent.

By the time he returned to Vermont, the Green Mountain Boys had assembled and were nearly ready to march on Ticonderoga.

"Mr. Mercier!" cried Ethan Allen, upon seeing him. "You almost missed the excitement! You are coming along, aren't you?"

"Wouldn't miss it," said Mercury, trying his best to express enthusiasm. "I love killing people over real estate."

The next morning they were trudging through the woods toward the mouth of Lake Champlain, and a week later they were in the town of Castleton, awaiting supplies and reinforcements. Ethan Allen had just called a war council of his officers in the town square when several men came galloping up horses. Mercury and the other men jumped to their feet, ready to square off against the newcomers, but it was clear from their clothing the men weren't Brits.

The leader, wearing the insignia of a colonel of the Continental Army, pulled up short. He looked to be in his mid-thirties, with an angular nose and small, piercing eyes. Mercury felt his gut tighten when he saw him. He'd seen this young colonel before, dressed in civilian clothes and drinking beer in an upper room in Boston.

"Greetings, gentlemen," said the man, handing the reins of his horse to an underling and stepping toward the assembly. "I am Benedict Arnold of the Continental Army. I've been empowered by the Massachusetts Committee of Safety to seize Fort Ticonderoga from the British."

Mercury edged backwards, trying his best to look inconspicuous.

"What, you and a dozen men?" cried Ethan Allen, regarding the small group on horseback.

"The rest of my contingent is back at the Massachusetts border," said Arnold. "We received word that your little band was planning an assault on Ticonderoga, and I came as quickly as I could. I'm afraid that I must insist that you delay your attack until my men arrive."

The entire assembly of Ethan Allen's men broke into laughter, Allen included. When he recovered, he clapped his hand on Arnold's shoulder and said, "I'm sorry, Colonel. You're completely right. As an officer of the Continental Army, you outrank me." He turned toward his officers. "Men, you heard Colonel Arnold. He's in charge now. Do whatever he tells you to do, alright? If he tells you to sit on your asses for a week so that his sorry collection of Massachusetts shopkeepers can catch up, you do that. Understood?"

"Understood, sir!" shouted several of the men in near-unison.

Allen sunk to one knee, removing his hat. "Kind sir," he said with mock pathos, "I would be honored if you would retain me as a member of your staff, perhaps as your official boot washer. But far be it from me to presume to usurp the judgment of a colonel of the Continental Army!" He drew a massive hunting knife from a sheath at his belt, and several of Arnold's men gasped in surprise or terror. But he then proceeded to hold the blade against his own neck. "Say the word, my colonel, and I shall slice my own head clear off and serve it to you on a platter. Although, now that I think about it, I should probably prepare the platter first, as I may not be in a position to garnish it properly after I've severed my own head. Men, find Colonel Arnold a platter!"

Hoots and catcalls rose from the group. "Tell him to get his own fucking platter!" shouted one of the men.

Ethan Allen sheathed the knife and got to his feet, putting his fists on his hips in feigned indignation. "Gentlemen, perhaps you didn't hear me," he growled. "I said that Colonel Benedict Arnold is now in charge of the Green Mountain Boys. Now say it back to me. Who is your leader?"

"ETHAN ALLEN!" howled the men without a moment's hesitation.

A smirk creeping across his face, Allen turned to Benedict Arnold, who was turning red with anger. "Sorry," Allen said, holding up his hands. "Nothing I can do. They won't submit to anyone else's authority. So," he said, his voice hardening, "I'm afraid I must insist you butt out of our business. Once we've taken Ticonderoga, you can try to take it from us, if you like—assuming your men ever show up."

"All right," said Arnold, who was fighting to remain calm. "We're all on the same side here. If you insist—that is, if you choose to press forward before the rest of my contingent arrives, then I certainly won't try to stop you. All that I would ask"—this clearly pained him to say—"is that you allow me and my men to accompany you in a support capacity."

Ethan Allen grinned broadly. "The more, the merrier," he said. Then, more quietly, "Just stay out of our way." He then turned back to his officers and launched into his tactical plan for the attack. Arnold and his men tied up their horses and joined the meeting. Mercury managed to slip away without Arnold getting a good look at him—or so he thought.

He observed the meeting from a distance, and it appeared that after their initial rocky start, Allen and Arnold were at least going to be able to cooperate on the assault without killing each other in the process. It was hard to say whether the small band of men—they now had just under a hundred, including Arnold's—would actually be able to take the fort from the British, but if not, the remainder of Arnold's contingent could probably finish the job in a few days. Mercury figured he'd done as much as he could to stoke the fires of war, and decided to slip away before Allen noticed he was gone.

But he hadn't gotten more than fifty paces from the town square when a familiar voice called to him from behind.

"Lord Squigglebottom!"

Mercury sighed heavily, stopped in his tracks, and turned to face Benedict Arnold.

"I knew that was you, even without the ridiculous wig," said Arnold, as he approached. It took Mercury a moment to process this statement. In fact he hadn't been wearing a wig the last time Arnold had seen him. He'd merely been wearing his own hair (which he'd grown to shoulder length) pulled back in a ponytail. Currently he was wearing a brown wig which he thought made him look French-er.

"I'm actually undercover here," said Mercury. "So if anybody asks, call me Monsieur Mercier."

"But why...?"

"Don't ask." In truth, there was no good reason for the different aliases (in Virginia, he was a German industrialist named Hermann Engel and in New York he was a Dutch investor named Marcus Uittenbroek[5]). It was often difficult to remember who he was supposed to be in a given location, but fortunately none of his portrayals of these different characters was particularly nuanced. In short, Messrs. Mercier, Engel, Squigglebottom and Uittenbroek shared every aspect of each other's personas except for their names, nationalities and choice in wigs.

"What is your involvement here, Squig—er, Mercier? I find it very strange that a man of your station should be found amongst a gang of ruffians such as this."

"Long story," said Mercury. "I bought a colonial in Boston. Nice place, but a bit of a fixer-upper. I asked around a bit for some advice on home furnishings and I ended out here in the wilderness with Ethan Allen and the boys."

"Cut the nonsense," said Arnold. "Sam Adams and those guys may have fallen for your charade, but I never bought it. I don't know who you are, but you're no Lord Squigglebottom or Monsieur Mercier. Where do you people come from? Are you even people?"

"I'm sure I don't—"

"I saw you *fly*, Mister. And it's not just you. I know there are others. Like that Mr. Rezon. He's one of you, isn't he?"

"Mr. Reason?" asked Mercury, confused.

"Rezon. R-E-Z-O-N. Lawrence Rezon. Don't play dumb."

"Honestly, I don't know what you're—"

Faster than Mercury could even blink, Arnold pulled a knife from his jacket and plunged the blade deep into Mercury's chest.

---

[5] Literally, "out of his pants." Surprisingly this is a perfectly acceptable surname in the Netherlands. Mercury liked the Dutch.

"Ow!" shouted Mercury. He looked down at the knife protruding from his chest. A dark stain was spreading outward over his shirt from the wound. "What in the name of Queen Victoria's third nipple do you think you're doing?"

"Just a little test," said Arnold. "You seem to be faring pretty well for someone who was just stabbed in the heart."

Mercury gripped the handle of the knife, took a deep breath, and yanked it out. He dropped the bloody knife to the ground and then fell backwards, his eyes rolling into his head. He hit the ground with a thud.

Benedict Arnold ran to his side, cradling his head in his arms. "Lord Squigglebottom!" he cried. "I'm so sorry! I thought…"

Mercury's lips moved as if he were trying to speak, and Arnold bent his ear close. "What is it, Your Lordship?" asked Arnold frantically. "Speak to me!"

A gurgle escaped from Mercury's mouth, followed by two syllables. "Ass…hole…" Mercury gasped.

Arnold pulled back and looked at Mercury, who was glaring at him angrily. "Excuse me?" Arnold said.

"I said you're an *asshole*," Mercury repeated, sitting up and brushing Arnold's hands away. "You can't just fucking stab someone like that, even if they *are* immortal."

"Aha!" exclaimed Arnold. "I was right!"

"Yeah, yeah," replied Mercury, getting slowly to his feet. "Congratulations. I would have told you if you had just asked, you know."

"You said you didn't know what I was talking about."

"I don't!" shouted Mercury. "That is, I have no idea who this Rezon guy that you mentioned is."

"Oh," said Arnold. "Well, I'll tell you all about him if you answer a few questions for me."

"Hey, why didn't I think of that?" said Mercury. "Oh, wait, I did. I was just about to suggest it when somebody *stabbed me in the fucking heart*."

"Oh," said Arnold sheepishly. "Sorry. That was pretty amazing, though."

"Glad I could entertain you," said Mercury. "Now, tell me about this Rezon character."

Benedict Arnold told Mercury what he knew. Mr. Rezon, it turned out, was none other than Lucifer himself. Arnold didn't know that, of course, and Mercury didn't tell him. But it was clear from Arnold's description—both of the man's physical traits and his slightly creepy yet oddly persuasive demeanor—who Rezon really was. Evidently this Rezon had also been posing as a wealthy British aristocrat who sympathized with the Americans, and Arnold had somehow deduced a link between Rezon and Mercury. Rezon had gone to Arnold shortly after the incident at Lexington to persuade him to take the offensive in the coming war against the British. Lucifer, who had a number of sleeper agents in Heaven, had apparently come into the same intelligence regarding British troop positions that Mercury's superiors had. So while Mercury was persuading Ethan Allen to attack Ticonderoga, Lucifer was trying to persuade Benedict Arnold to do exactly the same thing. Arnold, who needed permission from the Massachusetts Committee of Safety, had taken a little longer to get his act together, and had been nearly beaten to the punch by Allen.

"I don't understand," said Arnold, after Mercury had done his best to explain what had happened (without revealing any highly classified information). "If you and Rezon are working together, why would you send two independent groups of men to take a single fort? It was sheer luck and determination that got me here before the Green Mountain Boys launched their attack. It seems like terrible planning on your part."

"That's the thing," said Mercury. "We're *not* working together. At least not intentionally. There are different factions among my people, some good, some bad. Rezon's one of the bad guys." Mercury hadn't explained that he and Rezon were angels; he was technically not allowed to give that information to mortals, and in any case it would have just caused more confusion. He had told Arnold only that they were "supernatural beings from another world." That seemed to satisfy him as much as anything could.

"So Rezon is a bad guy," said Arnold.

"Correct."

"And you're a good guy," said Arnold.

"Correct again."

"And you're both on the same side."

Mercury frowned. "Well, I can see how you'd be a bit confused. To be honest, I don't fully understand it myself. Usually Rezon and I are on opposite sides, but occasionally stuff like this happens. He wants war for his reasons, and Heav—that is, my bosses want war for their reasons. So I guess everybody is going to be happy."

"So, Squigglebottom—"

"Call me Mercury."

"All right, Mercury. What makes you a good guy, if you want the same thing as the bad guy?" asked Arnold.

"Um," said Mercury. "It's not that we want the same thing. Generally speaking, Rezon wants war and mayhem, while my bosses want, well, peace and not mayhem. But in this particular instance our interests are aligned."

"And if I asked Mr. Rezon, would he say that he's the good guy and you're the bad guy?"

"I…" started Mercury. "Well, sure, I suppose, but that's like, you know… not really accurate."

"You seem like a smart guy, Mercury," said Arnold. "Do these questions not occur to you?"

"Honestly, I try not to think about it too hard," replied Mercury.

"It shows." He turned back toward the town square, where Ethan Allen's men were packing up. "Well, it looks like we're heading out," said Arnold. "Are you coming along for the attack?"

Mercury shook his head. "You don't need me. Between you and the Green Apple Gang, you've got Ticonderoga sorted. Anyway, I've got work to do elsewhere."

"Stoking the fires of war with your buddy, Rezon?"

"He's not my… fine, think what you want. Just take Ticonderoga, OK?"

Benedict Arnold smiled wryly and gave Mercury a sharp salute. Then he spun on his heel and walked back to the town square.

"Asshole," muttered Mercury.

# CHAPTER SEVENTEEN

*Somewhere in Wyoming; August 2016*

"So now what?" asked Suzy. She, Eddie and Mercury were sitting in a booth at a diner in a small town somewhere in Wyoming. For the first fifty miles they had been airborne, the Tercel skimming low over the hills of eastern Idaho. They touched down on the highway outside of Idaho Falls and drove into town, where Mercury somehow convinced an old potato farmer to trade his Chevy Suburban for the Tercel and what Mercury claimed was a solid gold potato that looked exactly like Richard Nixon. Whether it was really gold Suzy couldn't say, although it was certainly the heaviest potato she'd ever tried to lift. The resemblance to Nixon, though, was unmistakable.

The Suburban remained earthbound for the most part, but Mercury insisted on driving well over 100 miles per hour most of the time. She wasn't sure if he was just punching the accelerator to the floor or using the so-called "interplanar energy" to push the Suburban beyond its normal limits. Whatever the case, they had somehow covered 300 miles in the past two hours, and Mercury seemed satisfied that they had put enough distance between them and the cabin that no one would be looking for them here. His concern had been that the F-15 assault would be followed up with a squad of angels. Angels could manage a top flight speed of about 500 miles per hour, making them significantly slower than fighter jets, but they posed a much greater threat. There was no way

Mercury and Eddie could win a fight against five or six combat-trained angels.

"Don't ask me," said Mercury, in response to Suzy's question. "I'm just here for the pie."

Mercury had downed six cups of coffee and eaten four pieces of coconut cream pie in the ten minutes they'd been at the diner. Somehow Suzy found this more incredible than either the flying car or the gold potato.

"How can you stay so thin?" she asked incredulously. Mercury was built like a long distance runner.

"Angelic biology," said Mercury.

"That's no answer," said Suzy. "You can't violate the laws of physics. The food has to go somewhere."

Mercury shoved a forkful of pie into his mouth and looked at Eddie, rolling his eyes and making the crazy finger motion with his other hand.

"Can we stay on the subject?" Eddie asked. "We need to figure out what we're going to do. Obviously someone in the government has decided we're a serious threat."

"She's the threat," Mercury said around a mouthful of coconut cream. "You're just some Internet conspiracy nutcase, and I'm a manifesto-writing kook. Damn it!"

"What?" asked Suzy.

"I left my manifesto back there in the woods. Can we go back?"

"That strikes me as a fantastically bad idea," said Suzy.

"He's right, though," said Eddie. "We're just a couple of unaffiliated cherubim. You're the one they're scared of, because you know all about Brimstone. They want to silence you, at any cost."

"But I don't have any proof of anything!" she said. "It was all on that thumb drive, which is either destroyed or in the hands of the government."

"She's got a point," said Mercury. "What are they so scared of?"

"Us," said Eddie after a moment's reflection. "The three of us. They're worried we're going to go public."

"What do you mean?" asked Suzy.

"Rosenberg and I called it the 'nuclear option.' Probably not a great name, given the circumstances, but that's what we called it. A way of forcing the debate about the infiltration of the government into the open."

"You mean go public about the existence of angels," said Suzy.

"Yeah," Eddie replied. "It's never happened, not in the seven thousand years that angels and demons have been fighting it out on this plane. There have been rogue angels who have set themselves up as gods or used their powers for unauthorized purposes..."

Mercury seemed to be choking on a piece of pie.

"...but it was always generally agreed by everyone that no one's interests are served by giving human beings definitive proof of the existence of supernatural creatures. But we're desperate, and Michelle knows it. If Suzy reveals the truth about Brimstone, she'll be dismissed as just another disgruntled former government employee with an axe to grind. But if we explain that the government is overrun with angels, and offer proof..."

"Proof of the existence of angels," said Mercury. "What, like doing a press conference and bending a few spoons? Damn it!"

"Now what?" asked Suzy, exasperated.

"Left my trick spoon back there too. Are you sure we can't go back?"

"I was thinking something more along the lines of levitating a Buick, but yeah."

"Terrible idea," said Mercury.

"Why?" asked Suzy. "It's obviously what they're expecting us to do."

"Even worse," said Mercury. "Never do what anybody expects you to do. The phrase 'press conference' is synonymous with 'bullshit session.' They'll dismiss us as loonies and chalk up any miracles we perform to special effects." He waved his fork at a TV screen hanging in the corner of the diner. "Take this chick here, for example, blabbering about terrorists and nuclear bombs. Do you think anybody believes a word she's saying?"

Eddie and Suzy turned to look at the screen. A young blond woman was standing at a podium, addressing a group of reporters. She was saying "...thought to be a member of the terrorist group known as Chaos Faction. We have no information on her current whereabouts, but we do have solid intelligence that Chaos Faction has been planning an attack on a medium-sized American city. It has long been suspected that Cilbrith was involved in the theft of the Wormwood bomb, and law enforcement agents have had her under surveillance in the hopes of recovering the bomb. Early

Friday morning however, she disappeared, apparently with the help of several Chaos Faction operatives…"

"Hey, you never told me you're a terrorist!" Mercury exclaimed.

"I'm not!" cried Suzy.

A few of the diner's patrons glanced over at their table, but didn't seem to make the connection between Mercury's comment and what was happening on the TV screen. One man complained that the press conference had interrupted the Cornhuskers game.

"Then why did the blond lady on TV say it?" he charged, pointing his fork accusingly at her.

"Brilliant," said Eddie. "They smear Suzy, discredit the previous administration, cover up the Brimstone program, and create a mass panic, all in one fell swoop. Pretty impressive, in a Joseph Goebbels sort of way. And notice how they keep the threat vague, so they can justify doing whatever they want. I mean, they could probably institute…"

"…martial law in the following cities," the woman on the TV was saying. "Albuquerque, New Mexico; Nashville, Tennessee; Modesto, California…"

"How can they do this?" Suzy asked. "It's all lies! I didn't steal the bomb! They lost it and built another one, and they still have it! I've never even heard of this Chaos Faction thing. What the hell is going on?"

"All part of Michelle's plan to get complete control over the U.S., and then the rest of the world," said Eddie.

"You have to admit, though," said Mercury, "Blondie is pretty convincing. If I didn't know better… Damn it!"

"What did you forget now, Mercury?" asked Suzy, irritated. "Your toothbrush?"

"No," replied Mercury. "I just realized who that blond chick is."

"It's Gabrielle Gladstone," said Eddie. "The White House Press Secretary."

"Come on, Eddie," said Mercury. "The blond bob fooled me too at first, and I've never seen her in a suit before. Picture her with long brown hair, and wearing a white robe. Oh, and carrying a big-ass trumpet."

"Oh," said Eddie, his face going white. "Oh, no."

"What?" asked Suzy. "Who is it?"

"Her name really is Gabrielle," said Mercury. "But you probably know her by the male form of her name, Gabriel. The archangel."

# CHAPTER EIGHTEEN

*New York and Philadelphia; 1776 - 1779*

Benedict Arnold, Ethan Allen and their men had little difficulty taking Fort Ticonderoga from the British. Not having been informed that the continent was soon to be ravaged by a full-scale war, the Brits were caught completely off guard and surrendered the fort with minimal resistance. Seven days later, Arnold and fifty men went on to raid Fort Saint-Jean in Southern Quebec. It was Ethan Allen and the Green Mountain Boys who got most of the credit for these attacks, though, and Arnold's failure to achieve widespread popular acclaim or the accolades of Congress despite his consistently bold and clever military maneuvers was to be the defining theme of his career.

After these initial successes, Arnold found himself charged with the impossible task of forestalling a British naval invasion by way of Lake Champlain. Not having a navy, the Americans found themselves at a considerable disadvantage. Undeterred, Arnold summoned carpenters, sail-makers and gunners from Connecticut and Massachusetts, and over the summer of 1776 managed to build a fleet of three schooners, two sloops, three galleys, and eight gondolas. Facing the British Navy with such a fleet was comparable to staring down a charging rhinoceros with a sock full of marbles, but Arnold was undeterred.

He was encouraged in his efforts by the strange man—if he could be called that—named Rezon, who visited him occasionally over the summer. Rezon had a habit of asking Arnold if there were any particularly insurmountable difficulties he was facing, and Arnold would tell him about the sail-makers who were stuck in Connecticut because of a bridge that was out, or the schooner that couldn't be completed because of a shortage of nails. Rezon would listen quietly and then disappear as mysteriously as he had arrived, and more often than not Arnold found that somehow whatever problem had been plaguing his little ship works had been miraculously solved. The bridge would be repaired in the middle of the night, or an unscheduled shipment of nails would appear, and so on. Once in late August, three of the carpenters were miraculously healed of syphilis. Arnold accepted these gifts—if that's what they were—with aplomb, having little time to speculate on Rezon's motives. But in the back of his mind, he suspected that someday there would be a reckoning for his help.

Arnold proceeded with his ships down Lake Champlain to the north of Crown Point and situated them between Valcour Island and the western shore, so that both his wings were covered and he could only be attacked from the front. In this position he lay in wait for the British.

On October 11, 1776, Sir Guy Carleton's squadron approached, and the first naval battle of the war began. At sundown, after seven hours of brutal fighting, the British withdrew out of range, intending to renew their attack in the morning. Both fleets had been badly damaged in the fight, but the Americans were so badly cut up that Carleton expected to force them to surrender the next day. But Arnold's ships slipped through the British line in the foggy night and made for Crown Point as fast as the beat up fleet could travel. The enemy eventually caught up with him late the next day. Arnold sent most of his flotilla to flee to safety while he engaged three British ships in his schooner for four hours. His ship was badly damaged and her deck covered with dead and dying men when, having sufficiently delayed the enemy to allow the rest of his ships to escape, he ran the schooner aground and set her on fire. He and his men marched overland to Crown Point, rendezvoused with the fleet, and brought the whole force safely to Ticonderoga. Carleton did not press the attack.

Despite acquitting himself brilliantly in this battle, Arnold never received due acclaim for his efforts. A retreat—even one handled so impeccably as this—is still a retreat, and rarely receives the sort of accolades reserved for a victory. Arnold was passed over for promotion by the Continental Congress, and, adding insult to injury, personal rivals brought charges of corruption and malfeasance against him. He was acquitted of these charges—in fact, Congress ultimately found that he had gone deeply in debt in support of the war effort. But the damage was done. Bitter and feeling unappreciated, Arnold found himself in a dark corner of a Philadelphia tavern, brooding over his future.

It was in this dark moment that he was visited for the last time by the man he knew as Rezon. Rezon, who was in fact Lucifer, First of the Fallen, the original turncoat, had been doing some brooding of his own lately. His initial glee at the outbreak of war had turned to ambivalence as he realized that not only were the Americans going to win the war, but they were going to do it without reverting to a military dictatorship, a puppet state of France, or even a chaotic collection of rival colonies. It looked, in fact, that they were going to emerge stronger than ever, as the world's first constitutional republic. The Americans had among them a truly first-rate group of political thinkers, among them Jefferson, Franklin and Madison, and it was clear that these men intended to establish a government designed to make it almost impossible for someone like Lucifer to manipulate it. As a result, Lucifer decided a change in strategy was needed: he was now going to do everything he could to help the British win the war. And he knew just the man who could make that happen.

So it was that Lucifer settled in across from Benedict Arnold with the intent to reverse the course of both of their fortunes.

"Rezon," muttered Arnold. "You always show up at the worst times."

"I show up when you need me," said Lucifer. "But you're not doing so badly. They've put you in charge of Philadelphia and made you a major-general. And I hear you're courting a lovely young woman of a very fine family."

"How do you know about that?" demanded Arnold. "We've been very discreet, given her family's loyalist tendencies."

"I have ways of finding things out," replied Lucifer. "Although, speaking frankly, it's a shame you have to conceal your love for this woman merely because of a few prominent Tories in her family. What business is it of anyone who her family is? Love is love, is it not? And certainly you deserve some happiness, after all you've been through."

Arnold smiled wryly. "You do have a way with words, Rezon. Perhaps I could prevail upon you to exercise your persuasiveness with Congress. Somehow they've seen fit to promote five lesser men ahead of me, even though anyone with eyes could see that I should be second only to Washington himself, given what I've accomplished."

"Congress!" spat Lucifer. "An assembly of self-important baboons who think they have the right to play puppet master to truly great men, such as yourself. I wouldn't condescend to an audience with such a glorified mob."

"Why are you here, then," replied Arnold, "if you don't intend to grease the skids? I have no bridges in need of repair, other than the metaphorical type. Are you here at last to demand comeuppance for your aid?"

Lucifer held up his hands. "You affront me, sir! My assistance is offered without any expectation of reciprocation, in service to a greater cause."

"I'm beginning to realize that cause is not American independence, however," said Arnold.

Lucifer shrugged. "What about you, Benedict? What are you fighting for?"

"I fight in service of my country," replied Arnold.

"Which one?" asked Lucifer. "Up until a few scant years ago, you were a loyal British citizen. Now you've taken up arms against your former country at the whim of a noisome rabble. Tell me, Benedict, do you trust the fate of this continent to a Congress that promotes a jackal like Jedediah Wilkins over you?"

"What's your game, Rezon? Now you're suddenly rallying to the British cause?"

"I have my reasons for reassessing the situation," said Lucifer. "But you knew when I first came to you that my motives probably differed from your own. The question you need to ask is whether your interests are being served by your present course of action.

Someday this war will end. You'll be married, perhaps with children. Do you think your children will look up to a man who serves at the pleasure of a Congress that that has repeatedly scorned and ignored him? And what of your future wife's family? Do you think loyalists will be kindly treated in an independent America? You're a smart man, Benedict. I know you've asked yourself these questions."

"What would you have me do?" cried Arnold. "I've got responsibilities! I can't just…"

"You'll have responsibilities wherever you go," said Lucifer. "You're an important man, regardless of your circumstances. Someone of your wit and cunning will find a warm welcome anywhere talent and intelligence are appreciated. After all," Lucifer went on, "you do possess significant intelligence, do you not?"

Benedict stared into his beer, not speaking. The double-meaning of Lucifer's statement was not lost on him.

"I'm not here to strong-arm you," said Lucifer, getting up from the table. "But I do suggest you spend some time thinking about what's best for you and your future family. And your country, of course. Whichever country that may be. I will, of course, do whatever I can to assist you in any transition you see fit to make."

With that, Lucifer bowed slightly, turned, and walked out of the tavern, leaving Benedict Arnold to ruminate on his words.

# CHAPTER NINETEEN

*South Dakota; August 2016*

"Tell me again how you know where the bomb is?" Eddie said.

He and Suzy were back in the Suburban, barreling east on I-90 through South Dakota. Suzy had taken over driving, and Mercury was flying a few miles in advance to perform reconnaissance, in case Michelle had put up checkpoints to try to catch them before they got to Michigan.

"I worked on the damage assessment software," Suzy said. "We analyzed the potential effects of the detonation of a Wormwood-style bomb in seventeen American cities. The only city that Gabrielle mentioned that was also on our test list was Grand Rapids, Michigan."

"Hmm," replied Eddie.

"What?"

"That doesn't strike you as strange?"

Suzy bit her lip. It did, in fact, strike her as strange. "You think it's a trap."

"Well, they practically told us where to go to look for the bomb. Of course, it could be anywhere in the city...."

Suzy shook her head. "No, there was a very specific epicenter for each test. In Grand Rapids, it was on the roof of the Vanden Heuvel Building. The bomb does more damage if it's a few hundred feet above ground."

"What makes her so sure we're going to take the bait, though?" Eddie asked. "If we had any sense, we'd be on the other side of the planet when that bomb goes off."

"She's betting on my conscience," replied Suzy. "She figures that if I walked out of Brimstone because of ethical concerns, there's no way I'm going to let her actually detonate the bomb, if there's any chance I can do something about it."

"Is she right?"

Suzy sighed. "Yeah. Mercury said never to do what they expect you to do. I don't think he'd approve of this plan if he understood what we were doing."

"Hmm," said Eddie again.

"You think he knows we're heading into a trap?"

"Hard to say," replied Eddie. "Mercury is a strange one. One minute it looks like he's completely over his head and the next he's somehow made a fool out of everybody. I haven't figured out if he's putting on an act or if he's just incredibly lucky."

"Or maybe he just has good intuition," said Suzy. "Some people just seem to muddle through just by following their instincts."

"Could be," said Eddie. "Like I say, he's a strange one."

They both jumped as something thumped on the roof of the car. Mercury's face appeared, upside down, in front of the windshield, his silver hair whipping furiously in the wind. "Get off at the next exit!" he yelled. "Police cars up ahead. We're going to have to take back roads for a while."

Suzy nodded and Mercury shot into the air ahead of them. She took the next exit, which led to a two lane road that wound through the hills to the southeast. They remained on this road for the next three hours, when Mercury reappeared and told them it was safe to take the next left to get back on the highway.

In this manner, taking the highway unless warned to do otherwise by Mercury, they traversed the 1500 miles to Michigan. Suzy did most of the driving, even though she was dog-tired and Eddie, being an angel, didn't need to sleep. She liked Eddie but his driving made her nervous. He had a tendency to become interested in something on the horizon and then drift toward it, as if he had forgotten what he was doing. He wouldn't snap out of it until he either hit gravel or Suzy barked at him to straighten out. After the third time this happened, she insisted on doing the rest of the driving.

They didn't dare try to enter the city in the Suburban, since the National Guard had undoubtedly put up checkpoints on all the roads. They ended up ditching the vehicle outside of Kalamazoo and flying the rest of the way. They kept low to the ground, avoiding roads and houses, with Mercury carrying Suzy. It was a terrifying but exhilarating way to travel.

When they neared the outskirts of the city, the two angels landed and they walked for several miles. Suzy was so tired she could hardly put one foot in front of the other, and several times they had to make detours to avoid checkpoints or National Guardsmen walking down the street. Her mood was not helped by the banter of the two cherubim, who had spent twenty minutes arguing about what to call people from Kalamazoo.

"Kalamazooians," said Mercury.

"Kalamazooites," replied Perp.

"Kalamazoans," said Mercury.

"Ooh, I like that one," said Perp. "But wouldn't the plural be *Kalamazoa?*"

Mercury rubbed his chin. "My friend Bill is from Battle Creek, but Glen and Freda are Kalamazoa. Hmm."

"Kalamazooers?"

Finally they reached a motel and got a room. Suzy collapsed on one of the two beds while Mercury and Eddie sat on the other, trying to figure out what to do next.

"You realize, of course," said Mercury, "that this is a trap."

"So you figured it out too," replied Eddie.

"Of course I figured it out. How dumb do you think I am? Damn it!"

"What?"

"I did leave my toothbrush." He smacked his lips together. "My mouth tastes like road tar and gnats."

"Do you think she'll actually detonate the bomb?"

"Michelle?" asked Mercury. "Yeah. I mean, if she doesn't, it won't be because of any kind of moral scruples. Michelle's always had an authoritarian streak, and now that she's got nobody telling her what to do, all she's got left is her sense of order. She wants everything to be regimented, ordered, controlled. And if she's got to

141

cause a little bit of momentary chaos to bring that about, she'll do that."

"A nuclear blast in a city of half a million people is 'a little bit of momentary chaos?'" Eddie said.

"In the scheme of things, yeah. You nuke one city and suddenly everybody in the country is clamoring for more security. Look at what she's accomplished already, with just the threat of a nuclear attack: twelve cities under martial law. And nobody complains because Gabrielle is assuring them that it's temporary and only applies to a few cities. Except of course it isn't, and this is just the beginning. Michelle's not going to give up any power that she manages to get her hands on."

"So we have no choice," said Eddie. "Even if it is a trap. We have to stop that bomb from going off."

"Whoa, take it easy on the 'we,' there, buddy," said Mercury. "I told Suzy I'd get her here. I didn't say anything about defusing a nuclear bomb. I've already played that game, and it doesn't end well."

"So what are you going to do, leave?"

"Well, I'm not staying here in Blast Radius, Michigan, if that's what you're asking. Thought I might hang out in Portugal for a while."

"How can you just sit by while Michelle detonates a nuclear bomb in a city?"

"I can't. I have to fly to Portugal. Weren't you listening?"

"Thousands of people will die. Tens of thousands, probably. That bomb will take out most of downtown Grand Rapids."

"Thousands of people die every day," said Mercury. "Mostly from war and famine. Most of the world is in chaos."

"You sound like you're defending Michelle."

"I'm not defending her; I'm just saying this is the way things are. The world is in tension between order and chaos. It's always been this way. Sometimes things swing too far to the side of chaos. Maybe it's time for a correction."

"Time for a... it's a nuclear bomb, Mercury! The fallout and radiation alone..."

"Not much fallout with a bomb like Wormwood. I did some research on these bombs after I got blown up by one. Turns out one of the advantages of ultra-grade plutonium is that there's relatively little radiation released. I mean, you're not going to want to be downwind of this place for a few weeks, but most of the damage is in the initial blast. And it's a painless way to die. You're atomized before you even know what hit you."

"Unless you're on the outer edge of the blast," said Eddie coldly.

"Well, yeah. Third degree burns and probably some radiation poisoning. A slow, painful, gruesome death over the course of a few days or weeks. Damn it!"

"You forget your dental floss too?"

"Huh? No, floss is in my pocket. It's unwaxed, though." He shuddered at the thought. "So, you really want to do this? Walk right into Michelle's trap?"

"I just don't see how we have any choice, Mercury. We're the only ones in a position to do anything about the bomb. If we don't stop it, we'll have the deaths of thousands on our hands. I'd rather try and end up in Michelle's secret prison than just run away."

"Yeah, yeah, fine," said Mercury. "I get it. There's not enough beer in Portugal to make a guy forget about people dying from radiation sickness. So what's the plan?"

"Um," replied Eddie.

"You're going to make me come up with the plan, aren't you?"

Eddie smiled.

"All right," said Mercury. "First, we need to identify the weak link in their organization."

# CHAPTER TWENTY

*New York; 1779 - 1780*

Lucifer's poisonous words slowly worked their evil in Benedict Arnold's heart, until one day in the April of 1779 he penned a letter to the British General, Sir Henry Clinton. Written in disguised handwriting and under the signature of "Gustavus," the letter described its author as an American officer of high rank, who, due to disgust at the French alliance and "other recent proceedings of Congress," might be persuaded to switch sides in the war. Congress having recently spent a fair amount of time dithering over the latest trumped up charges to be made against Arnold, there was little doubt as to the identity of this "officer of high rank."

This initial letter led to a correspondence between Arnold and Sir Henry's adjutant-general, Major John André. At first Arnold offered only his personal allegiance to the crown, but once he had begun to think of himself as a British agent rather than an American officer, it was but a small step for him to decide to take advantage of his position for the benefit of his new masters. He entreated General Washington to put him in charge of West Point, and Washington, who had long defended Arnold against the trifling charges that plagued his career, did not hesitate to entrust his friend with this strategically important post.

Arnold wasted no time in betraying Washington's trust, conspiring to meet with André to develop a plan for turning West Point over to the British. It was agreed that Arnold would furnish the British with descriptions of the fortresses and information regarding the disposition of the troops, as well as arrange for the American troops to be in positions such as to make capture by the British as easy as possible. And so it was that the British co-conspirator, Major John André, found himself riding across an open field just northwest of White Plains, New York, a scant three miles from the British lines, with his boots lined with stationery from the desk of Benedict Arnold.

A betting man observing this situation would have given at least ten-to-one odds of André reaching his destination and handing over the intelligence to Sir Henry Clinton. And given this eventuality, the odds of the British successfully taking West Point, forcing the surrender of 3,000 American troops, and winning the war for the British, would have been very good indeed. But history is riddled with accidents—fortuitous or calamitous, depending on your point of view—and one of these accidents occurred to Major John André. An objective observer might be forgiven for thinking that this particular accident was part of some grand plan by a divine authority to bring about an American victory. Or it might have been simply have been pure chance.

Or something in between.


"This way!" cried Mercury, steering his horse to the left. The other six men hesitated.

"Are you sure you know what you're doing, Long-Drink-of-Water?" one of the men called after him. "The tracks indicate the ruffians fled this way." He pointed to the left.

"That's a false trail," said Mercury, straightening his war bonnet. "If I had a bead for every time I almost fell for a false trail, I'd own Manhattan. Follow me!" He charged off down the path to the left.

The men behind him grumbled but followed after. They'd been convinced of Mercury's bona fides as a tracker when he managed to skewer a pigeon at three hundred yards with his eyes closed, but now so far he'd had little success in pinpointing the gang of ruffians the men had been chasing all morning. Some of them were beginning to doubt whether he was even a real Mohican. He wasn't going to be able to keep up the ruse much longer.

Fortunately, he didn't need to. "Look!" cried Mercury, pointing at a lone horseman crossing the field toward them. "Yon ruffian!"

There was no reason to believe the man was one of the ruffians they'd been chasing; there were half a dozen of them, and they'd been heading in the opposite direction. Still, a man traveling alone through disputed territory was worth investigating.

Mercury approached close enough to positively identify his target and then held back, allowing his compatriots to take the lead.

The stranger stopped short as the men approached and dismounted. He hesitated, but then smiled slightly as he noticed the Hessian overcoat worn by the leader.

"Gentlemen," said the stranger. "I hope you belong to our party."

"What party?" asked one of the men.

"The party of England," replied the stranger.

"We do," answered the leader.

"Very good," said the stranger. "I must tell you then, that I'm a British officer, and must not be detained."

"Is that right?" asked the leader. "Did I say that we're British? I meant American."

The stranger's face went white. He swallowed hard. "Then I meant I'm an American officer." He produced a passport signed by Benedict Arnold. "You must understand, I claimed to be British only because I thought you were."

"Yeah?" said the leader. "And what's an American officer doing this far from the American lines?"

"Please," said the stranger. "You can have my horse. And my watch. Just let me walk the last few miles to White Plains."

"I have a horse," replied the leader. "And I already know what time it is. Search him."

The stranger was stripped, and the papers were found in his boot.

The leader looked over the papers, which were damp from the stranger's sweat. After a moment he held them to his nose.

"Smells like treason," he said.

Mercury sighed and turned away, leaving the men to arrest Major André. He felt bad for the man; he was only doing his job, and he'd likely be hanged for it. As would Benedict Arnold, if he could be caught. After all Arnold had done for the American cause, it seemed grossly unfair to Mercury. How could one mistake wipe out all the good he had done? If only he hadn't listened to Lucifer.

Having been through a lot of wars, this wasn't the first time Mercury had witnessed such a betrayal, and at first he couldn't figure out why this one was hitting him so hard. He had no personal interest in this war. He'd only seen to the capture of Major André because Heaven had decided that an American victory was definitely in their interest. If the British could take West Point with minimal bloodshed and end the war, it would have been fine with Mercury.

Ultimately he came to realize that he held himself personally responsible for Arnold's moral failure. If Mercury had been able to come up with better answers to Arnold's questions, maybe he wouldn't have switched sides. Arnold had glimpsed the angelic machinations behind the war and must have felt like a puppet to forces beyond his control. If his mysterious benefactor had seen fit to change sides, who was Benedict Arnold to question him? Would it have changed anything if Mercury had told him that Rezon was really Lucifer? Lucifer was just a name, after all. Had he given Arnold any reason to trust an angel named Mercury over one named Lucifer? Angels and demons were all playing the same game. It wasn't Arnold's fault that he had seen through the charade.

# CHAPTER TWENTY-ONE

*Grand Rapids, Michigan; August 2016*

Zion Johnson made his way slowly across the rooftop of the Vanden Heuvel Building, flanked by four heavily armed men in gear that was designed to camouflage them against the gray gravel of the roof. He was moving slowly because he was using crutches, and in his left hand he carried a heavy black duffel bag. His right knee was completely immobilized by a cast, and with every movement pain shot through the whole right side of his body. It wasn't hot out, but droplets of sweat were pouring down his brow. Zion Johnson wasn't big on pain medication, particularly when he was working.

He could have had someone else handle this part of the job, but Zion Johnson wanted to see the mission through. He'd made sure that the bomb had fallen into the hands of Chaos Faction, and prevented the army truck that the terrorists had inexplicably driven across the country from being pulled over by any law enforcement agencies. With any luck, they'd driven to the coordinates he'd provided and were preparing the detonated the Brimstone bomb at the agreed-upon time. He mentally went over the note he had left them for the hundredth time, concluding for the hundredth time that the instructions could not possibly have been any clearer: the blueprints of the Vanden Heuvel were merely a ruse; they were to be left somewhere near Grand Rapids to lead the authorities to think that the terrorists had planned to attack the city. Meanwhile, the bomb would actually detonate harmlessly several miles away, scaring the shit out of the city's half million residents but causing few, if any, casualties.

Sure, there had been that frustrating Internet exchange with the one called Nisroc, but Zion Johnson was fairly certain Nisroc was the dimmest of the group. That Izbazel didn't seem so bad. Yes, he had bungled the truck hijacking, but everything had turned out OK. Except for all those dead men, of course, but they knew what they were getting into. Well, not *exactly* what they were getting into. It's not like they knew they were guarding an illegal nuclear bomb whose owners had plotted to hand it over to terrorists. But they knew, *in general*, the sort of thing they were getting into. Anyway, that whole episode was the result of a simple misunderstanding. Izbazel had thought the men in the truck were just going to hand over the bomb without a fight. Zion Johnson had made a point of telling Nisroc the bomb would be heavily guarded, but he hadn't specifically told him that the guards would shoot at anyone trying to take the bomb. It was his own mistake, really. He'd have to communicate more clearly in the future.

This line of thinking let Zion Johnson to wonder, for the one-hundred-and-first time, whether his note had been clear enough. Realizing that he was engaged in a circular train of thought, Zion Johnson focused on his mantra.

*Superior attitude, superior state of mind.*
*Superior attitude, superior state of mind.*
*Superior attitude, superior state of mind.*

The four men had completed recon of the roof and the ranking officer gave Zion Johnson the all-clear sign. He nodded and signaled for the men to fan out across the roof. They did so, hiding themselves behind air ducts and vents so thoroughly that an ordinary person could walk within five feet without noticing anything amiss—not that an ordinary person had any reason to be strolling across the top of the Vanden Heuvel Building.

Zion Johnson set the duffel bag down in the middle of the roof, unhooked a walkie-talkie from his belt and held it a few inches from his face, surveying the empty roof. "This is Big Dog," he said. "The package is in place and the roof is secure. Shut down the elevators and get some men in the stairwells. I don't want anybody getting up here from below."

Zion Johnson took a last look around. Nothing to do now but hope that this Mercury fellow takes the bait. He hobbled back to the stairwell.

# CHAPTER TWENTY-TWO

*Grand Rapids, Michigan; August 2016*

Nisroc moved quietly from desk to desk, emptying trash bins into the garbage bag hanging from a janitor's cart. He liked this sort of work. It was soothingly repetitive. Good, honest work, too. Imagine what would happen if nobody ever emptied the trash bins. He shuddered to think. It would be nice if Chaos Faction could do more work like this, he thought. It seemed like a better way of making a living than blowing up noses, but then what did he know? Nisroc always seemed to get in trouble when he made decisions for himself. He was better at following orders.

As he reached under a desk to pick up an errant gum wrapper, he was jolted out of his ruminations by a loud squawking in his ear. He'd forgotten about the earpiece, and in his terror he jumped straight up, banging his head on the bottom of the desk.

"Nisroc, what's your position?" the voice squawked.

"On the floor," moaned Nisroc, holding his head.

"Well, get up!" said the voice. It was Izbazel. "Have you planted the bomb yet?"

Nisroc crawled out from under the desk and got slowly to his feet. Still holding his head, he spoke into the microphone hidden in his shirt. "Not yet," he said. "I'm still working on the trash."

"The *trash?*" asked Izbazel. "Forget about the trash and plant the bomb at the red X!"

"That's the thing," said Nisroc. "I've been all over this floor, and I don't see the red X."

"It's not going to…" Izbazel started. "Never mind. Just leave the cart anywhere. It's doesn't matter if it's not right on the X. It's a nuclear bomb, for Pete's sake. It's going to take out the whole downtown area."

"OK," said Nisroc. After a moment he added, "Over and out."

Nisroc wasn't really very keen on the whole nuclear bomb idea. He didn't quite grasp why anyone would want to take out the whole downtown area. It seemed to him that it would just make a big mess, and if Izbazel kept shuffling Chaos Faction from one secret mission to the next, Nisroc probably wouldn't be around to help clean it up. Too bad. Nisroc liked cleaning things up.

He let out a heavy sigh and reached into the bottom of the big black garbage bag. Finding the little switch cover with his fingers, he pulled it open and flipped the switch.

OK, so that was done. The bomb was armed and it would detonate in thirty minutes. Plenty of time for Nisroc and the rest of Chaos Faction—who were waiting in a coffee shop down the street from the Vanden Heuvel building—to get out of the blast radius. In fact, Nisroc thought, probably enough time for him to empty a few more trash bins. He wheeled the cart to the next desk and leaned over to pick up the bin, which was brimming over with crumpled papers and yogurt containers.

The something struck him on the back of his head and everything went black.

Some time later, he regained consciousness tied to a chair inside what appeared to be a janitor's closet. A single fluorescent panel overhead lit the small room. Judging from the brands of the cleaning products on the shelves, he was still in the Vanden Heuvel building, but it was impossible to say what floor. He thought he sensed someone behind him. He strained against his bonds, but they were too tight for him to wriggle free. Next he tried to grab hold of some interplanar energy in the area to weaken the cords, but found that something was interfering with his efforts.

"Not going to work," said a man's voice. It sounded strangely familiar, but he couldn't place it. "I'm not going to let you get a handle on the energy," said the man.

"What do you want?" asked Nisroc. "I was just doing my job."

"Doing your job!" cried a woman's voice, which he didn't recognize. How many people were in this supply closet? She went on, "You know who else was just doing their job? The Nazis!"

Nisroc thought about this for a moment. He supposed it was true. The Nazis must have had janitors, after all. What if all the janitors in Germany had refused to empty the trash bins of any Nazis? Eventually the offices of the Third Reich would have been so clogged up with papers and banana peels that the whole war machine would have shut down. Was that what the woman was implying? That by emptying the trash bins on the thirty-fifth floor of the Vanden Heuvel Building, he was facilitating some vast enterprise of evil? Pangs of guilt struck his heart, making it hard for him to think. This is what always happened when he started thinking for himself.

"We know about the bomb," said the woman. She walked around to stand in front of Nisroc. Nisroc felt like he should recognize her, like he'd seen her on a TV show recently. She didn't look like an actress, though. She was kind of short and a little too well-padded to be the lead in a TV show. She might have played the fat friend, but she wasn't quite heavy enough for that. She was in that awkward range of height-to-weight proportion that put her squarely in the demographic that made up seventy-five percent of the female population that wasn't allowed to be on television. Also, her hair was purple.

"Oh, the bomb!" exclaimed Nisroc. He had forgotten about the bomb. He wondered what time it was.

"Don't play dumb," snapped the purple-haired woman.

"I'm fairly certain he's not playing," said the man, walking into view. Nisroc was confirmed in his belief that he had met this man before. It was when he and Ramiel were guarding that condo in Glendale, the one with the interplanar linoleum portal.

"Hey, you're..." Nisroc started.

"Ederatz," replied Eddie. "Used to work for the Mundane Observation Corps. You can call me Eddie."

"Who do you work for now?" asked Nisroc.

"A better question is, who do *you* work for now?" Eddie replied.

"Well," said Nisroc. "We call ourselves Chaos Faction."

"What?" asked the woman. "*You're* Chaos Faction? The terrorist group?"

"Not just me," replied Nisroc. "There are four of us. Well, there are more, but most of us are in prison."

"So," Eddie said. "Michelle has her agents working with Chaos Faction, to make it look like the bombing is an act of terrorism."

"Michelle?" asked Nisroc hopefully. "You mean *the* Michelle? So we're the good guys, then."

"You're about to detonate a nuclear bomb in the downtown area of a major city," the woman said. "Does that sound like something the good guys would do?"

Nisroc frowned. It did sound pretty bad when you just came out and said it like that.

A phone rang and Eddie pulled it out of his pocket and answered it.

"Yeah," he said. "On the roof? What does it look like? Uh-huh. Uh-huh. Yeah, that's what I thought too. OK."

He hung up the phone.

"Did he find it?" asked the woman.

Eddie shook his head. "He says there's a black duffel bag on the roof."

Nisroc's brow furrowed. He didn't know anything about a duffel bag on the roof. Izbazel never told him anything.

"But you don't think that's it?" asked the woman.

"Mercury thinks it's too obvious," said Eddie.

"Isn't that the point? They planted the bomb right where we expected them to."

"Mercury thinks it's a decoy. If we try to grab it, Michelle's agents will swoop in and arrest us. He also says there's a Balderhaz field emanating from somewhere near the top of the building."

"A what?"

"There's a device called a Balderhaz Cube that prevents angels from performing miracles within a given range. It complicates our efforts to dispose of the bomb."

"But you said you don't think the bomb is on the roof," said the woman. "So where is it?"

"Ask Mr. Just-doing-his-job," said Eddie.

Nisroc bit his lip. He wasn't happy about the whole nuclear bomb situation, but his feelings of loyalty to Chaos Faction made him reluctant to divulge the location of the bomb.

156

"Look," said the woman. "You seem like a decent guy. My guess is that you just got mixed up with the wrong crowd. I know how it goes. I was on the team that helped build that bomb. I didn't fully realize what was going on until it was too late to stop it. But it's not too late to keep the bomb from going off. You just have to stop following orders and do the right thing."

Nisroc shook his head. "It *is* too late," he said.

"What do you mean?" asked the woman.

"I flipped the switch. The bomb is armed. It will explode in thirty minutes. I mean, thirty minutes after I flipped the switch."

"Holy shit," said the woman.

Eddie glanced at the cell phone. "It's been fifteen minutes since we nabbed you. How long before that did you flip the switch?"

"Oh, not long," said Nisroc. "Maybe a minute or two."

"Where is it?"

Nisroc figured it didn't make much difference at this point. If there was a Balderhaz Cube at the top of the building, there was no way they were going to get the bomb out of the building in time. "In the janitor's cart," he said. "Under the trash."

Eddie hit a button on the phone. "He's not answering!" he said after a moment.

Nisroc heard a door open behind him. "Wow, it's cozy in here," said a voice. "Got room for one more?"

"Mercury!" exclaimed the woman. "The bomb is in a janitor's cart on the thirty-fifth floor. It's going to detonate in less than fifteen minutes!"

"Hmm," said Mercury.

"Hmm? All you have to say is 'hmm'? Go get the bomb!"

"The problem is," said Mercury, "they've shut down the elevators and they've got guards in the stairwells to keep anybody from getting to the roof. Normally that wouldn't be a problem, but with that Balderhaz cube up there, I can't get past them. Can't fly up there either. The cube seems to have a range of about a hundred yards."

"So, what?" asked the woman. "We just sit here in a supply closet until the bomb goes off?"

"Hmm," said Mercury again. "Hey, what's that stuff on the bottom shelf? Is that spray paint?"

# CHAPTER TWENTY-THREE

*New York; Autumn, 1780*

Such had been Arnold's reputation among his fellow officers that when incriminating documents were found bearing his signature, he was not immediately suspected of foul play. The papers found their way into the hands of Colonel John Jameson, who commanded a cavalry outpost a few miles from White Plains. Assuming the documents were part of some elaborate ruse on the part of the British, Jameson wrote a letter to Arnold, explaining what had happened. Rather than send the letter directly to Arnold, however, he sent it by courier along with another—with similar contents—addressed to General Washington. Washington was traveling at the time and ended up taking a different route than was expected, with the result that the courier missed him. The courier delivered the letters to a residence where Arnold was supposed to be meeting Washington and several other officers for breakfast. If Washington hadn't tarried to examine some defensive fortifications before the meeting, it would have been a very awkward breakfast for Benedict Arnold indeed.

As it was, Arnold read the letter and, with admirable composure, finished his croissant, took a sip of tea, and excused himself from the table. He said goodbye to his wife and infant son, ran to the yard, leaped on a horse, and galloped down to the river, where he took a barge to the British sloop called, rather ominously, the Vulture.

Washington soon received the letter addressed to him and, having learned of Arnold's flight, quickly deduced what had happened. He alerted the men of West Point to the possibility of an attack, thus undoing the British advantage. As Washington dined that evening in the very room Arnold had fled in the morning, he received a letter from the traitor insisting on his wife's innocence in the matter. Summoning one of his officers, the broken-hearted general said quietly, "Go to Mrs. Arnold and tell her that though my duty required no means should be neglected to arrest General Arnold, I have great pleasure in acquainting *her* that he is now safe on board a British vessel."

Having evidently exhausted Lucifer's use for him, Benedict Arnold never saw his mysterious benefactor again. It became clear to all concerned shortly after the West Point debacle that the British cause was lost, and it can be assumed that Lucifer decided his energies were best spent elsewhere for the time being. This is not to say, though, that Arnold was never visited by another angel. In fact, while brooding on his fate on the deck of the Vulture that night, he noticed a familiar figure leaning against the railing.

"Pretty nice sloop," the man said. "One of the better sloops I've seen, and I've seen some sloopy sloops. I think this sloop is the sloopiest sloop."

"What do you want, Lord Squigglebottom? Or is it Mercier today? Or Mercury? Or Long-Drink-of-Water?"

"Just Mercury," said the man. "Sloop is a great name. Almost as good as man-o-war. What's your favorite kind of ship, Bennie?"

"Frigate," said Arnold.

"Watch your mouth," chided Mercury. "It was an innocent question."

Arnold sighed. "So are you here to add to my torment? To tell me I was wrong to betray the American side?"

"Nah," said Mercury. "I'm pretty sure your conscience is going to be eating at you for the rest of your life, so I don't really see the point in piling on. If it makes you feel better, that Rezon guy was actually Lucifer. You know, Satan? You're not the first person he's tempted to doing something they later regretted."

"Yeah," said Arnold. "I had deduced as much myself."

"Really? And you went along with his plan anyway?"

Arnold laughed bitterly, staring out at the moonlight reflected in the calm water. "You know why they hang traitors?" he asked.

"Um," replied Mercury. "Something to do with loyalty, I think."

"If an American officer is captured by the British, they treat him like a houseguest. Same thing for a British officer captured by the Americans. It's all tea and crumpets and no hard feelings. Neither side would ever dream of executing an officer just for being on the wrong side. It's universally considered barbaric. So why the gallows for a man who switches sides?"

"Um," replied Mercury again. "I'm sticking with the loyalty thing."

"Because the traitor reveals the inherent absurdity of war," Arnold went on. "If the British are all just basically good men doing their jobs and the Americans are all just basically good men doing their jobs, then switching from one side to another should raise eyebrows no more than a man walking down the street to save a farthing on a loaf of bread. But allowing officers to change sides at the drop of a hat would make a mockery of the whole idea of war, so we create this elaborate fiction around the idea of 'treason.' The traitor's only crime is to listen to his conscience rather than blindly accept the absurd contradictions of war."

Mercury raised an eyebrow at this. "Conscience?" he asked. "Is that what you're calling it?"

Arnold sighed heavily. "Perhaps my conscience is faulty," he admitted. "Perhaps I'm not so much following my own inner voice as rebelling against the decrees of small-minded men. I don't like my actions being dictated by the whims of fools."

Mercury had no response for that. He didn't particularly like it either.

"In the end, though," said Arnold, "I suppose I'm just a pawn in a game that's beyond my grasp. Tell me, Mercury, how does it all end?"

"What all?" asked Mercury.

"America," he said.

"You mean, do the Americans win?"

Arnold thought for a moment. "Yes, that, I suppose. But I'm really wondering whether, in a bigger sense, the American ideal survives."

"The American..."

161

Arnold laughed. "Ah, never mind," he said, wistfully. "Someone in your position, on the outside, you can't see it. There is something special about this place, though. And about the people. Something about the combination of the British love for law and order and this wild, untamed country. You can see it in the best of America's citizens, like Washington himself. If this country can follow his example, and not fall victim of the sort of petty backbiting and narrow self-interest that has befallen me—and which I, to my regret, have engaged—this country could become something the world has never seen. A beacon of freedom and justice. I want to know whether that could really happen, or whether men like Washington and Jefferson are doomed to be disappointed by what this country becomes."

To this, Mercury had no answer, and for a long time the two stared quietly out across the water.

"Sloop," said Mercury quietly at last. "Sloopy sloop."

# CHAPTER TWENTY-FOUR

*Grand Rapids, Michigan; August 2016*

The silver-haired figure burst from the clouds and plummeted toward the roof of the Vanden Heuvel Building. At first he fell limply, as if he were asleep, but as he approached the roof, he began to look around frantically, as if suddenly realizing where he was. But by then it was too late: he was caught in the Balderhaz Field, making it impossible for him to exert control over the interplanar energy fields. His eyes went wide as the roof grew steadily bigger. On the roof, almost directly under him, was a black duffel bag. He wondered what was in it. He wondered if he could make himself hit the duffel bag, and whether it would break his fall.

Fortunately, he didn't have to worry about the pain caused by hitting the roof, because when he was still about a hundred yards up, he was riddled with automatic weapon fire. It seemed that hiding behind various ventilation ducts had been several men wearing camouflage that made them virtually indistinguishable from the gravel of the rooftop.

The figure hit the roof about three feet from the duffel bag, which, holding only a cinder block, wouldn't have done much to break his fall anyway. He lay unmoving as the men ran out from their hiding places, their guns still trained on him. The door to the stairwell burst open and Zion Johnson ran out to examine the main. He pulled out a cell phone and punched a button.

"It's me," he said into the phone after a moment. "We got him. I'm sure, yeah. My guys tore him up pretty bad, but there's no mistaking the hair. So far, he's the only one who's shown up, but we're working on tracking down the other two. When this guy comes to, we'll put the screws to him."

Zion Johnson hung up the phone. Michelle had told him Mercury was the ringleader of the group, the one they needed to capture at all costs. The other one, Eddie, was a mild nuisance at worst, and Michelle was convinced that without Mercury he was no threat. Suzy was nothing to worry about either; they'd already gotten the thumb drive with the Brimstone data on it, so she had no proof of anything. Mercury was the one big x-factor, the fly in the ointment of Michelle's plan.

He grimaced as he approached the bloody figure on the roof. Zion Johnson had been given mug shots of Mercury, but there was no chance of identifying his face in this condition. If it weren't for that ridiculous hair, there'd be no way of knowing it was really him.

Zion Johnson grabbed a walkie-talkie from his belt. "This is Big Dog. Quicksilver is in the bag. I repeat, Quicksilver is in the bag. Send the elevator to the roof. Let's get moving."

One of the men threw the silver-haired figure over his shoulder and they made their way to the elevator. They took the elevator down to the parking garage, where they loaded the limp body into an unmarked van and got inside. The driver had been waiting for them; Zion Johnson threw his crutches inside and managed to climb into the passenger's side. The van peeled out, heading for the exit.

"Bomb... in... garbage..." moaned the silver-haired man in the back. One of the men kicked him in the ribs.

"Shut up!" yelled Zion Johnson. "And don't try anything. I've got this cube thing." He pulled the Balderhaz Cube from his pocket and regarded it. He couldn't help but laugh, despite the pain in his leg. "You guys aren't so special. All it takes to bring you down to our level is this little black cube."

The tires screeched and the Balderhaz cube jumped out of Zion Johnson's hand as the van came to a sudden stop.

"What the hell?" said Zion Johnson. But when he looked up it was clear why the driver had stopped. He'd been just about to pull out of the garage when a couple had walked in front of the van.

164

And not just any couple: a weasely-looking guy and a chick with purple hair. They were standing in the middle of the sidewalk, momentarily paralyzed with fear.

"Apprehend those two pedestrians!" growled Zion Johnson.

The van door swung open and four of the men jumped out.

Eddie and Suzy took off running, but they didn't get far. The men tackled them, ziptied their hands, and dragged them back to the van. They were hoisted into the back of the van along with the silver-haired man. Zion Johnson's men climbed in after them and slammed the door shut. The van pulled onto the street.

"Ha!" exclaimed Zion Johnson, looking behind him at the trio tied up in the back of the van. "I not only got the big fish, I got the two little ones too."

"…garbage…" the man in the back murmured.

"Yeah, good job on that," Suzy sneered at him. "You're like some kind of tactical genius."

"Suzy!" snapped Eddie.

"What?" said Suzy. "It's too late for him to do anything about it. It's up to Mercury to stop the bomb now."

Zion Johnson felt a sinking feeling in his gut. It was possible this was some sort of ruse, but it didn't feel like one. He jumped out of his seat, grimacing as pain jolted through his leg. "Out of my way!" he yelled at the men crowded into the van, as he clawed his way toward the man lying curled up in the back. He leaned over the man and grabbed his hair, yanking his head back so he could see his face. But it was no use; the man's face was still badly beat up and covered with blood. He understood that these BIOS—Beings of Indeterminate Origin, that's what they were calling them—healed at an extremely accelerated rate, but maybe the cube thing was interfering with that ability.

He pulled his hand back and found it sticky with blood and… something sparkly? It smelled like solvent. He turned to Suzy. "Is that… spray paint?" he asked, already knowing the answer. The sinking feeling had become more of a plummeting-in-free-fall-without-a-net feeling. He drew his gun—a Desert Eagle .44 magnum—and held it to the man's temple. "Who are you?" he demanded.

"…bomb…" the man with the spray-painted hair murmured.

"His name is Nisroc," said Suzy. "He's from Chaos Faction."

"But then…" said Zion Johnson, "Chaos Faction is *here?*"

"You seriously didn't know?" asked Suzy.

Zion Johnson said, "They were supposed to be… I mean, I thought they were…"

"They're here," said Suzy. "And they've got the bomb."

"…couldn't find the red *X*…" the man with the sticky silver hair murmured.

"Shut up," Zion Johnson growled, and shot Nisroc in the face.

# CHAPTER TWENTY-FIVE

*Grand Rapids, Michigan; August 2016*

Mercury crashed through a window on the top floor of the Vanden Heuvel Building, hitting the carpet and rolling several times, finally coming to a halt as he slammed into a heavy wooden desk.

"Ergh," he said, as he lay on the floor trying to orient himself. He'd waited as long as he dared for the men with the Balderhaz Cube to leave, but knowing that the bomb could go off any minute, he'd had to make the last fifty feet or so of the flight inside the field. He'd had to get up to a hundred miles an hour and aim slightly above the window to compensate for gravity, since he would be relying on momentum to get him the last fifty feet. He was a little amazed it actually worked.

He groggily got to his feet and looked around. He was in a reception area, beyond which was a maze of cubicles. "If I were a cute little nuclear bomb," Mercury mused, "where would I be?"

After a moment he remembered that Nisroc had said the bomb was in a janitor's cart. He sprinted down a hall between two rows of cubicles and turned at random down another. The cart was nowhere to be seen. He sprinted down another hall, but still didn't see the bomb. Realizing too late that he should have used a more systematic method, he made another turn and found himself back where he had started. Or was he? All of these posters selling PERSEVERANCE and DEDICATION and AMBITION looked alike. It seemed to Mercury that anyone who possessed any of those traits wouldn't be stuck in a place like this, but maybe that's why they had so many of them. Had he passed that seashore already? That mountain range looked familiar.

While trying to get his bearings, he literally stumbled on the janitor's cart, banging his knee against it while he was trying to make out whether a distant poster read DELIVERANCE or PERVERSITY. He rooted through the trash, finding at the bottom a lumpy, almost rectangular mass of components wrapped in brown plastic, about the size of an Oxford dictionary. Mercury shuddered. It looked just like the Wormwood bomb. He could try disarming it, since now he knew which wire not to disconnect, but he didn't want to take the chance that they'd swapped the wire colors for the Mark II bomb. There was no visible timer on this one, so it was impossible to know when it was going to detonate. It was also impossible to determine why the bomb smelled like gasoline, but that was a question for another time. He tucked the bomb under his arm, sprinted across the floor, and crashed through the nearest window.

And immediately began plummeting toward the ground.

Mercury had taken so long to find the bomb that he'd assumed the agent carrying the Balderhaz Cube would be well out of range by the time he jumped through the window, but apparently he'd been mistaken. He managed to get ahold of enough interplanar energy to slow his descent a bit, landing with a crash on the roof of a parked Buick sedan, shattering the windows and crushing the roof canopy. It was late enough that the streets were mostly deserted, but the few pedestrians in the area stopped and gaped at him.

"Hey, it's that terrorist from TV!" somebody yelled. "And he's got a bomb!"

This struck Mercury as a little unfair. Even if he was a terrorist, there was no way anyone could know that what he was carrying was a bomb. He didn't even think it particularly looked like a bomb. It could be a box of blueberry muffins for all they knew. Mercury wished it *was* a box of blueberry muffins instead of a device for starting an uncontrollable nuclear reaction that would level twenty blocks. He loved blueberry muffins.

Mercury leaped off the Buick onto the street and began sprinting down the street away from the Vanden Heuvel building. If he was going to get airborne, he needed to get farther away from the Balderhaz Cube. When he was half a block from the building, he shot into the air, to the abject surprise of the pedestrians.

Soaring above the buildings, Mercury gained velocity as he left the Balderhaz field behind. His greatest fear was that the bomb would go off while he was only half a mile or so up. He'd done enough research after his experience with the Wormwood bomb to know that a ten kiloton bomb would actually do far more damage if it detonated several hundred yards up than at ground level. That had presumably been the reasoning behind putting the bomb on the thirty-fifth floor of the Vanden Heuvel. If Michelle had really wanted to maximize destruction, she'd have had someone carry it a few hundred yards higher into the sky, right above downtown— exactly like Mercury was doing right now. The Little Boy bomb, which had destroyed Hiroshima, was of comparable explosive power, and it had been designed to detonate at 1,900 feet for maximum impact.

He assumed that whenever the bomb went off, it was going to take him with it. He didn't particularly like the idea of being blown to a billion pieces far above western Michigan, but it was a painless way to disincorporate, and of course it wouldn't be permanent. His angelic life force would gradually reassemble his body over the course of the next several hours, and he'd be as good as new. The same was true for any other angels caught in the blast radius. Human beings, of course, would not be so fortunate.

When he was about half a mile up, he began to think he might just make it far enough away to save most of the residents of the city. In the interest of making better time—and out of concern for the residents of Lansing, about an hour downwind to the east—he turned north toward what looked like a mostly forested, unpopulated area. He continued to climb gradually, and soon was a mile up and about five miles from downtown Grand Rapids. He'd made it. If the bomb went off now, it was far enough away from the city to cause minimal damage. Maybe Michelle's people weren't as smart as he had figured.

He wasn't sure what to do with the bomb, though. He could try to stash it somewhere and maybe use it as leverage against Michelle, but what if they had some way of tracking it? He could destroy it, but he wasn't sure how to do that without either detonating it or spreading highly radioactive material all over the place. He could put it into orbit, but that would be a catastrophe waiting to happen. He could bring it to the Moon, but that would take days. And really, hadn't he done enough damage to the Moon?

He'd finally settled on the North Pole when the bomb went off in his hands.

# CHAPTER TWENTY-SIX

*Apocalypse Bureau Building, Heaven, 1783 A.D.*

"Enough!" cried Mercury, to the astonishment of Uzziel, who jumped nearly out of his chair.

Uzziel had been expounding on Heaven's latest plans for America. The war had been won, but now Heaven had turned its sights to France, where Tiamat was stirring up rebellious sentiment. It was thought that if there was a revolution in France, war could spill over into Britain. If America joined the French cause, it could be very bad for the prospects of parliamentary government in Western Europe. So now Mercury was to be tasked with the precise opposite of his previous mission: he was to stoke the fires of American affection for the mother country. It was thought by the higher-ups that pro-British sentiment could dampen the Americans' enthusiasm for the cause of *Liberté*, *égalité*, and *fraternité*. Not that there was anything wrong with *Liberté*, *égalité*, and *fraternité per se*. Heaven was all in favor of *Liberté*, *égalité*, and *fraternité* in principle, but it was generally agreed that France wasn't quite ready for a big helping of all three at once.

Mercury, though, was thoroughly fed up and for once simply refused to follow orders. "First of all," he growled, "I've got nearly ninety years of vacation time saved up, and at the rate you've got me working I'm going to hit the century mark pretty quick. You know payroll won't let me bank more than a hundred years, which means that I'm going to lose that time. Don't make me file a report with the Wage and Hours Commission."

Before Uzziel could respond, Mercury went on, "Second, I'm sick to death of interfering in these complex political situations. First nobody wants war. Then Lucifer wants war, but we don't. Then we want war too. Tiamat doesn't care one way or another, but she pretends to help bring about war so that she can take over France. War breaks out and everybody's happy, except for me and all the guys getting shot to death, of course. Everybody except George Washington is convinced that the British are going to win, but for some reason we support the Americans anyway. Then Lucifer changes his mind and decides to support the British. The British lose and Lucifer gets distracted by something shiny in South Africa. Meanwhile we're just thrilled about the American victory for about five minutes, when we realize that, hey, big surprise, Tiamat has *fucking taken over France*. So now suddenly we have to get the Americans to remember that they're best pals with the country that a few years earlier had hired a bunch of Germans to kill them. It's insane! How do you not see this?"

"I'll admit it's a complex situation..." started Uzziel.

"A round robin tournament of monkeys playing Parcheesi in bumper boats is a complex situation," yelled Mercury. "This is a fucking disaster! How can anyone with an ounce of sense think that getting involved in this sort of situation is a good idea? There are so many alliances and counter-alliances and double-crosses, it's completely impossible to foresee the outcome of anything you might do anyway! What is the point, man?"

"Well, that's just the thing," said Uzziel. "Lucifer and Tiamat aren't going to stay out of the situation even if we do, so we've got to have some presence on the ground. And while it's true that in a chaotic system it can be difficult to anticipate—"

"What if we all just stayed out?" Mercury asked.

Uzziel's brow furrowed. "What do you mean?"

"I mean, Lucifer and Tiamat don't understand the situation in America any better than we do. What if we all just got together and agreed to stay the hell out of their business?"

"That would free up their demons to do a lot of damage in Europe and Asia..."

"And it would free up a lot of angels to counteract them," finished Mercury. "Look, I get we're supposed to be doing what we can to bring about the Divine Plan, and we've got a lot of vested interests in Europe, the Middle East, and plenty of other places on the Mundane Plane. But we don't really have much going on in North America yet. It's mostly just me running up and down the eastern seaboard changing wigs. Lucifer has pulled out most of his guys, and Tiamat's focused on France these days. Why couldn't we all just agree to let the Americans decide their own fate?"

Uzziel shook his head. "That's not the way it works," he said. "We're charged with unfolding the Divine Plan on the Mundane Plane, and currently that means we're supporting the cause of representative government in the New World. That means boots on the ground."

"Do you even hear yourself talking?" Mercury asked. "What part of 'representative government' do you not understand? How can you say you're in favor of 'representative government' while simultaneously being opposed to letting the American people govern themselves without our interference?"

"I get the point you're trying to make, Mercury…"

"Do you? Because it kind of seems like you don't. It seems like you're all 'rah-rah democracy' until someone wants to actually have a fucking democracy."

"What has gotten into you, Mercury?" asked Uzziel. "It's not just the vacation days, I can see that."

"I'm tired, Uzziel. Tired of messing with people's lives for no good reason. What's wrong with letting people make their own decisions for once?"

Uzziel sat back in his chair, regarding Mercury somberly. The fact was, Uzziel was right: there was something that had prompted him to make this suggestion—some*one*, actually. But it would help matters if Uzziel knew that. It was best if Uzziel thought Mercury had come up with the idea on his own.

"I'll float the idea up the chain," Uzziel said at last. "No guarantees."

"Fantastic," said Mercury. "That's all I'm asking."

"All right," said Uzziel. "Now get out of here. Take a few days off. You look terrible."

# CHAPTER TWENTY-SEVEN

*Near Grand Rapids, Michigan; August 2016*

The man who had abducted Suzy and Eddie—his name was apparently Zion Johnson—lost no time in reacting once Suzy told him about the bomb. Whatever could be said about this guy, thought Suzy, he was decisive. He threw poor, beat-up, bleeding, spray-painted Nisroc out the door of the van, got back in his seat, and started barking orders. The van peeled out of the garage and got onto the road, the engine roaring and horns blaring as smaller vehicles scattered to get out of its path. Suzy tried to figure out where they were headed, but Zion Johnson also had her and Eddie fitted with cloth hoods that prevented them from seeing where they were going. After a lot of squealing tires, honking horns, and rolling around on the van floor, the van screeched to a stop, the door was thrown open, and she was lifted bodily out of the van and carried to another vehicle nearby. From the sounds it made, she was pretty she was in a helicopter. Somebody strapped her in, and she felt someone—presumably Eddie—being strapped in next to her. She heard the pitch of the engine increasing as the rotors spun faster and faster. After a few seconds, she felt the vehicle leave the ground. Suzy was strapped tightly into her seat, which was good because her hands were tied, making it difficult for her to brace herself against the movements of the cabin.

"Don't bother to try any fancy tricks," barked Zion Johnson over the whine of the motor. "I've still got the Balderdash Cube, so your magic powers won't work."

"Balderhaz," muttered Eddie.

"Shut up!" yelled the man, and she felt Eddie jerk backwards as if being struck. Then he went limp and stayed quiet.

The helicopter pitched forward and began to pick up speed. They arced to the right and then continued straight for some time, rapidly gaining altitude. Then everything became very quiet, as if the motor had suddenly cut out. Suzy felt the tiny hairs on her arms stand up and the cabin became suddenly warm, as if being showered with bright sunlight.

"Get us the fuck—" yelled Zion Johnson. The rest of his words were drowned out by the whoosh of a sudden wind, followed by a deafening boom. The helicopter pitched forward and Suzy was thrust back against her seat. Eddie stirred next to her.

There was another moment of eerie near-silence, in which only the hum of the rotors could be heard. The helicopter began to fall.

Another rush of wind followed, this time pulling them backward. Suzy felt the helicopter pitch and roll crazily.

"We're going down!" yelled a man farther away, whom Suzy took for the pilot.

"Wha... happened?" murmured Eddie.

"I think the bomb went off," Suzy said urgently. "We're falling! Is there anything you can do?"

"Ungh," said Eddie. "Balderhaz."

They were now losing altitude rapidly, the helicopter wobbling lazily from side-to-side in the chaotic wind.

"Can't you get the rotors going?" barked Zion Johnson.

"EMP must have fried something," said the pilot. "Everything's dead!"

"Jesus Christ," growled Zion Johnson. "Whose idea was it to take a fucking helicopter? We could be in a fucking Cadillac right now. I bet an EMP wouldn't take out a Cadillac. And if it did, who cares? You're in a fucking Cadillac. You pull over and wait for fucking Triple A."

The helicopter continued to fall.

"Drop the cube," said Suzy suddenly.

"What?" snapped Zion Johnson.

"Drop the Balderhaz Cube! Eddie can save us if you get rid of the damn cube!"

"Not a chance," said Zion Johnson. "He'll use his powers to escape."

"He'll escape for sure if we crash," replied Suzy. "We'll all be killed, but he'll escape. Is that what you want?"

There was a momentary pause, in which Suzy wondered whether the regimented stupidity of military thinking was going to prevent Zion Johnson from making the only possible correct decision.

"Throw out the cube!" he barked at last. "Now!"

"Yes, sir!" shouted another man.

"OK, it's gone," yelled Zion Johnson. "Do something!"

"Take my hood off," said Eddie. There was some commotion next to Suzy. "Hers too," Eddie said. Suzy's hood was jerked off.

"Alright, now do something!" shouted Zion Johnson. He was a gruff-looking man who seemed to be in his early fifties. His left leg was encased in a cast. Besides Zion and the pilot, there were two other young men in combat gear in the helicopter.

"Can't," said Eddie.

"Why not?" demanded Zion Johnson.

Suzy chanced a look down and could just make out a farmer on a tractor in a cornfield staring up at them. The farmer waved.

"We're falling almost as fast as the cube," said Eddie. "I can feel the field weakening, but I'm going to need a few more seconds."

"We don't have a few more seconds!" Zion Johnson yelled.

Eddie shrugged. "Should have taken a Cadillac," he said. "Or not detonated a nuclear bomb."

Suzy saw that the farmer had gotten off his tractor and was now fleeing through the cornfield. She could make out individual ears of corn. She had remembered hearing something a few years back about some mutant strain of corn that was taking over South Africa. She wondered whatever happened with that.

The helicopter continued to fall. She could feel Eddie straining his muscles next to her, as if he were using every cell in his body to try to stop their fall. Then she felt a strange tingling, as the hairs on the back of her neck were being pulled upward. She felt the descent of the helicopter slow.

"OK, now land us," said Zion Johnson, drawing his sidearm. "And don't try anything or I'll shoot the girl."

"Doing... my... best..." Eddie gasped. "Cube... right... below us...."

"He can't set us down," Suzy said. "The closer we get to the cube, the weaker his power is." She turned to Eddie. "Can you get us higher? Or move us horizontally away from the cube."

Eddie's face had turned red and sweat was pouring down his brow. "All I can... do... to keep us... in air."

They were now floating a little over a hundred yards off the ground. The helicopter's rotors were spinning so slowly that Suzy could see the individual blades. A fall from this height would kill them as surely as a fall from ten miles up.

"Rope!" yelled Zion Johnson. The other man handed him a bundle of rope, securing one end to a metal clip in the floor. Zion Johnson tossed the rope out the door and it unwound as it fell. The end of the rope hung about thirty feet off the ground.

The man who had handed Zion Johnson the rope shrugged. "That's all we have," he said apologetically.

"Are you shitting me?" asked Zion Johnson. He turned to Eddie. "Can you drop us another thirty feet?"

Eddie stared at the man in horror, his whole body trembling. His face was purple and his clothes were drenched with sweat.

"I think that means no," said Suzy. "I mean, he can drop us, but we'll keep dropping."

"Alright," said Zion Johnson. He turned to the other man. "Get down there."

"Sir?"

"Climb down the goddamn rope until you run out of rope. Then fall to the ground. Find that cube and get it as far away from us as possible. Preferably before we crash into you."

"Yessir!" The man gripped the rope and lowered himself to the helicopter's landing gear. Then he disappeared from view.

Suzy moved closer to the door so she could see what was happening.

"Don't try anything!" growled Zion Johnson.

"Like what?" demanded Suzy, holding up her hands, which were still bound with a zip-tie. "Falling to my death?"

The young man had made it about halfway down the rope, and was continuing to move hand-over-hand toward the ground. The helicopter jerked suddenly and fell a few heart-stopping feet before halting its descent again. Suzy looked over at Eddie, who looked like he was about to pass out. "Just a little longer, Eddie!" she said. "You can do it!"

The man had now reached the end of the rope and was looking uncertainly at the ground, which was still a good twenty feet below him.

"Jump!" yelled Zion Johnson. "We don't have time for this! Jump, Newton!"

The young man, evidently named Newton, let go of the rope, plummeting to the cornfield. The ground looked rather soft and muddy from the helicopter, but Suzy supposed it didn't feel that soft when you fell onto it from twenty feet up.

Newton yelped in pain, rolling to his side and gripping his ankle.

"Find the cube!" shouted Zion Johnson.

The man got on his knees and began crawling around the cornstalks.

"I can't..." Eddie gasped.

"Just hold on a little longer, Eddie!" Suzy cried.

Down below, Newton was still crawling around in the mud, trying to find the Balderhaz cube.

"Got it!" he shouted at last, holding a black object about the size of a Rubik's Cube.

"Get away from the helo!" yelled Zion Johnson.

Newton began crawling away.

Eddie continued to shake, and he eyes began to glaze over. He looked like he was having a seizure, but the helicopter remained levitating just over a hundred yards up.

Newton had managed to get on one foot and was hopping as quickly as he could away from the helicopter.

Eddie's eyes began to roll back in his head. The helicopter pitched forward began to lose altitude.

"Eddie!" Suzy cried. But Eddie had passed out, slouched over in his seat. The helicopter was in freefall. "Eddie!" Suzy screamed again, slapping him across the face.

"Eh?" said Eddie, looking around crazily.

"We're falling!"

"Oh," said Eddie.

Then the helicopter hit the ground.

It landed head-first, throwing Suzy against her restraints and knocking the wind out of her lungs. The windshield shattered and the cockpit crumpled. Then the helicopter rolled onto its left side, rocked a few times, and was still. Suzy was dazed but conscious, as were Zion Johnson and the pilot. Eddie had passed out again. She could only assume that Eddie had managed to break their fall at the last moment. There was no other explanation for why they were still alive.

Suzy managed to free herself from her restraints and then unfasten Eddie's.

"Don't try anything," said Zion Johnson, who was lying sprawl on the wall of the helicopter, still holding his gun on her.

"Will you stop saying that?" Suzy snapped. "I get it, you have a gun. I don't. Now will you help me get Eddie out of here?"

Zion Johnson nodded to the other men. The pilot climbed out the door of the helicopter, which was now overhead. The other man grabbed Eddie around the middle and hoisted him onto his shoulder. The pilot grabbed Eddie's belt and dragged him on top of the helicopter. Then he gave Eddie's limp body a shove, and Eddie slid across the top of the fuselage to the ground, landing with a thud.

"Hey!" cried Suzy. "Be careful! He just saved your life!"

The man next her shrugged.

Zion Johnson went next, managing to climb out with minimal assistance despite his immobile left leg. When he was out of the way, the two men helped Suzy out. She scrambled down the fuselage to the ground, followed by the other man. Eddie was lying crumpled on the ground, moaning. Zion Johnson and the pilot stood nearby. The man who had fallen from the rope, Newton, was nowhere to be seen.

"Newton!" yelled Zion Johnson. "Get back here!"

Suzy helped Eddie sit up. He lay blinking in the sunlight. "Wow," he said, staring into the distance.

It didn't take long for Suzy to figure out what Eddie was looking at: the remnants of a mushroom cloud hung in the sky. "The city…" she gasped.

Eddie shook his head. "Too far away. He did it. Mercury saved Grand Rapids."

"Newton!" yelled Zion Johnson again. "Get back here with that cube!"

"Eddie," whispered Suzy. "Can you walk? If we can get far enough away from that cube…"

Eddie nodded, glancing over at the three men, who were still staring into the cornfield.

"Where the hell is Newton?" growled Zion Johnson.

Eddie quietly got up and the crept away between two rows of corn.

"Hey!" yelled Zion Johnson. "Didn't I tell you not to try anything?"

Suzy stopped, raising her bound hands above her head. They turned to face Zion Johnson, who was training his gun on them.

"If you fire that gun, I'll make it blow up in your face," said Eddie.

"Why wait?" replied Zion Johnson with a smirk. "Just make it blow up now. Go ahead, do it."

Eddie glared at him.

"You won't," said Zion Johnson, "because you can't."

As he spoke, Newton crawled out from a wall of corn stalks. His face was ashen, and in one hand he clutched the Balderhaz Cube. He dropped it and fell face-first into the mud. His left ankle was bent at a completely unnatural angle.

"Now here's what we're going to do," said Zion Johnson, plucking the Balderhaz Cube out of Newton's hand and handing it to the man to his left. "Purple-hair and Jenkins are going to go for a nice walk to that tractor over there. Eddie, you're going to fix Newton's ankle and my leg. If you try anything funny, Jenkins is going to shoot Purple-hair in the head." He glanced at Jenkins, who nodded and drew his gun. "Then, assuming we're all still alive and ambulatory, we're going to walk to that farmhouse and commandeer a vehicle with four fucking wheels and some drink holders. Everybody on board with that?"

181

# CHAPTER TWENTY-EIGHT

*Heaven, Washington, D.C., and Plane 4721c; 1789 - 1793*

To Mercury's astonishment, his plan of angelic non-involvement in North America met with some interest in the higher reaches of the Heavenly bureaucracy. The main concern was the difficulty of enforcing the agreement. If Heaven pulled its agents out of North America, it would have no way of knowing whether Lucifer and Tiamat had done the same.

Another problem was that various Heavenly agencies not involved in military intelligence insisted that it was necessary for them to have free reign in North America. Prophecy Division, for example, claimed that it was a violation of their charter to agree to any sort of neutrality treaty. Mercury's own organization, Apocalypse Bureau, also expressed misgivings about going along with an agreement that would limit its ability to manifest the Divine Plan.

Mercury's solution to this problem was to limit Heaven's activities only in regards to political endeavors. He argued that there was no reason both Prophecy and Apocalypse Bureau couldn't fulfill their obligations without attempting to directly influence political decision-making. They'd be free to do whatever they wanted in the nascent country except to partake in the process of governing or manipulate political officials. He called it the Separation of Angels and Government.

Prophecy was skeptical, but Uzziel said he thought he could sign off on the concept if Lucifer and Tiamat could be convinced to go along with it. Presumably Uzziel assumed that would never happen—a safe assumption, given the fact that Lucifer and Tiamat rarely agreed on anything, and almost never agreed with Heaven. But Mercury pulled some strings with the Diplomacy Corps, and ultimately a meeting was set up on neutral ground[6] between the archangel Michelle, Tiamat, and Lucifer. The meeting was rancorous and vitriolic, but after three days the three parties had hammered out a basic agreement.

It was Tiamat, surprisingly, who offered a solution to the problem of enforcement. Tiamat had for centuries been experimenting with ways of manipulating interplanar energy to bend the fabric of space and time. She'd had limited success with this, but in the course of her research she had learned a great deal about the nature of the mysterious energy that permeated every plane of the multiverse. Angels, although they instinctively know how to use interplanar energy to bend the laws of physics, generally know about as much about the nature of this energy as fish know about the nature of water. Tiamat had realized early on that if she could discover the basic principles by which this energy operated, she might very well exercise dominion over all the other angels, who were so thoroughly dependent on it.

The most brilliant angel in her employ had been an eccentric cherub named Balderhaz, the inventor of the Balderhaz Cube.[7] Balderhaz had left Tiamat's employ not long before, having been recruited by Michelle to be her chief weapons supplier. Tiamat knew that when Balderhaz left, he had been working on another sort of device based on the technology used to create the Balderhaz Cube. He called it the Meta-Energy Oscillation Weapon, or MEOW. MEOW would create a field like that emitted by a Balderhaz Cube, but instead of cancelling out the Interplanar Energy, it amplified it and altered its frequency. The result was that

---

[6] Plane 4721c, known for its delicious cheeses.

[7] A Balderhaz Cube, as you may recall, is a device that emanates a "no miracle" zone within a given radius. There are believed to be about a dozen Cubes in existence, one of which was causing Ederatz the cherub a great deal of trouble at present.

any angel within range of MEOW would not only be unable to harness the energy; he or she would also experience a constant ear-splitting screech that sounded like a cat being slowly turned inside out.

Tiamat also knew, though, that Balderhaz had run into apparently insurmountable technical difficulties with MEOW. She divulged this fact at the meeting—as well as making the claim that Tiamat herself had found the solution. Michelle, who had been hoping to use MEOW against Tiamat, was loath to reveal anything about the new weapon, but she was even more concerned that Tiamat might successfully build one before Heaven did. Tiamat, who was missing some key components and the brains behind most of the development, had similar fears about Michelle. Tiamat suggested that she and Balderhaz meet to complete the design, and that the first working device be placed in the capital city of the United States. The effect would be to prevent any angels or demons from entering the city limits. There would be nothing preventing them from attempting to influence politicians outside of this sphere, but it was thought that making the capital itself completely off-limits to supernatural influence would prevent the most blatant attempts at manipulation. Lucifer knew nothing of MEOW, but he was happy to go along as he didn't currently have the manpower to try to corrupt the entire U.S. Congress.

So Balderhaz and Tiamat met and hammered out the technical details, and a few weeks later they had a working prototype. After testing indicated that the device caused excruciating pain to any angel within a one-mile radius, it was decided that it was ready for deployment. By this time Washington, D.C. had been selected as the location for the U.S. capitol, and designs were being finalized for the Capitol Building. Mercury arranged for the device to be hidden inside the cornerstone of the capitol, which was laid on the first of March, 1793. From that date until late in 2001, neither angel nor demon came within a mile of the U.S. Capitol.

And then something changed.

185

# CHAPTER TWENTY-NINE

*Somewhere in the Eastern Atlantic Ocean; August 2016*

Some time after being blown into a billion pieces by a nuclear bomb, Mercury found himself in a bar called La Traviata on an island in the Azores. If asked, he probably wouldn't have been able to answer precisely when he reincorporated or how he got to the bar exactly. Being vaporized tended to wreak havoc on one's short-term memory, and having eighteen beers in the course of four hours didn't help either.

He supposed that he ended up here because it was a familiar place, a sanctuary of sorts. He'd sought refuge here several times in the past. He came here when he was in danger, or when he was feeling at loose ends. Right now, he was both.

He should feel good about saving Grand Rapids. That had been a good thing. But Eddie and Suzy were now Michelle's captives. At least, he assumed they were. Eddie had sent a transmission via Angel Band shortly before the bomb went off indicating that Michelle's men had found them. Eddie said that they had a couple of Chaos Faction members with them, so Eddie decided not to put up a fight and risk hurting Suzy. That was the last Mercury heard from them. He had no idea where they were or what Michelle planned to do with them. And even if he did, what chance did a lone cherub have against Michelle's massive security apparatus? She had the whole U.S. government at her disposal, not to mention hundreds of angels. Perhaps it was best just to lay low. Eventually the truth would come out about what Michelle was doing, and then she wouldn't be able to get away with it anymore. He was a little fuzzy on who was going to stop her and how, but presumably things would work out in the end. They always had in the past. Like during World War II, when it looked like the Nazis were going to take over the whole world, but then Michelle and her angels... OK, well, that was a bad example. It was more like the Cuban Missile Crisis, when it looked like the U.S. and Russia were going to get into a full-on nuclear war, but at the last minute Michelle...

It occurred to him that he couldn't think of an example of a potential worldwide catastrophe that hadn't been forestalled at least in part by Michelle and her Heavenly army. That was back when Michelle was taking orders from the Heavenly Senate, though. When the job was done, she was always called back to Heaven to await the next crisis. Now there was no one to call her home, and no home for her to go to. Michelle was the ultimate authority on Earth, and there was no one who could challenge her. Well, *almost* no one. But there were some possibilities that were even more horrific to consider than an all-powerful Michelle.

"Hey, Jorge," said Mercury to the bartender. "Can you turn that off?" The talking heads on the news had been blathering non-stop about the explosion near Grand Rapids. They kept showing shaky video of the blast and then three pictures: Eddie, Suzy and Mercury. Eddie's looked like a security camera photo; Suzy's was her employee ID photo from the Brimstone project; and Mercury's was a composite drawing that made him look a little like the lead singer of Coldplay. He resented this almost as much as the implication that he was some kind of terrorist. Various government officials were blaming Chaos Faction, the Babcock administration, and lax security protocols for the blast, and crediting "quick-thinking federal agents" for getting the bomb out of the city in time. It was repeatedly stressed that other attacks, perhaps with chemical or biological agents, were expected. Martial law would continue indefinitely in the high-risk cities, and the list of high-risk cities was expected to grow as more intelligence was gathered.

Jorge shut off the TV and handed Mercury another beer. Nobody in the bar complained; apparently all the other patrons were sick of hearing about it too. There wasn't anything anybody could do about nuclear bombs going off halfway around the world, so there was no point in obsessing over it. At least, that's the general impression Mercury got of the sentiment in the bar. Being rather addled at this point, he may not have been the best judge.

In fact, it seemed that he was now hallucinating. For he was looking at what appeared to be a small child wrapped in an overlong coat, nursing a beer in the corner of the bar.

"Do you see that?" he asked Jorge.

"What?" Jorge replied.

"That little guy over there." Mercury blinked several times, but he still saw the diminutive figure.

"Sure," Jorge said. "That's Pete. He's been coming in here almost every day for the last three years. Odd looking guy, but nice enough. Just don't ask for his advice on anything."

"Why's that?"

"He never shuts up once he gets started. Always talking about how to unstick zippers or keep mushrooms fresh or something."

"You don't say," replied Mercury, regarding the tiny figure. He realized why he hadn't noticed the weird little guy before: the overcoat covered most of the stool, giving the impression that he was a full-sized person. He wasn't hallucinating; he was suddenly seeing things as they really were.

Mercury stumbled over to the table where the little person sat. "This seat taken?" he asked, indicating a stool on the opposite side of the table.

"Portugal is a free country," said the little figure. "For a little longer, anyway. Power corrupts. Absolute power corrupts absolutely."

Mercury took a seat. "Your tips have gotten a bit more philosophical," he said, setting his beer down on the table.

"I don't have much practical advice to give these days. Everything seems so... Mercury!"

Mercury grinned. "Good to see you, Perp. What are you doing in Portugal? For that matter, what are you doing on the Mundane Plane?"

Perp sighed. "I've been here for three years. When I opened that portal to get your friends back here, I decided to slip through myself. Not that I didn't trust you to defuse that bomb..."

"You made the right call," said Mercury. "Who knows what would have happened to you if you'd stayed in the planeport."

"What happened to *you?*"

"Er," Mercury said. "Hard to explain. I've sort of been on vacation. I got summoned back here by some idiot wannabe Satanists."

"Should have known when that bomb went off in Michigan," replied Perp. "Stuff explodes wherever you go. That's two nuclear blasts you're responsible for. And you imploded most of Anaheim. Plus the Moon thing. What is it with you and explosions?"

"Technically Anaheim and the Moon were *im*plosions. And I'm pretty sure the second nuke was Chris Martin from Coldplay," said Mercury. "How did things get so screwed up, Perp?"

Perp shook his head. "Those who would give up essential liberty to purchase a little temporary safety deserve neither liberty nor safety."

"But where did it all go wrong, Perp? I was here. I was around when Lucifer was infiltrating the U.S. government with his agents. How did I not notice? How did he manage to get demons into D.C. in the first place? What happened to the barrier?"

"Flight 93," replied Perp quietly.

"Huh?" asked Mercury.

"September 11, 2001. Flight 93 was one of the four planes that were hijacked. Two of them hit the World Trade Center in New York and one hit the Pentagon. Those were distractions, though. Flight 93 was the important one. That's the one that hit the Capitol Building."

"Holy shit, Perp, that's it!" cried Mercury. "It must have damaged the MEOW device. How did that not occur to anybody?"

"It did," replied Perp. "Lucifer was fully aware of it, obviously, since he was the one behind the attacks. But he was clever about it. Rather than send in his agents right away, he waited for Heaven to figure out the barrier was down. He suspected that Michelle would try to take advantage of the situation by infiltrating D.C. with her own agents. In fact, he knew exactly which angels she would likely send, since they were mostly double agents working for him. Once Michelle had her agents in place, Lucifer knew she was in no position to insist that the Non-Involvement Agreement of 1791 be honored. Over the next several years, he filled dozens of key advisory posts inside the government with demons. Having planned for this for over a decade, he was much better prepared to seize the reins of government than Michelle, and by the time Michelle realized she'd been hoodwinked, it was too late for her to say anything. The best she could do was to secretly plot against Lucifer behind the scenes, trying to turn his agents against him. Her recruiting efforts were not very successful."

"Until Lucifer was captured. And Michelle was stranded on this plane."

"Right. She was perfectly situated to take over where Lucifer had left off. And although Lucifer had managed to fool her once, she's quite a bit more capable than he, as you well know."

"So that's it, then," said Mercury. "We're screwed. Lucifer put the machine in place, and now Michelle is running it. There's no stopping her from taking over the whole world and ruling it with an iron fist."

"It doesn't look good," Perp agreed. "Most regimes built around the personality of a charismatic leader collapse when the leader dies. But with Michelle..."

"Yeah." Mercury sighed heavily. "I wish there was something I could do about Suzy and Eddie, at least."

"The terrorists who hang out with Chris Martin?"

"They don't hang out with Chris Martin!" Mercury protested. "They're friends of mine. They helped me get that bomb out of Grand Rapids. But they got captured, and now I don't know where they are."

"Well," replied Perp. "I can tell you where they're likely to end up. Possum Kingdom."

"They're going to end up in a Toadies song?"

"Possum Kingdom is a state park in Texas, about half an hour outside Dallas. A few years ago, a huge cave was discovered not far from the park. The authorities put fences up around the area, supposedly because the ground is unstable and could cave in. But a geologist from the University of Texas claimed that was a bunch of bunk. And then a hiker uploaded pictures of the fences they erected: thirty foot tall electrified chain-link fence topped with razor wire. There are two fences, about fifty feet apart—one with the razor wire facing out, and one with the razor wire facing in. Oh, and nobody knows what happened to the guy who took the pictures."

"So what?" asked Mercury dubiously. "They're running some kind of top secret underground prison?"

"Have you heard of Chaos Faction?"

"Yeah, they're the ones the government is blaming for the bomb in Michigan."

"Exactly. The government keeps trying to play up Chaos Faction as this big, bad terrorist organization, blaming them for every kidnapping in Baghdad or natural gas explosion in Pasadena. But I know for a fact that Tiamat and most of her minions were captured during an attempted attack on Fort Knox."

"Wait, Tiamat is part of Chaos Faction?"

"Of course!" Perp exclaimed. "It's her organization! She started it to cause problems for Michelle, to put a few speed bumps on the road to world domination. But Chaos Faction is a shell of its former self. All the key members, including Tiamat, have been captured. Which raises two key questions: first, who the hell is really running what's left of Chaos Faction these days? And second, where the hell are Tiamat and her minions?"

"Well, we know the answer to number one," said Mercury. "Michelle has co-opted the group for her own purposes."

"And I'll bet you anything Tiamat and her minions are in Possum Kingdom. And if your friends aren't there yet, they soon will be. Along with Chris Martin and anybody else Michelle considers a threat."

"Where do you hear all this stuff?" Mercury asked.

"You know me," said Perp. "I find things out. But most of this stuff is available online. BitterAngels.net broke the story about Possum Kingdom last year, but none of the mainstream news organizations picked it up. I'm not sure if the news organizations are in Michelle's pocket, or if they're just incompetent and lazy. Either way, the information is out there, but hardly anybody seems to care."

"Maybe they just don't know what to do," offered Mercury.

"Maybe," said Perp. "But what's the difference?"

Mercury nodded. It was true, as long as nobody stood up to Michelle, nothing was going to change. But what could anyone do? Mercury was an angel who had powers far surpassing those of an ordinary mortal, and he didn't have a clue what to do. Not about

Michelle's plan for world domination, anyway. There was one thing he could do, though.

"So," he said, "Let's suppose you're right about this Possum Kingdom place. How would you go about breaking someone out?"

Perp grinned at him. "Fools rush in where angels fear to tread," he replied.

# CHAPTER THIRTY

*Costa Rica; August 2016*

The next day Mercury and Perp found themselves in the remote jungles of Costa Rica. Perp claimed to have a lead on an idea for breaking into Possum Kingdom, and Mercury, though dubious, had little choice but to go along.

"How do you even know where this place is?" asked Mercury, as they trudged through the jungle. Well, Mercury trudged, while Perp fluttered. They were on a sort of path, but it was fairly overgrown and occasionally Perp would make a slashing motion and a vine or branch would fall as if severed by an invisible machete.

"I told you," said Perp. "I know things. Avoid eating bright red berries."

"Nice to know you're back to your old self," replied Mercury. "Philosophical Perp was starting to get on my nerves."

"I think it's just ahead," said Perp.

"OK," said Mercury. "But for the record, I'd like to say that I don't trust anyone who lives by himself in a remote cabin in the wilderness. It's not normal. Also, those places smell terrible."

"Agreed," said Perp. "Nobody ever accused Balderhaz of being normal."

Eventually they came upon the cabin, which turned out to be a mansion compared to Mercury's now-obliterated hovel. The place was so well-camouflaged, though, that Mercury didn't realized he was looking right at it until he was less than fifty feet away. It was a multi-leveled structure with an irregular, tiered roof that seemed intended to mimic the jungle from above. Knowing Balderhaz, the visual aspect was only one small part of the structure's camouflage. He'd probably constructed the place with sound absorbing walls and heat signature dampeners, as well as some kind of device to hide any fluctuations in the interplanar energy levels that his work might cause. If Balderhaz didn't want to be found, he was going to make damn sure he wasn't found.

Which made it all the stranger that Perp seemed to know exactly where he was. Was this some sort of elaborate trap to lure Mercury into Michelle's clutches? After all, Balderhaz had been working for Michelle up until not too long ago, when he disappeared. There were rumors that he had gone rogue and was hiding out somewhere on the Mundane Plane, but maybe that was just a cover story. Maybe he was still working for Michelle. Or, worse, Tiamat. Was Perp leading him into a trap?

Mercury paused, regarding the structure. No movement was visible inside. The place appeared deserted.

Perp stopped in mid-air when he realized Mercury wasn't following. "What is it, Merc? Something wrong?"

"Nah," said Mercury, and continued after Perp. If he couldn't trust Perp, then he might as well pack it in.

Perp fluttered up to the door of the building. He knocked three times, paused, knocked twice more, paused again, and knocked six more times. "Secret knock," he said.

Mercury nodded enthusiastically.

The door suddenly swung open, and a man with a long beard and long, dirty hair appeared. He wore nothing but a loincloth that appeared to have been constructed from a paisley necktie and Christmas-themed bath towels. "What are you doing out here?" he cried. "Get inside!"

Perp and Mercury hurried inside and the man slammed the door. The interior of the building appeared to be one big room, filled with tables and benches that were covered with vials, beakers, microscopes, stacks of paper, books, computers, various electronic components, and hundreds of other random items.

"What's wrong?" asked Mercury.

"Why?" asked the man. "Didn't you want to come inside?"

"Well, yeah," replied Mercury. "But—"

"Then nothing's wrong," the man said. "Hi, Perp. Who's Mr. Longshanks here?"

"His name is Mercury," said Perp. "He's a friend. Mercury, Balderhaz. Balderhaz, Mercury."

"We have the same name, but backwards!" exclaimed Balderhaz, gripping Mercury in a hug.

"No, it's not..." Mercury started, but when Perp cast him an anxious look, he dropped it. Balderhaz showed no signs of intending to let him go.

"It's, um, nice to meet you as well," said Mercury.

"It's like meeting my twin brother for the first time," said Balderhaz. Mercury felt something damp on his chest and realized that Balderhaz was weeping.

"Yeah, it's pretty great," said Mercury, patting Balderhaz on the back. "I'm familiar with some of your work. The Balderhaz Cube, that was some impressive stuff."

"Get ahold of yourself, man!" said Balderhaz, pulling himself away from Mercury. "Uh-oh. Where's Marcus Aurelius?" Balderhaz was scanning the interior of the building.

"Marcus Aurelius?" asked Perp. "The Roman Emperor?"

"No," said Balderhaz. "Marcus Aurelius the white-headed capuchin monkey. He floats sometimes. Ah, there he is!"

Indeed, Mercury saw that about eight feet overhead, just below the peak of the vaulted ceiling, a capuchin monkey was floating. The monkey seemed mildly irritated but not really surprised, like someone who had just gotten a parking ticket for parking three feet too close to a hydrant.

"What are you doing up there, Marcus Aurelius?" demanded Balderhaz. He turned to Mercury. "It's really not his fault, you know. I broke the laws of physics."

"You did what?" asked Mercury.

"The laws of physics. I accidentally broke them a while back."

"Isn't that what we do whenever we perform miracles?" asked Mercury.

"Eh? No, no. We *bend* the laws of physics. They always snap back. Not this time, though. This time they're broken."

"But... you can fix them?"

"You can be assured that if anyone can, I can!" exclaimed Balderhaz.

Suddenly the monkey squealed and fell to the ground. It landed on all fours, shrieked at Mercury, and ran off.

"Does he just do that at random?" asked Perp.

"What, fall?" said Balderhaz. "No, the falling is perfectly ordered and natural. It's the floating I can't predict. What can I do for you boys?"

"We need to break someone out of Possum Kingdom," said Perp.

"Possum Kingdom!" cried Balderhaz. "The Toadies song?"

"That's what I said!" exclaimed Mercury.

"The secret underground prison," said Perp.

"Oh!" said Balderhaz. "That's good, because there's no escaping that Toadies song. I've got just the thing." Balderhaz dived under a table and began rooting through a cardboard box that appeared to be filled with Circus Peanuts. After a moment he produced something that looked like a hair dryer and handed it to Mercury.

"What is it?" asked Mercury.

"Anti-Balderhaz Field Gun. It temporarily cancels out the effects of a Balderhaz Cube within a limited range. I make them out of hair dryers. Try it."

Mercury pointed the gun and pulled the trigger, releasing a blast of hot air.

"My mistake," said Balderhaz. "That one's still a hair dryer. But imagine, instead of hot air, a sort of invisible magic field being released!"

Mercury released the trigger and examined the device. "How does it work without being plugged in?"

Balderhaz frowned at him. "You just saw a floating monkey, and it's the battery-powered hair dryer you're having trouble with?" He went back to the box and found another device, which looked identical to the one Mercury was holding. "Here."

Mercury took the gun and handed the hair dryer to Balderhaz. He pulled the trigger, but nothing happened.

"Aha!" cried Balderhaz. "See? I told you. Invisible magic field."

"If you say so," replied Mercury.

"We can't really test it here, because I don't have a Balderhaz Cube. Ironic, right? Everybody's got one these days except old Balderhaz. But what it does is, it cancels out the effect of a Balderhaz Cube in a conical pattern, extending about fifty feet. It creates an anti-no-miracles zone, allowing you to manipulate interplanar energy even within a Balderhaz field. They've undoubtedly got a Balderhaz Cube in Possum Kingdom, to prevent the likes of you from doing what you're planning on doing. But with this baby, you can perform all the miracles you like, as long as you're standing more-or-less directly in front of the gun, and you're between twenty-eight and fifty-two feet away."

Mercury regarded the gun dubiously.

"You're sure this one isn't a hair dryer?" asked Mercury.

"Did it blow any air when you pulled the trigger?"

"No."

"Then it's not a hair dryer. Or the battery's dead. But I'm pretty sure it's not a hair dryer. Anymore. Uh-oh. Where's Pliny the Elder?"

"Pliny the Elder the white-headed capuchin monkey?" Perp ventured.

"No, Pliny the Elder the albino boa constrictor."

# CHAPTER THIRTY-ONE

*Near Possum Kingdom State Park, west of Dallas, Texas; August 2016*

Mercury and Perp approached the fence in near complete darkness. They had been mostly hidden by a few scraggly trees until they got within about fifty feet of the fence, but now they were completely in the open. They'd watched from the trees long enough to determine that there were two guards on duty, walking the perimeter of the fence at regular intervals. The outside fence was roughly square, about 300 yards on a side. Centered inside the fence was a small concrete building that presumably concealed the entrance to the cave. Next to the building was a thirty foot pole with an array of spotlights angled in several different directions, lighting up most of the yard inside the inner fence. The plan was to break through the fences, take out one of the lights, and then sprint to the building before they were seen.

"I don't like this," said Perp.

"What's not to like about breaking into a secret underground prison in the middle of the night?" asked Mercury.

"I'm serious," said Perp. "It's too obvious. There's no way they aren't going to be ready for us, even if that hair dryer thing works. We have no idea who or what's inside that building. What if Michelle's got angels standing guard?"

"You think she's got angels to spare?"

"To guard Tiamat and God-knows-how-many other demons? I think she could spare a few."

"Ugh," said Mercury. "Alright, back to the trees."

They crept back under cover.

"So now what?" asked Mercury.

"Well, it's a cave, right?" said Perp. "There have got to be other ways in."

"I don't know," said Mercury. "They've got a pretty big area fenced in. What if the cave only extends inside that area?"

"Could be," said Perp thoughtfully. "But I get the impression it's a pretty big cave. There could be side tunnels that reach outside that area."

"Alright, then," replied Mercury. "How do we find one?"

Perp smiled. "Trial and error."

"Ugh," said Mercury again. "Sounds incredibly boring."


It was incredibly boring. Worse than the Toadies' second album, even. They walked along the edge of the Balderhaz field, occasionally attempting to levitate a small twig or pebble to gauge its strength. The boundary of the field lay some distance outside the outer fence, where the light from the spotlights didn't reach. It was unlikely they'd be spotted in the moonless dark, but when a guard came within a hundred feet or so, they would lie down until the threat had passed.

Perp's theory was that the fences were mostly for show, and that the real barrier to anyone trying to get in or out of the prison was the Balderhaz field. Well, that, and several hundred tons of sand and rock. When Perp saw what he identified as a "promising spot"—using criteria that were a complete enigma to Mercury—just inside the Balderhaz field, he would stand some thirty feet away from Mercury and aim the hair dryer at Mercury while Mercury harnessed interplanar energy to drill a small hole in the ground. The idea was that if the cave extended underneath them, eventually he would reach an air pocket and he would feel a sudden decrease in resistance.

It seemed like a good idea in theory, but Mercury wasn't cut out for what he called "mind-numbing manual labor."

"Can't we just storm the building?" he whined. "This is literally the worst job I've ever had. And I had to sit and watch Job scrape his boils with pot sherds for six weeks."

"Focus, Merc!" snapped Perp. "If we want to get your terrorist friends out of prison, this is how we're going to do it. I never promised it was going to be exciting. It is, after all, boring work."

"If you make that joke one more time," said Mercury, "I'm going to pull your wings off."

"To get rid of garbage disposal odors," Perp retorted, "drop in a cut-up lemon, some salt and a few ice cubes."

"Super helpful," grumbled Mercury.

Finally, when Mercury had burrowed almost twenty feet down on his sixteenth hole, he felt something give.

"Hey!" he exclaimed. "I think I've got something!"

"Shh!" whispered Perp, pointing to a guard heading their direction. The two huddled on the ground, not moving, while the guard strolled by, waving his flashlight lazily around in front of him.

"OK, dig it out," said Perp.

Mercury harnessed as much interplanar energy as he could to weaken the bonds of the rock, turning it to sand and levitating it out of the way, while Perp kept the hair dryer trained on him. Mercury was making the hole just big enough for them to climb through, but as he got ten feet or so down, it was all he could do to keep the sand moving.

"Are you sure that thing is working?" he whispered to Perp.

"If it wasn't working, you wouldn't be able to move the rock at all," answered Perp. "You're probably getting closer to the Balderhaz Cube. Most likely they've got it underground, somewhere near the center of the cave."

Mercury grunted in response. He was sweating from the effort of breaking up the rock.

They had to hunker down twice more as one of the guards passed by, but finally Mercury managed to hollow out a tunnel that connected to the cavern below. Cool air flowed out of the opening.

Without waiting for further advice from Perp, Mercury slid down the tunnel, dropping to a cold stone surface some eight feet below the bottom of the shaft. Perp followed after, falling to the floor of the cave with a thud.

"Damn it," grumbled Perp. Perp hated not being able to fly. He never walked anywhere if he could help it; his chubby little legs weren't built for it. But inside the Balderhaz field, neither of them could perform any miracles without the help of the Anti-Baldherhaz

Field Gun, and flying counted as a miracle, Perp's vestigial bird-like wings notwithstanding.

They now found themselves in the complete darkness of the cave. Angels have extremely sensitive vision, but even they can't see in total darkness. Unfortunately, neither of them had thought to bring a flashlight. One of the drawbacks of ordinarily being able to count on violating the laws of physics was that you tended to overlook certain mundane necessities.

"Point the thing at me," said Mercury.

"It won't work," said Perp. "You have to be like thirty feet away."

"OK, then back up thirty feet and point the thing at me."

"Back up where?" Perp cried. "I can't see where I'm going! I could fall into a chasm!"

"OK, fine. I'll try moving forward."

Mercury took a step, tripped on a rock, and fell face-first onto the stone floor.

"I'm going to try crawling," he said.

A dim light appeared in front of them. "Can I be of assistance, gentlemen?" a woman's voice asked.

"Oh, no," groaned Mercury, getting to his feet.

"What kind of greeting is that?" asked the woman. She was holding a small flashlight in her hand. She was flanked on either side by a large demon. It was too dark to identify either of them, but Mercury couldn't mistake the one in the middle. Tiamat.

"Look, Tiamat," said Mercury. "We're just looking for some friends of ours who got thrown in here by mistake."

"By mistake!" cried Tiamat. "No one gets thrown in Possum Kingdom by mistake! There's a very strict process for vetting new occupants, consisting of that insufferable little harpy Michelle deciding whether you're a big enough threat to take up some space in her precious secret prison. Let me guess, you're looking for that twerp Ederatz and the chick with the purple hair."

"Are they here?" asked Mercury.

"They're here," said Tiamat. "Good luck finding them, though. This place is like a maze. Speaking of which, how did you... oh!" She had spotted the hole in the ceiling. "Does that lead... outside?"

"Yes, but..." Mercury started.

"Gamaliel!" Tiamat barked to the demon on her right. "Round everybody up. We're getting out! And do it quietly. If we alert the guards, we're screwed."

"Wait!" said Mercury. "Get Suzy and Eddie too, or I start yelling for the guards."

"If you do that, we'll all be stuck here. Not a smart move, Mercury."

"Your choice," said Mercury. "Either we all get out or we all rot in here forever."

Tiamat regarded Mercury with a bemused look on her face. "How did you get in here? There's no way you drilled through twenty feet of solid rock without somebody noticing, unless you used interplanar energy. But that's impossible inside the Balderhaz field."

Mercury said nothing. Perp remained standing quietly behind him, holding the hair dryer behind his back.

"Unless you found some way to counteract the field," said Tiamat, peering around Mercury and shining her flashlight on Perp.

"I'll tell you whatever you want to know," said Mercury. "Just get my friends out of here."

"Merc!" hissed Perp. "You can't..."

"Deal," said Tiamat. She turned to Gamaliel. "Get the twerp and the girl too. And hurry."

# CHAPTER THIRTY-TWO

*East of Dallas, Texas; August 2016*

"I can't believe you made a deal with Tiamat," said Perp.

"What choice did I have?" asked Mercury. "It was the only way of getting Suzy and Eddie out of there."

"Remind me who Tiamat is again?" asked Suzy.

She, Perp, Mercury and Eddie were sitting at a picnic table at an otherwise deserted rest stop on Interstate 20, just east of Dallas. Well, three of them were sitting at the table. Perp was sitting cross-legged on top of the table, which was the only way he could remain at eye level with the others without levitating. Tiamat and Gamaliel were sitting at another table, kitty-corner to them, presumably plotting the resurgence of Chaos Faction. The rest of Tiamat's minions, and whoever else had been in the prison—there were a lot of prisoners, and it had been pretty dark—had scattered to the four winds. Evidently Tiamat had instructed them, wisely, to split up in case of an escape, to rendezvous at some predetermined place and time in the future.

"The one sitting over there," said Mercury. "The one who looks like she'd steal the silverware from your wedding reception."

"She's a demoness," said Eddie. "A bad one. She's come pretty close to world domination a few times. If there's anybody on Earth more dangerous than Michelle, it's Tiamat. She's the leader of Chaos Faction."

"And we just let her out?" asked Suzy.

"Like I said, no choice," said Mercury.

"Uh, you could have left us in there," replied Eddie. "I mean, don't get me wrong, that place was awful. Dark and wet and cold and filled with terrifying characters, but I'm not sure I want Tiamat's release on my hands."

"It's not on your hands!" Mercury snapped. "It's on mine. It was my decision, OK? I couldn't let Suzy spend the rest of her life in that place. No offense, Eddie, but you're immortal. You'd have gotten out eventually. But if we didn't break Suzy out, she was going to die in there. That's not OK in my book. Also? Whatever you think about Tiamat and her gang—and I'll admit she's a malicious, hateful bitch who deserves to be thrown into a dank pit for the next thousand years—the fact is that it's not Michelle's job to decide who gets thrown in prison forever. Nobody in Heaven or Earth gave her that responsibility. I don't even know who most of those people in that prison were, or what crime they were supposedly guilty of. I mean, obviously they were never convicted of anything in a court, or they'd be in a regular prison. If we give Michelle the power to lock up anybody she wants, sure, she'll start with loathsome, putrescent maggots like Tia..." He paused as uncomfortable looks came over the faces at everyone at the table. "She's standing right behind me, isn't she?"

"Don't stop on my account, Mercury," said Tiamat. Gamaliel, who had been talking with Tiamat a moment earlier, was nowhere to be seen. "Other than some regrettable rhetorical flourishes," Tiamat went on, "you were doing quite well. You're exactly right about Michelle. She's a usurper and a tyrant. And while I'll admit to occasionally acting on some dictatorial impulses of my own in the past, my goal in forming Chaos Faction was not world domination, but the precise opposite. I've come to the sad conclusion that I'm simply in no position to take over the world, given the current disposition of angels on this plane. Michelle now commands not only her own army—the bulk of which was trapped on Earth along with her—but also Lucifer's intelligence structure, and by extension, most of the U.S. government. We can't beat her on her own terms. The only solution is asymmetrical warfare."

"You mean terrorism," said Suzy.

"Terrorism is a word used by the strong to denigrate the only tactics available to the weak," said Tiamat. "But let's not get into a semantic discussion. My point is that we are all on the same side."

"We're not terrorists!" yelled Suzy.

"That's not what I've heard," said Tiamat. "But again, semantics. We all want to see Michelle's security apparatus disbanded, correct?"

There was general agreement around the table.

"And if I'm not mistaken, you possess a device capable of counteracting the effects of a Balderhaz Cube, correct?"

Perp glanced at Mercury, who nodded. Perp pulled the Anti-Balderhaz Field Gun from his diaper and set on the table. Mercury and Suzy both shuddered.

"A hair dryer?" asked Tiamat.

"It's had some modifications," replied Mercury.

"Balderhaz," said Tiamat.

Perp was looking at the ground. Mercury said nothing.

"Come on," Tiamat said. "It has to be Balderhaz. Nobody else could do something like that."

"So what if it was?" asked Mercury.

"If you know where Balderhaz is, I know how we can stop Michelle."

"Bullshit," said Mercury. "Hey, where'd Gamaliel go?"

"I sent Gamaliel on an errand," replied Tiamat. "I've got a lot of demons to look after. He's tying up some loose ends. Now answer my question. Where's Balderhaz?"

Mercury and the others regarded Tiamat dubiously.

Tiamat laughed. "I don't blame you for being skeptical, but you have to believe me. This is the only chance we have to stop Michelle. Balderhaz and I built the MEOW device that used to keep the angels and demons out of Washington, D.C., you know. The place is only overrun now because that plane hit it. All we have to do is build another one. Balderhaz and I can do it."

"Even if you could," said Mercury. "And we could get it to Washington, D.C. and activate it, all it would do is chase Michelle's agents out of D.C. This isn't the eighteenth century. They have phones and email now. Michelle can run the government just as well from the suburbs in Maryland."

"Sure, she probably could, eventually. But her hold over Lucifer's agents is already tenuous. And don't forget that these demons are undercover as advisors and secretaries. What do you think will happen when they all run screaming from their offices simultaneously and are never seen in the city again? That's a career-ending move, even in Washington, unless you're Dick Morris. Even if nobody ever figures out what actually happened, Michelle's shadow government will be ruined. She'll still be a threat, of course, but she won't be running the federal government anymore."

"What's in it for you?" Mercury asked.

"I told you, I don't want Michelle in control of this plane any more than you do."

"Because you want to be in control of it yourself."

"Well, obviously," said Tiamat. "But first things first. We can go back to being enemies as soon as we've dealt with Michelle."

Mercury glared at Tiamat, ruminating on her words.

"Merc," said Perp. "You can't tell her where Balderhaz is. He trusted me. I'm one of the few people who knows about his hideaway. If I had known you were going to—"

"Will you pardon us for a moment?" Mercury said to Tiamat. He grabbed Perp around the waist and carried him far enough from the group for them to have a private conversation.

"Stop that!" Perp spat, as Mercury set him down.

"Sorry, Perp. Can't have you flying in public, and we don't have time for niceties. We have to bring Tiamat to Balderhaz."

"No!" Perp cried. "He'll never forgive me!"

"Perp, the fate of the entire world is at stake here!"

"You've already played that card like three times, Mercury."

"Because the fate of the world keeps being at stake! It's not *my* fault! How long do you think he's going to be able to hide anyway? You know what Michelle's capable of. She'll have this whole continent under martial law within six months. How long do you think it will take her to get to Costa Rica? You know she's got to be looking for him right now. And what happens when she finds him? Michelle holds all the cards, that's what. She'll have her army, Lucifer's intelligence network, the U.S. military, and Balderhaz, all in her pocket."

"Balderhaz would never..."

"I know you like the guy, Perp, but he's a few sandwiches short of a picnic. I don't think it will take that much for Michelle to convince him to come to work for her. And even if you're right, and he holds out, they'll just lock him away for the next ten thousand years. I don't trust Tiamat any more than you do, Perp, but we have no choice. If there's any chance she and Balderhaz can build another MEOW, we've got to take it."

Perp's brow furrowed and his lips pursed in concentration. Mercury knew he was trying to think of some objection, some reason not to betray Balderhaz, but there wasn't anything to say.

"Put eggs in warm water to bring them to room temperature before using them for baking," Perp offered at last.

"I hear you, brother," said Mercury. "I hear you."

# CHAPTER THIRTY-THREE

*Provo, Utah; August 2016*

Gamaliel touched down just outside Provo, Utah. He could easily have walked the last few miles, but it was easier just to accept a ride. Single women tended to pull over when they passed Gamaliel by the side of the road. He was built like the guy kicking sand in the wimp's face in the back of old comic books.

So he rode into town in a RAV-4 with a chatterbox single mom with a bad dye job and lips full of collagen. She offered to buy him a drink, but he demurred, having her drop him in an unkempt industrial area about a quarter mile from the nondescript building that was his destination. The RAV-4 lingered by the curb for a good minute after he got out, and Gamaliel shuddered as he imagined the over-primped woman leering at his hindquarters. Human women could be downright creepy.

Eventually she sped off to whatever soccer game or AA meeting she was on her way to, and Gamaliel turned toward the building. The building was surrounded by a twenty foot chain link fence topped with barbed wire. Two armed guards stood at the entrance, but Gamaliel didn't slow down or say a word to them. He glanced at one of the guards and the gate swung open. He walked through the gate and approached the building.

It was one of the ugliest buildings he'd ever seen; a great big concrete block with a sagging pitch roof and walls coated with some kind of weird façade of river pebbles. There were no windows, and the doors were of the flat steel variety, badly dented and painted an uninviting shade of brown. It was, in sum, about the last place one would expect to find a technological innovation that was about to change the world.

Gamaliel approached one of the doors and knocked. Just below eye level, at a slightly cockeyed angle, was a label that appeared to have been created by one of those little clicky label makers you can buy for three dollars at an office supply store. It read:

## MENTALDYNE

After a couple of minutes, the door opened and a pasty, balding young man beckoned Gamaliel to come inside. He wore a nametag that read "Zanders." A tablet computer was tucked under his arm.

Gamaliel and Zanders walked past several clean rooms and laboratories where technicians wearing anti-static suits labored on various projects, finally reaching another steel door. Zanders punched a code into a pad near the door and then opened it. They stepped inside a small vault lined with shelves. The shelves were empty except for a single small cardboard box.

"This is the first batch," said Zanders, motioning to the box.

Gamaliel picked it up. "How many?"

"Two hundred," said Zanders. "That's what she asked for. Will that be enough?"

"More than enough, I should think," replied Gamaliel. "Have they been tested?"

Zanders frowned. "They've gone through the same testing as the other chips."

"That's not what I mean," said Gamaliel. "I want to know if you've tested the... additional feature."

"Oh!" exclaimed the man with a smile. "Of course."

"And?"

"I'll let you judge for yourself." He pulled a cell phone from his pocket and made a call. "Tracey?" he said after a moment. "I need you to come down to vault six. Right now, please."

Less than a minute later, a young woman dirty blond hair appeared at the door to the vault. She was cute in a mousey sort of way. "Sir?" she asked quietly. "You asked for me?"

"Hello, Tracey," said Zanders. "This is Mr. Gamaliel. He's a very important Mentaldyne investor. Mr. Gamaliel, this is Tracey Bowen. She works on the assembly line for us. How long have you been with Mentaldyne, Tracey?"

"Eight years, sir."

"And do you like it here?"

"Yes, sir. It's steady work and the management treats us nice."

"Very good, Tracey. How old are you?"

"I'm thirty-three."

"Kids?"

"Two, sir. Max is ten and Lily is eight."

"Are you married?"

"No, sir. My boyfriend… he left two years ago."

"But you're doing OK? You and the kids?"

"We get by alright. Especially since that bonus last month." Tracey grinned, revealing a mouth full of sparkling but slightly crooked teeth.

Zanders turned to Gamaliel. "Tracey volunteered to test the new chip. We gave her a small token of our gratitude."

Gamaliel nodded impatiently. "Could we dispense with the small talk and move on to the test?"

"Just establishing a baseline," replied Zanders. "I want it to be completely clear that Tracey is just a typical Mentaldyne employee who has not received any coaching or preparation for this test."

"Sir," said Tracey, "am I going to be taking some kind of test? I'm not very good at tests."

"Yes," said Zanders, "but there's no need to worry. This is a going to be a very easy test. You're just going to do what feels natural to you. Do you think you can do that for me?"

Tracey's brow furrowed. "I guess?"

"Excellent," said Zanders. "Tracey, could you please flap your arms and cheep like a baby bird asking its mommy for a worm?"

Tracey's face instantly flushed a deep purple. She took half a step backward, seeming to want to run from the room. "S-s-sir?" she stammered, on the verge of a full-fledged panic attack.

"Just a joke," said Zanders with a reassuring smile. He pulled the tablet computer from under his arm.

"Oh," said Tracey weakly. "OK." She didn't look very reassured, but the abject panic had passed.

Zanders tapped a few keystrokes on his tablet computer and then handed it to Gamaliel. Gamaliel frowned, looking at the screen. It looked like this:

---

# Myrmidon Control System Version 1.1

## Target:

○ Single chip:        | 000000034329 (Tracey S. Bowen) |

○ Group ID or range:  |                                |

○ All chips

## Target command:

○ I want to...    ○ I feel...    ○ I am...

|                                                     |
|                                                     |
|                                                     |

[ Submit Command ]

---

"What the hell is this?" asked Gamaliel.

"It's exactly what you think it is," said Zanders. "You've seen what happens when I give Ms. Bowen a simple verbal command to do something she feels uncomfortable doing. Now try it with the Myrmidon system."

Gamaliel frowned. "You want me to try to make her cheep like a bird?"

"Well, I was hoping you'd be a little more imaginative than that," replied Zanders.

Gamaliel regarded Tracey, who was watching him suspiciously. "Like what?" he asked.

Zanders shrugged. "Anything you like."

Gamaliel stared at the screen. He wasn't used to coming up with ideas. Usually he just followed Tiamat's orders. After a moment's thought, he clicked the I want to... radio button and then typed:

## kiss mr. zanders

He tapped the **Submit Command** button at the bottom of the screen.

Without a moment's hesitation, Tracey walked up to Zanders and planted a kiss right on his mouth. Then she stepped backwards, a look of horror creeping over her face. "Oh my god," she said hoarsely. "I don't know why I did that. Mr. Zanders, I'm so sorry!"

Zanders had turned almost as red as Tracey had been earlier. "Er, that's, um, OK, Tracey," he stammered. He turned to Gamaliel, trying to reclaim his businesslike demeanor. "As you can see, the subject takes full responsibility for her actions. She has no sensation of being manipulated whatsoever. As far as she is concerned, she simply decided of her own—say, what are you doing now?"

Gamaliel was giddily typing something else into the tablet.

"Give me that!" snapped Zanders, grabbing the tablet. "You've had your—"

"Hey!" exclaimed Gamaliel. He had intended to type "Kiss everyone in this building," but Zanders had caused him to brush the **Submit Command** button before he was finished. He had gotten as far as "Kiss everyone."

Tracey took a step toward Gamaliel, wrapping her hands around his neck and pulling his head toward her. She gave him a long, very enthusiastic kiss. The she let go and ran out of the room screaming, "Oh my god I'm so sorry!"

Her remorse lasted until she ran into a rotund woman with a clipboard in the hallway. Tracey bent over, pulled the woman's head back, and planted a kiss on her mouth. The she ran off again, screaming apologies.

"Nice to see Tracey coming out of her shell," observed Zanders.

"Remarkable," said Gamaliel. "How long will she keep doing that?"

"Until she collapses from exhaustion," said Zanders. "Then she'll get up and continue on her quest to kiss everyone."

"Everyone?"

"That's what you typed. *Everyone.*"

"Can you override the command?"

"Of course. But I think this might be good for morale. Anyway, the urge to kiss everyone will fade as she gets farther away from the transmitter."

Somewhere down the hall, Tracey screamed another apology.

"Where is the transmitter?"

"For testing purposes, we're using a very small one here in the building. Its range is only a few miles, so Tracey will most likely limit her kissing spree to the Provo area. Obviously the production transmitter has a much greater range."

Gamaliel nodded. "Good work, Zanders," he said. "When will you be able to start mass producing them?"

"We're converting the machinery now," Zanders said. "By the end of next week we'll be producing ten thousand a day."

"All right," said Gamaliel. "That should do for now. Depending on how things go over the next few days, we may need you to bump up those numbers."

"Bump up the numbers?" asked Zanders, shocked. "How many people do you plan on…?"

A glare from Gamaliel silenced him. "That's not your concern," he said. "Just be ready for a big increase in demand."

# CHAPTER THIRTY-FOUR

*Costa Rica; August 2016*

Balderhaz's reaction to the arrival of Tiamat and the rest of the group was anticlimactic, in that it was precisely the reaction he'd had to the arrival of Mercury and Perp a few days earlier: he rushed them inside and then proceeded to deal with whatever animal happened to be on the ceiling at the time.

Mercury tried to explain how Michelle was using Lucifer's intelligence apparatus to create a worldwide totalitarian state, but Balderhaz didn't seem particularly interested. It wasn't that he was apathetic, but rather that he was so paranoid already that nothing Mercury told him seemed particularly remarkable. Balderhaz had long ago had enough of conspiracies, double-crosses, and plans for world domination, which was why he was hiding deep in the jungle of Costa Rica. What Mercury had first taken as a symptom of insanity was in fact merely good planning.

The eccentric angel's ears perked up when Tiamat started talking about building another MEOW device. Balderhaz had apparently been rather proud of his success with the last one, and had been a bit put out that it had been destroyed in a terrorist attack. In fact, he seemed to view the destruction of the MEOW device as the chief tragedy of that day, which solidified Mercury's impression that Balderhaz's moral compass was a bit off. If Michelle ever got her hands on Balderhaz, she'd likely be able to convince him to do just about anything as long as he found it an interesting technical challenge. Mercury made a note not to let that happen.

Balderhaz and Tiamat began working on the device that same day, leaving Mercury, Eddie, Suzy, and Perp to entertain themselves. Balderhaz had at one point given up inventing to become a fairly respectable tennis instructor, and he remained an aficionado of the game, but he hadn't had room in his Costa Rica hideaway for a court. The best he could do was a ping-pong table in the basement, which served as the primary source of recreation for the group for the next three weeks. Suzy was virtually unbeatable, which frustrated Mercury, who was himself a mediocre player despite his unmatched wingspan. Mercury resorted to cheating, using minor miracles to increase the spin of the ball or change its shape suddenly before it hit Suzy's paddle. Suzy responded by enlisting Eddie and Perp in her defense. Eddie nullified Mercury's attempts to harness interplanar energy for his own benefit, and Perp went on the offensive, causing the ball to miraculously pass through Mercury's paddle. Rather than admit defeat, though, Mercury responded with a series of complex rules governing the use of miracles during gameplay. The situation continued to escalate, culminating with Suzy's paddle being turned into an angry lobster. This is what passed for entertainment while Tiamat and Balderhaz perfected the new MEOW device.

Finally they did finish it: a metal box just a little bigger than a typical Balderhaz Cube. Mercury could hardly believe such a tiny device was capable of ridding Washington, D.C. of angels, but then he didn't think much of the hair dryer at first either. Tiamat and Balderhaz seemed to work relatively well together. There was some arguing toward the end of the project that had Mercury concerned, but they seemed to have worked it out, whatever it was. Now the question was how to get the device to Washington, D.C. and activate it.

There was general agreement that Mercury would be the one to deliver it, since everybody more-or-less trusted him, but activating it was going to be a problem. The device had to be activated manually, but any angel in the vicinity of the device at the time of activation would be rendered completely incapacitated by it. The effect of the MEOW device decreased as one got farther from it; those a hundred yards or so away would most likely be able to get out of the area, but any angel closer than that wouldn't even be able to think clearly enough to put one foot in front of the other. At a distance of about a mile, the device's output faded to a barely tolerable screech.

In any case, it was going to be impossible for any of the angels in the group to activate the device and then get safely out of the area. Tiamat wouldn't have blinked an eye at sacrificing any one of them, but nobody was about to volunteer to be trapped indefinitely in a place within the excruciating emissions of the MEOW device. That left only one possibility.

"Fine," said Suzy. "I'll do it. But can I take a commercial jet to D.C.? I'm kind of over the whole flying-by-the-seat-of-my-pants thing." Mercury had carried her from Texas to Costa Rica, and her hair still hadn't recovered.

"Sorry," said Mercury. "You're on the no-fly list for sure. You're lucky you know some angels, or you'd never fly again."

"I don't feel lucky," said Suzy. "So what do I do with this thing, exactly? Just flip a switch and drop it in a planter somewhere near the Capitol?"

"No, no!" exclaimed Balderhaz. "It has to be permanent! You can't put it anywhere somebody can just pick it up and walk off with it."

"He's right," said Tiamat. "That's why the original was in the cornerstone of the Capitol. Nobody could remove it without attracting a whole lot of attention."

"Well, we can't very well put it back where it was," said Eddie. "They've already repaired the cornerstone. And we can't get it inside the Capitol or any other important building, like the White House, because it will set off the metal detectors. They'll think it's a bomb."

"It doesn't have to be anyplace special," said Mercury. "We're not going for symbolic value. It just has to be someplace central in D.C. Find a construction site where they're pouring concrete and toss it in."

Suzy wasn't entirely convinced it was going to be as easy as Mercury made it out to be, but she reluctantly went along with the plan, in part because she was promised a full makeover as part of the deal. Her hair was going to be a disaster after flying halfway across the world again, and in any case her current coloring would make it far too easy for the authorities to identify her. Undoubtedly she was on the FBI's Most Wanted list by now.

Mercury flew her to Alexandria, Virginia, where she had her hair and nails done—she opted to go with a soft pink for the nails and a dark brown for her hair that was close to her natural color, along with hair extensions, since Mercury was paying. She wasn't sure where Mercury came up with the cash; she suspected he was literally creating it out of thin air. Which was, as she understood it, basically what the Federal Reserve did, so it was all the same to her.

Next they went clothes shopping. Mercury had little patience for shopping and his taste ranged from garish to godawful, but Suzy did acquiesce to his demands to "dress more like a chick." In college and then at Brimstone she had gotten so tired of being hit on by socially inept dweebs that she had somewhat unconsciously adopted a style somewhere between disaffected Goth and committed lesbian. She wasn't feeling the bright red leather miniskirt Mercury insisted would somehow "bring out her eyes," but they compromised on a suitably cute-but-professional jacket-and-skirt ensemble. She then picked out a purse, the primary purpose of which was to hide the MEOW device, a pair of serviceable flats, and a pair of dark sunglasses.

They flagged down a cab and Mercury instructed the driver to drop him off at Arlington Cemetery.

"You're not even going into the city with me?" asked Suzy.

"I don't really want to be within a mile of that thing when you turn it on," said Mercury. "You know what to do. Just meet me back at Arlington when you're done."

"How will you know when it's on?"

"Trust me," said Mercury. "I'll know. I was about six blocks away when they activated the first one." He shuddered. "I could feel it in my molars."

Suzy nodded. His reluctance to be near the device was understandable.

"So," she said. "You do this kind of thing a lot?"

"Well," replied Mercury, "not this particular thing."

"Right, but foiling diabolical plans for world domination?"

Mercury shrugged. "Sometimes the plan is to destroy the world," he said. "Michelle's a dominator. Well, dominatrix, I guess.

Like Tiamat. They're dominatrices. Lucifer's a destroyer. Thankfully he's in custody."

"In Heaven."

"Last I knew, yeah. He was trying to deliver a nuclear bomb there—the Wormwood bomb. But this FBI guy and a friend of mine pulled a switch on him, so Lucifer ended up in Heaven empty-handed."

"You have a friend?" asked Suzy. She didn't mean it as an insult; she just had a hard time imagining anyone putting up with him for an extended period of time. Perp didn't count; that guy was even weirder than Mercury.

"*Had*," corrected Mercury.

"Oh, I'm sorry," said Suzy.

"No, no," said Mercury. "She didn't die or anything. My understanding is that she got sent back in time by a glass apple filled with croutons."

"She what?"

"It's hard to explain," said Mercury, in a tone that indicated he didn't really want to go into it.

Suzy couldn't help smiling.

"What?" asked Mercury, seeing the odd look on her face.

"You miss her, huh?"

Mercury shrugged. "I've been around a long time. I don't get too close to humans. They don't stick around long enough to make it worthwhile." He turned to look out the window.

She didn't press the issue, but for some reason she suddenly felt better about this crazy mission they had embarked on. Mercury put on a good act, but underneath the bombast and sarcasm, he was pretty human himself.

A few minutes later, they reached Arlington Cemetery. Mercury got out of the cab and Suzy directed the driver to drop her off in front of the Capitol Reflecting Pool. The plan was to find a construction site somewhere within the area between the Capitol and the White House.

She paid the cab driver with a couple of Mercury's crisp Andrew Jacksons and set off on a self-guided walking tour of Washington, D.C.

# CHAPTER THIRTY-FIVE

*Washington, D.C.; August 2016*

By the time Suzy had spent three hours walking every inch of sidewalk between the White House and the Capitol, she decided the shoes had been a mistake. Plenty of those high-powered political types wore sneakers on their lunch breaks, after all. At least she'd had the sense not to pick the stiletto heels she had her eye on. If she'd have been wearing those, the free world would have had to just pack it in.

The best location she'd found for the MEOW device was a half-finished overpass a few hundred yards northwest of the Capitol building. Large cylindrical supports had been set in concrete, and Suzy thought if she could reach the top of one, she could drop the metal box down inside one. Assuming the supports were hollow all the way to the concrete, it would be very difficult to get it out of there without tearing out the column. The supports were a good twenty feet tall, but part of the concrete had been poured already, forming a roughly step-like structure. She was going to attract some attention climbing up there, but it couldn't be helped.

She waited until the street was mostly clear, then slipped off her shoes, grabbed the MEOW device from her bag, and hopped onto the first tier of concrete. As soon as she did so, a police car rounded the corner.

"Shit!" she yelled, making her way across the narrow strip of concrete to the next section, which reached to her waist. The car's flashers went on. Suzy scrambled on top of the concrete block and continued to the next section.

The car pulled up a few yards from the overpass and the driver got out.

"Miss," said the young man who'd stepped out of the car. "Please get down from there."

"It's a free country!" shouted Suzy, who was now on the third tier of concrete and was starting to get vertigo from the height.

"It's a safety issue, Miss," said the police officer. "You could fall."

"Why don't you go arrest a corrupt Congressman or something," Suzy yelled.

"Miss, the next time a corrupt Congressman climbs up an unfinished overpass at great risk to his own personal safety, I promise you I will do whatever I can to address the situation. What do you have in your hand?"

"None of your business!" Suzy shouted, clambering onto the fourth tier. From here she thought she could reach the top of one of the supports.

"Miss, please show me your hands."

Suzy ignored the officer, daring neither to look down nor at him. She assumed he was pointing a gun at her. So much for her personal safety. She slowly got to her feet, with both arms wrapped around the metal column.

"Show me your hands!" So much for "please."

The top of the column was still a good two feet over her head. Suzy felt like crying. There was no way she could reach.

She turned to the cop, who did indeed have a gun pointed at her. "Look," she said, holding out the MEOW device. "It's just a metal box. It's nothing."

"Miss, set down the box."

Suzy sighed. She was becoming resigned to the fact that she'd have to settle for just flipping the switch and hoping for the best. The device would still work; it just wouldn't take very long for Michelle to get rid of it. Presumably she had at least a few human agents in the area; all she had to do was pinpoint the location of the device and dispose of it. Balderhaz had designed it so that the once the device was turned on, it couldn't be turned off. It could be destroyed, but it would take quite an impact—like being hit by a 747, for example.

Of course, first she had to open the lid of the box and flip the switch. Which could be difficult if Officer Public Safety actually intended to shoot her.

"OK," she said. "I'll get down. You can even arrest me, if you want. Or shoot me, whatever you need to do. But I have to do something first. I have to open this box and flip a switch."

"Miss, set down the box! Don't make me shoot you!"

"I'm not going to *make* you do anything!" shouted Suzy. "If you decide to shoot me because I'm flipping a switch, that's on you."

"I can't take a chance, Miss. It could be a bomb. Set it down."

"It could be anything!" Suzy yelled. "You have no idea what it is. Why would you assume it's a bomb? Have you asked yourself that? Why do you look at a perfectly innocent little metal box and think 'yep, probably a bomb.' Maybe if I open this box and flip the switch, hundreds of beautiful butterflies will fly out. Maybe it plays Peter Gabriel's "Shock the Monkey." Or maybe, just maybe, this little box is the solution to what's so fucked up in this country right now."

She opened the box and flipped the switch.

In the distance, someone screamed.

The cop turned, startled, and in that instant Suzy flipped the box lid closed, gripped the box in both hands, and jumped as high as she could, slamming the cube through the top of the column. Then she landed with one foot halfway off the concrete and fell backwards to the dirt below.

She lay for a few seconds on the ground in intense pain, unable to move. At first she feared that she'd broken her back, but when she was able to move her fingers and toes she concluded she'd merely had the wind knocked out of her. Fortunately she had fallen on the side of the wall opposite the cop, and he hadn't made it around to her yet. Hopefully he was dealing with whoever had screamed. Whoever was *screaming*, she corrected herself. It was still going on. Every few seconds the person—or angel, presumably—would pause to take a breath and then resume screaming. The poor bastard got caught just a few blocks from the MEOW device when Suzy had turned it on. Either that, or he was being stabbed repeatedly in the kidney.

227

She got slowly to her feet. Her back hurt and she was having trouble breathing deeply, but she seemed to have avoided any broken bones. She hobbled away as quickly as she could manage, not stopping to look whether the cop was following. Apparently he wasn't, because she made it to the next intersection without him threatening to shoot her again. She flagged down a cab and got in. "Arlington... cemetery," she gasped, and lay back against the seat. Every muscle in her back seemed to be seizing up.

The cab pulled away from the curb and made its way toward Arlington. They were heading west on Constitution, not far from the White House, when Suzy heard another scream and the driver slammed on the brakes. Suzy pitched forward into the seat ahead of her. There was a thump as the cab hit something.

"What the hell?" Suzy snapped.

"No, no, no!" cried the driver, a young Middle Eastern man wearing a turban. He threw open his door and got out of the cab.

Suzy looked around. She'd been zoning out, exhausted from her ordeal, but now she was fully alert. The cab was stopped in the middle of the street. Around them, cars whooshed past, honking.

Suzy got out and walked to the front of the cab. The driver was bent over a small figure lying on its back in the street. "No, no, no!" he cried again, turning desperately to Suzy. "Help!"

Stepping around the driver, Suzy gasped as she got a better look at the body: it was a little African-American girl, no older than fourteen. Suzy couldn't see any sign of injury, but the girl appeared to be unconscious.

Now what? She couldn't leave the girl in the street, but if she waited around for an ambulance, the police would figure out who Suzy was. Even if Michelle was no longer in power in Washington, Suzy would still be on the Most Wanted list. She'd probably rot in prison for years before anybody figured out that she'd been set up.

Suzy didn't want to move the girl in case she had a spinal injury, but when the girl began to stir and try to sit up, she decided to take the matter into her own hands. She picked the girl up, carried her to the cab, and lay her in the backseat. Suzy got in and cradled the girl's head in her lap. The girl was semi-conscious and kept moaning and shaking her head back and forth as if having a nightmare.

The driver leaned in the door and raised his hands. "What is the matter?" he asked.

Sirens could be heard in the distance.

"I don't know," Suzy said. "Head injury, maybe." But the girl wasn't bleeding and Suzy didn't feel any bumps or abrasions on her scalp. "Just get us out of here."

"OK, OK," said the driver, closing the door and getting behind the wheel. He slammed his own door and the cab squealed away. The girl continued to moan and squirm. As they crossed over Arlington Memorial Bridge, she seemed to relax a bit. The cab pulled up in front of the cemetery, and there was Mercury, as promised. He was wearing a ridiculous curly black wig and sunglasses with round lenses, which had the unfortunate effect of making him look like Howard Stern.

Mercury walked up to the cab and opened the door. "Took you long enough," he said. "I was starting to think you... holy shit!" He was looking at the girl resting on Suzy's lap.

"I know," said Suzy. "It couldn't be helped. She just ran out in front of the cab, and I couldn't leave her there..."

"The hell you couldn't!" cried Mercury. "Do you know who that is? It's Michelle!"

Suzy looked from Mercury to the girl and back again, unable to follow what Mercury was saying. "Wait, what? You mean Michelle..."

"The archangel, yes. The one who tried to nuke Grand Rapids. The one who had you thrown in prison."

Suzy stared aghast at the young girl lying in her lap. She looked perfectly innocent, with soft brown skin and beautiful long chestnut hair.

"You didn't tell me Michelle was a little black girl," Suzy said, in a slightly accusatory tone.

"It didn't seem relevant!" cried Mercury. "Just get her out of here. Drop her off at the cemetery and let's get the hell out of here before she wakes up!"

"Tiamat," Michelle murmured. "Running... D.C."

"What does that mean?" asked Suzy.

"She's delirious," answered Mercury. "Having a nightmare about running from Tiamat or something. Just—"

"What... have you done?" Michelle said, her eyes fluttering open and affixing on Mercury.

"What have *I* done?" asked Mercury. "You're one to talk. All I did was—"

"Put Tiamat in charge of Washington," said Michelle, sitting up. She held her hands to her ears as if trying to block out a noise. "Driver," she barked. "Get us out of here. Head west."

Without a moment's hesitation, the driver threw the car in gear and began pulling away from the curb. Suzy didn't blame him. There was something in Michelle's voice that communicated that very bad things would happen to those who disobeyed her.

"Wait!" yelled Mercury, who was still standing outside. The driver hit the brakes long enough for him to catch up and jump in the front seat, then peeled away.

"Whatever game you're playing, Michelle," said Mercury, "it's not going to work. The jig is up. We've flushed out all your agents in D.C."

Michelle sighed. "All *my* agents, yes," she replied. "But not Tiamat's. Did you really think she was going to let you activate another MEOW device if she didn't have a way around it? You've just given her the keys to the kingdom."

# CHAPTER THIRTY-SIX

"Thank God you're here," said President Danton Prowse as the door to the Oval Office opened. "Something very strange is… oh."

"Expecting someone else?" asked Tiamat sweetly as she entered the room.

"Who the hell are you?" demanded the president. "How did you get past the—"

"Save the hysterics, Prowse. My name is Tiamat. I'm Michelle's replacement. The organization is undergoing a bit of a restructuring at present."

Prowse frowned. "I… see," he said at last.

"Don't act so put out," said Tiamat. "Nothing has changed, as far as you're concerned. You remain the leader of the free world. I'm merely filling in for Michelle as your advisor."

"What happened to her?" asked Prowse. "She ran out of here screaming. It was… disturbing. And my press secretary and several advisors seem to have disappeared as well."

"St. Patrick drove the snakes out of Ireland," replied Tiamat. "I drove the weasels out of Washington, D.C. It's true that we've lost some manpower, but I think you'll find that the D.C. shadow government is now a much more streamlined and efficient organization."

"Um," said Prowse. "What do you mean by 'efficient'?"

"What I mean," replied Tiamat, "is that there will be no more half-measures. No more of this gradual, halting progress toward fascism. From here on, we're going all out. Tell me, Mr. President, are you familiar with a company called Mentaldyne?"

"Hmm," said Prowse. "Sounds familiar."

"It should," said Tiamat. "They make the RFID chips that federal prisons have been implanting in convicted felons since 2013."

"Ah!" said Prowse. "That's it. The Federal Felon Tracking Program. One of my most popular initiatives. I've been meaning to buy stock in that company."

"It's privately owned," said Tiamat. "I should know, since I own it. Mentaldyne is the sole provider of implantable RFID chips for the federal government. Do you know how that happened?"

Prowse shrugged.

"Mentaldyne underbid every other company by at least seventy-five percent. We lose nearly three hundred dollars on every chip we sell."

Prowse frowned. "That doesn't, um, sound like very good business."

"It isn't. We did it to get a monopoly on the market. And do you know why?"

"I have no idea."

"The Mentaldyne chips have an undocumented feature. They can receive radio signals and convert them into neural impulses."

"Neural impulses? You mean, like…?"

"Mind control. I can manipulate the thoughts and actions of anyone with one of those chips implanted, with radio signals. Remote control human beings."

"What?" cried Danton Prowse. "That's horrific! And why would you want to have an army of remotely controlled felons anyway?"

"The prisoners were just a trial run, to get used to the idea of implanting chips in people. Nobody complains about the government violating the rights of criminals. Who gives a shit, right? They're criminals. They *should* be tracked. It only makes sense. You put a chip in them while they're in prison and justify it as a security measure, and then you leave it in after they get out as a concession to 'public safety.' After all, we already strip felons of the right to vote and the right to own firearms, so why not track them while we're at it? But I don't need to tell you this. The tracking program was part of your big 'tough on crime' agenda."

Prowse shrugged again.

"And then, after the criminals," she continued, "you move on to people accepting food stamps or living in public housing. And again nobody complains, because after all, you have to make sure these people aren't taking advantage of the system. You don't want to be subsidizing a bunch of drug dealers. If you've got a tracking chip in their heads, you can see exactly where they are at any time of the day, and who they're associating with."

"Hey, I fought against those requirements!" protested Prowse.

"Of course you did," said Tiamat. "You liberals push to get these programs in place, and then the conservatives push for 'accountability.' The conservatives don't have the votes to get rid of the program, and the liberals don't have the votes to override the demands for these additional restrictions. And just like that, you've got several million people who have effectively ceded their rights to the government in return for a little cash or security. It's beautiful. And once you've managed to convince the public that people who are accepting 'public assistance' need to be tracked by the government, you've got everybody by the balls. After all, isn't Medicare 'public assistance'? Or veterans' benefits? Or Social Security? Or federally subsidized student loans? Or corporate tax breaks? Practically everybody in this country is on some kind of 'public assistance' if you define the term broadly enough. Hell, you could argue that federal highways are a form of public assistance. All these damned freeloaders need to be tracked!"

"Hmm," said Prowse. "I think you're oversimplifying things a bit. And in any case, I assure you that if I had known about this whole 'mind control' program you've got going, I'd have fought it every inch of the way."

"Oh, that's adorable," gushed Tiamat. "You're fine with tracking people everywhere they go, but you draw the line at actually *controlling* them, because that would be *wrong*. God, I love you ethical types. Where were your ethics when that nuclear bomb nearly took out Grand Rapids? Were they out sick that day?"

"That was not my fault!" Prowse snapped. "Michelle said she'd remove me from power and find another president willing to go along with it. It would have happened no matter what I did!"

"OK, good," said Tiamat with a smile. "So you know where you stand."

Prowse paled as he realized what he'd just told Tiamat: that he'd do anything she asked as long as he remained in power.

"So what's your end game, Tiamat?" asked Prowse bitterly. "Who else do you want to implant these chips in?"

"Everybody," said Tiamat.

Prowse frowned. "Now, when you say everybody," he said, "you mean…"

"*Everybody*," Tiamat said again. "Every man, woman and child in America. And then the rest of the world."

"What, you're just going to start grabbing people off the street?"

"No, no," said Tiamat. "It has to be done in an orderly fashion. It's one thing to force something like this on prisoners and welfare queens, but when you start picking on Joe Middle Class, you're going to get some pushback. That's when you ratchet up the threat level, to dramatize the consequences of not tracking everybody. Michelle's already done a pretty good job of that with her little demonstration in Grand Rapids. Scare the shit out of everybody and then tell them you can keep them safe if they submit to the very minor inconvenience of having a tiny little tracking chip implanted in their skulls. I mean, who could argue against that? Why wouldn't you want the government to know exactly where you are at all times? If you're not doing anything wrong, you have nothing to be afraid of."

Danton Prowse frowned. "But the mind control chips… Is that really necessary? It seems like Michelle and Gabrielle were doing a pretty good job manipulating public opinion without resorting to such extreme tactics." It was true; between Michelle's fabricated security threats and Gabrielle's massaging of the media, mind control was almost redundant. Prowse had been particularly impressed by the way Gabrielle had managed to dredge up "experts" to defend whatever absurd and illegal policy the Prowse administration happened to be pushing at the time. Often these people were major stakeholders in defense or security companies, or they were officials from the Babcock administration who had been thoroughly discredited years earlier. Some were bona fide war criminals. In many cases, they were all three. These supposed "experts" would banter back and forth with some fringe journalist or pointy-headed lawyer from the ACLU, the moderator would intone that it was definitely "a serious issue on which people had some strong opinions," and then cut to a commercial featuring a lizard selling car insurance.

"The problem," said Tiamat, "is that public opinion is a capricious and unpredictable beast. It requires a constant effort to keep people worried about inconsequential issues and unconcerned with important matters. And while it's true that most people are sheep, easily led and controlled, there's always a fringe element out there, stirring up trouble. Like those guys running that BitterAngels.net site. Since the Grand Rapids incident, the traffic on that site has soared a hundredfold. With the right catalyst, a few dedicated, independent-thinking individuals can get the sheep to look up. And once that happens, it's going to take more than a few press conferences and cable news appearances to smooth things over. Of course, you've already made great inroads into the fringe element by chipping felons, the poor, and people committed to mental institutions. But there's always a threat from those people who are right on the edge of sanity. The ones who manage to stay out of any serious trouble, but who don't quite fit in with the sheep. *Those* are the people we need to get to. But there's no simple way of doing that without chipping everybody."

"So, what now?" Prowse asked.

"It will be done in stages, of course," said Tiamat. "We start with Grand Rapids. Chip everybody in the city. And then, when that program is a smashing success, we'll roll it out to some of the other 'high-threat' cities."

"And when you say that it will be a smashing success, you mean..."

"I mean we get a bunch of locals who had been opposed to the chips to go on national television and tell everybody how wrong they were, and how much safer they feel now that everybody in the city is chipped. This is the beauty of a mind-control program. The most vocal opponents suddenly become strident supporters."

"And you don't think anyone will see through that?"

235

"Sure, some people will. But whoever complains the loudest will be next in line for chip implantation. Eventually we'll have silenced every critic either by directly controlling them through the chip or through the power of sheer intimidation. Either way, dissent is silenced. After we chip the residents of a handful of key cities, the tide of public opinion will have turned. But we've got to do it fast, before any organized resistance can form."

Prowse sighed heavily. "And you're sure this is going to work? That we'll be able to get most of the country chipped before people realize what's going on?"

"Absolutely," Tiamat said. "There's only one loose end. And that's being taken care off as we speak."

# CHAPTER THIRTY-SEVEN

*Costa Rica; August 2016*

Gamaliel and his team had just gotten into position when he received word that Tiamat's coup had been successful. Michelle and every angel and demon loyal to her had fled Washington, and Tiamat and her agents now held the executive branch. Soon they'd begin the process of chipping everyone in the U.S. The only weak point in the plan was that Balderhaz was still at large. If anyone could throw a wrench in Tiamat's plan, it was Balderhaz—which was why Gamaliel and his team of a dozen combat-trained demons were about to abduct Balderhaz and drag him to the Mentaldyne facility in Utah. Tiamat hoped that Balderhaz could be put to work designing weapons for her, but at the very least he'd be negated as a threat.

Gamaliel wasn't sure what Balderhaz could do to interfere with Tiamat's plan at this point, but Tiamat wasn't taking any chances after all the work she'd done to get this far. The only reason she'd suggested the MEOW device in the first place, some two hundred and thirty years earlier, was that she was fairly certain she could come up with a way around it. She was right, but it had taken a bit longer than she'd expected: it wasn't until the advent of neural implant chips in the early twenty-first century that she'd been able to devise a way to block the MEOW device's emissions.

Tiamat had founded Mentaldyne in the late 1990s, when the technology was still cutting edge and the original MEOW device was still in place. The destruction of the MEOW device on September 11, 2001 had been a serious setback, and she had been on the verge of shutting down the whole enterprise: there was no point to devising an override for a weapon that no longer functioned. But she couldn't shake the feeling that the chips had potential for uses far beyond blocking the MEOW emissions.

The chips worked by tapping into the brain stem and sending a neural signal that was essentially the mirror image of the MEOW emissions. Like noise-canceling headphones, the chip counteracted the frequency of the debilitating neural impulses caused by the MEOW device, allowing the chipped angel to function normally within the range of the MEOW device.

But if you can send one sort of neural signal, Tiamat reasoned, you should be able to send others as well. Specifically, you should be able to override the signals sent by the brain to the body, to get the individual to do something they didn't actually want to do. (Initially the testing of the chips had been on angels, as humans weren't affected by the MEOW device, but for the mind control feature, Mentaldyne started with mice and worked their way up to dogs, cats and monkeys, and, finally, human beings.) At first the signals sent through the chips were simple motor movement, like "raise your right hand." The human trials went better than anyone expected: not only could the subject be forced to raise his right hand against his will; the subject was actually convinced that raising his right hand was *his idea*. Receiving countervailing neural transmissions at the brainstem level was so confusing to the brain that the brain reacted by rationalizing the end result as borne of its own intention. The subject would vehemently insist that although he had originally intended not to raise his hand, he had subsequently changed his mind. No matter what contrary evidence was presented, the subject remained blind to the obvious fact that his mind had been changed for him, vehemently insisting that he had raised his hand of his own volition.

It was a small step from that point to actually inserting intentions and preferences into the subject's mind. One man, who had a life-long aversion to cantaloupe, was convinced that cantaloupe was now his favorite food in the entire world. He drove directly from the testing facility to a local farmer's market, where he bought sixty-eight ripe cantaloupes and ate nothing else for the next three weeks. One woman was converted from Judaism to Islam. An Oakland Raiders fan was convinced to root for the 49ers.

With a few hundred of these chips implanted in the skulls of influential individuals, Tiamat could rule the world. The problem, of course, was that the people she most wanted to control—the rich and powerful—were the least likely to submit to having a chip implanted. Mentaldyne had a hard enough time finding vagrants who would go along with it—and succeeded in this only by virtue of cash bribes and blatant lies about what the chips actually did.

But the increased interest in security after 9/11 gave her an idea: she'd have Mentaldyne add a tiny radio transmitter to the chip and market them as tracking devices. Mentaldyne's first contract was with a supplier of veterinarian supplies, who marketed them as a way of preventing little Fido or Fluffy from running away. Not long after that, some of the more conservative states like Texas and Alabama began implanting them in prisoners. Danton Prowse, who had to work hard to overcome the impression that he had been "soft on crime" when he was governor of Connecticut, gave in to an advisor's suggestion that he support a nationwide Federal Felon Tracking Program. That advisor, of course, had been a demon— one of Lucifer's agents whom Tiamat had managed to turn.

So what had started out simply as a means of circumventing the MEOW device had turned into a full-fledged secret mind control program. There were two different types of chips: the ones implanted in angels and the ones implanted in humans. They differed only in the respect that the angel chips included the anti-MEOW feature. Both types of chips had the RFID and the mind control functionality—although Tiamat neglected to mention this to her minions. She insisted that the chips that were being implanted in her demonic underlings were solely for protection against the MEOW device, and that the mind control and tracking functionality had been disabled. Whether any of them actually believed her was a function of how well they knew her.

Gamaliel, for his part, didn't, but then he pretty much did whatever Tiamat wanted anyway, and if he was going to continue to be her second-in-command, he would need the chip to protect him from the MEOW device. The actual implantation was quick, easy and relatively painless: a technician at Mentaldyne had implanted one in Gamaliel and then instructed him on how to implant the chip in Tiamat's agents in Washington. You simply held the implantation device—which, oddly, resembled one of those little clicky label makers you can get for three dollars at an office supply store—at the base of the subject's neck and pulled the trigger. The subject would feel a sensation like a bee sting and that was that: the tiny cilia-like neural conductors would latch onto the subject's brain stem. Gamaliel had managed to meet with Tiamat and twelve of her other agents in Washington to implant them with chips before returning to Costa Rica. She had many more agents, of course, but they were outside the MEOW zone awaiting further instructions. The plan was for Gamaliel to nab Baldherhaz and then return to Washington to chip the rest of Tiamat's minions. When that was done, Tiamat would be unstoppable.

Gamaliel gave the signal and the demons moved in, three on each side of Balderhaz's compound. Tiamat was taking no chances: although there were only three angels inside—Perp, Eddie, and Balderhaz—and none of them were a match for any of Gamaliel's commandos, she had erred on the side of caution. Each of Gamaliel's men carried an AK-47, in case their sheer numbers weren't enough to tilt the odds in their favor.

As the three other groups closed on the sides and back of the compound, respectively, Gamaliel and the two demons flanking him approached the front door. The two demons held back, pointing their rifles at the front of the building, while Gamaliel kicked the door in.

"On your knees!" Gamaliel barked. "Hands in the air!"

But the laboratory area was deserted.

"They're downstairs," Gamaliel said. "In the rec area."

He led his two men into the basement while the others kept an eye on the lab. But downstairs he found only an abandoned ping-pong table. On the table, underneath one of the paddles, was a sheet of paper. Gamaliel picked it up and looked at it. The note read:

*HOW DUMB DO YOU THINK I AM?*

*- MERCURY*

# CHAPTER THIRTY-EIGHT

*Washington, D.C.; August 2016*

The Cadillac pulled into a dark alley and stopped about twenty paces from another car, which had approached from the opposite direction. The driver got out of the car, grabbed a pair of crutches from the trunk, walked to the passenger side, and opened the door. Zion Johnson stepped out, irritably taking the crutches. Eddie had done a half-assed job repairing his knee, fusing the kneecap together but leaving a mass of torn ligaments and scar tissue. It had been enough to get Zion Johnson out of the cornfield, but it was far from healed and the pain was getting worse. After the walking he'd done on it, he'd had to get another cast put on to immobilize the joint. It made walking difficult and driving impossible. For someone who prided himself on self-reliance, that was hard to take.

On top of that ever-present annoyance, Zion Johnson was furious at himself for falling for the spray-painted hair trick, not to mention trusting those Chaos Faction morons to set the bomb off at the right location. It had been a miracle that the bomb hadn't gone off in the city. He had Mercury to thank for that, he supposed, but he wasn't disposed to be very complimentary of Mercury right now, given the way Mercury had hoodwinked him. Grudging respect as a worthy adversary was the best he could manage at present.

Zion Johnson limped on the crutches toward the other car as a woman exited the back seat and walked toward him. They met in between the two cars, in the blinding glare of headlights.

"So you're the one in charge now," said Zion Johnson.

"I'm just an advisor," said the woman. "My name is Tiamat."

"An advisor, huh?" said Zion Johnson. "Who are you advising?"

"Right now?" asked the woman with a smile. "I'm advising you to watch your step, Mr. Johnson. My people tell me you're the one to go to if I want to get something done. Is that correct?"

"I do what I can to serve my country," said Zion Johnson.

"Patriotism," said Tiamat with a barely concealed sneer. "Such an old-fashioned value. Useful, though. Mr. Johnson, your country needs your help with some security arrangements."

"Where?"

"Grand Rapids, Michigan. I believe you know the place."

"Was just there, as a matter of fact," said Zion Johnson. "They had a bit of a terrorism scare recently."

"Indeed," said Tiamat. "You'll be happy to hear that I've come up with a plan to prevent anything like that from happening again."

"To prevent it from happening in Grand Rapids, or from happening anywhere?"

"First Grand Rapids, then everywhere else," replied Tiamat. "I'm hoping that the plan is such a brilliant success in Grand Rapids that there will be little resistance in the rest of the country."

"So what is this plan?"

"We call it Project Myrmidon," said Tiamat. "We're implanting RFID chips in everyone within the city limits. You enter the city, you get chipped. Once everybody is chipped, a terrorist attack will essentially be impossible, because we'll be able to track everyone all the time. Tracking algorithms will be used to flag suspicious movements, so we can stop crimes before they ever happen."

"Interesting," said Zion Johnson. "And these chips, would they be similar to the ones that are being used on felons and mental patients?"

"Very similar."

"Implanted at the brain stem," said Zion Johnson. "Some have postulated that such a chip could theoretically be used to control behavior. Theoretically."

"Is that right?" asked Tiamat. "Well, I'm sure that capability is years off. And we'll put safeguards in place to prevent those sorts of abuses from occurring, in any case."

"Oh, of course," said Zion Johnson. "Manipulating the behavior of ordinary citizens would be unethical."

Tiamat smiled wryly. "You're very perceptive, Mr. Johnson. How would you like to be in charge of Myrmidon?"

Zion Johnson frowned. "Why me?"

"I've read your file, Mr. Johnson. You're a man of discipline. You abhor disorder, crime, and weakness of the will. You'd love more than anything to make the world a better place, but you're stymied at every turn by corruption and stupidity."

Zion Johnson didn't know who put together this file she was talking about, but he'd like to commend them on their accuracy. "So that's it?" he asked. "I'm a control freak, so you want me in charge?"

Tiamat laughed. "No, it's what *makes* you a control freak that I care about. Your affinity for order and your aversion to chaos. I believe you understand what's at stake here. The world has strayed too far toward chaos, and I need someone who can help me pull it back from the brink. Is that you, Mr. Johnson?"

"Yes, ma'am," said Zion Johnson, without a second thought.

"Good," said Tiamat. "Catch the first flight tomorrow to Grand Rapids. Put things in order there, and then we'll talk about the plan for the rest of the country." She turned to go, but then stopped. "Oh, and Mr. Johnson," she said, "when you get there, you will of course get a chip implanted yourself. The leaders have to set the appropriate example."

"Yes, ma'am," said Zion Johnson again.

"Very good," said Tiamat, with a smile. "Oh, and you should have that cast taken off."

Tiamat walked back to the car and got inside. The car backed out of the alley and drove off, leaving Zion Johnson standing alone in the headlights of the Cadillac. His leg had suddenly stopped hurting, and he had no doubt that if he had the cast removed, he'd find it had been completely healed. Just in time for his new assignment. Working for Beings of Indeterminate Origin had its downsides, but you couldn't beat the medical benefits.

Something was still bothering him though, and it irritated him that he couldn't seem to pinpoint what it was. He was still upset with himself for the Grand Rapids debacle, but things had turned out OK in the end, and in any case Tiamat either didn't know or didn't care what had happened with the bomb. He was still angry with that Mercury character, but that wasn't it either. He was a little disconcerted that the United States government was apparently now in the hands of a narcissistic megalomaniac, but this was hardly the first time that had happened.

No, what bothered him, he realized, was that he had just been given the assignment that he had been working toward his entire life, and it scared the shit out of him.

# CHAPTER THIRTY-NINE

*Somewhere in Missouri; August 2016*

Unfortunately, Mercury seemed to be nearly as dumb as Tiamat and Gamaliel thought he was. While he'd foreseen that they would attempt to abduct Balderhaz, he hadn't anticipated Tiamat's scheme to make her agents immune to the effects of the MEOW device. So while Balderhaz, Eddie, and Suzy had escaped, Tiamat remained in control of Washington, D.C. And there didn't seem to be much any of them could do about it.

They'd regrouped in one of Michelle's safe houses—a rundown old farmhouse in Missouri. Mercury hadn't had much choice but to trust Michelle; they needed a place to hide where they could figure out what to do next. Mercury had sent word of what had happened to Perp via Angel Band, and instructed Perp's group to meet him at the safe house as soon as possible. Mercury, Michelle and Suzy arrived early in the evening, and a few hours later Perp, Balderhaz and Eddie showed up.

"What a dump!" Balderhaz exclaimed as he strolled inside the house. Eddie and Perp followed close behind. Mercury, Suzy and Michelle were sitting in the living room. An ancient TV flickered against one wall, showing the latest news from Grand Rapids and the other cities that were still under martial law.

"I'm less concerned about the décor and more concerned about the company," said Eddie. Perp nodded in agreement.

Michelle, sitting on an easy chair in a corner of the room, seemed amused at Eddie's distaste.

"Yeah, I get it," said Mercury. "Competing plans for world domination make for strange bedfellows. I'm not thrilled about it either, but Tiamat's double-cross means we're stuck with Michelle for the time being."

"This sorry bunch of rejects isn't exactly my first choice of allies either, you know," said Michelle. "This morning I had the President of the United States under my thumb, and now I'm stuck in Podunk, Missouri with the morons who put her in power."

"We didn't put her in power!" snapped Suzy. "You did! You're the one who set up this whole shadow government, and you're the one who made it necessary to create another..."

"MEOW device," finished Mercury.

"Yeah, I refuse to use that name," said Suzy, dropping onto the couch next to Mercury. "It's idiotic."

"And in Michelle's defense," said Mercury, "it was Lucifer who set up the shadow government. Michelle just took it over. And now the reins have unfortunately passed to Tiamat."

"Because you gave them to her!" yelled Michelle.

"You tried to nuke Grand Rapids!" yelled Suzy. She nearly jumped off the couch at Michelle, but Mercury held her back.

"OK," said Eddie. "This is getting us nowhere. We've all made some mistakes—"

"Putting another MEOW device in Washington was not a mistake," Mercury protested. "Michelle forced our hand. We had no way of knowing—"

"You made a deal with Tiamat!" cried Michelle. "What did you think was—"

"Stop!" shouted Eddie. "Enough! From here on out, nobody says anything unless it's an idea for getting Tiamat out of Washington!"

An eerie quiet fell over the farmhouse. It seemed that no one had any ideas.

"Do we even know how she's counteracting the MEOW emissions?" asked Perp. "Balderhaz?"

"Eh?" said Balderhaz, who had been transfixed by a pair of dust bunnies blowing across the hardwood floor.

"Any idea why Tiamat's agents aren't affected by the MEOW device?" asked Perp.

"Oh," said Balderhaz. "Um, no?"

"Hey, turn it up!" Mercury suddenly yelled. On the TV a reporter was holding up what looked like a tiny computer chip.

Suzy turned up the volume on the TV. The reporter was saying that given the ongoing threat of a terrorist attack, all residents of Grand Rapids were going to be required to have a small computer chip implanted so that security officials could track their movements. When the reporter was done explaining how safe and innocuous the chips were, he handed the one he'd been holding to a smiling man wearing a Homeland Security uniform. The smiling man put the chip into a device that looked surprisingly like one of those little clicky label makers you can get for three dollars at an office supply store. He pressed the label maker thing against the back of the reporter's neck. There was a click, and the reporter winced.

"What do you think?" said the Homeland Security officer.

"Better than a tetanus shot!" said the reporter.

They both chuckled, and then the reporter said, "And now, Donna with the weather!"

Suzy turned the TV off. "Sickening," she said. "Why do people put up with this shit?"

"It's for their own good," said Michelle. "If you're not doing anything wrong—"

"Don't say it!" screamed Suzy. "I don't care if you *are* an archangel. If you say, 'if you aren't doing anything wrong, you have nothing to worry about,' I will pull those gorgeous brown locks right out of your fucking head!"

"Try it," said Michelle, with a smirk.

Suzy glared at her. "Are you seriously trying to argue that the government has our best interests at heart when you know full well that the government is in the hands of a *demon*?"

"Because *you* put her there!"

"You're missing the fucking point!" screamed Suzy. "You're an *archangel*. The best of the best. The highest moral authority on this planet. And when you were in charge, you tried to detonate a fucking nuclear bomb in one of your own cities!"

"The plan," said Michelle icily, "was to detonate the bomb *near* the city. Which is exactly what happened."

"No thanks to you and the gang of knuckleheads you entrusted with the bomb," snapped Suzy. "Not to mention the fact that you seem to think it's totally cool to detonate a nuclear bomb *near* a major city."

Michelle stared daggers at Suzy.

"And as utterly fucked up as that is," Suzy went on, "I'm willing to accept that this Tiamat character might actually be an even more heinous bitch than you are. But that's not the point. The point is that *nobody should be trusted with that sort of power.* Once you've got the capability to track people's movements twenty-four hours a day, the temptation to try to control their behavior is too great."

"Hmm," said Mercury. Everyone's eyes turned to him.

"What do you mean, 'Hmm,'" said Suzy.

"Does it seem strange to anyone else that Tiamat would be pushing this RFID thing right now?" Mercury said. "I mean, what's the point?"

"Security," said Suzy. "She wants to know where everyone is at all times."

"Everyone in Grand Rapids, Michigan."

"For starters," said Suzy. "Presumably she'll move on to other cities."

Mercury shook his head. "Something doesn't add up."

"I agree," said Michelle. "Tiamat is overplaying her hand. She has to know there will be major pushback against something like this."

"Unless there isn't," said Mercury. "Balderhaz!"

Balderhaz stepped out from behind a curtain. "Eh?"

"Do you know anything about these tracking chips?"

"Mmm," said Balderhaz. "Neural implant chips. Hack right into the central nervous system. Very bad."

"Oh, shit," said Eddie suddenly. "Rosenfeld was working on a story about this for BitterAngels.net. I thought he was going a bit off the reservation, so I didn't pay much attention. But I remember him talking about some plot to get these chips implanted in everybody. He said the tracking part was just a Trojan horse."

"Ugh," said Mercury.

"What?" asked Suzy.

"Nothing," said Mercury. "Bad memories. I mean, the *smell*. You have no idea. Go on."

"Anyway," Eddie went on, "Rosenfeld said the RFID thing was just to trick people into getting the chips implanted. He said the real purpose was mind control."

"Mind control?" asked Suzy dubiously.

"That fits," said Mercury. "Tiamat's an even bigger control freak than Michelle. No offense."

Michelle shrugged.

"She's going to chip everybody in Grand Rapids," Mercury went on. "There won't be any complaints about the chips, because when she's done, they'll all be her puppets. And when the rest of the country sees how happy, well-adjusted and secure the Grand Rapidians are, they'll be lining up for their own chips. Diabolical. Grand Rapiders."

"Grand Rapidites," offered Eddie.

"Grand Rapitians," said Mercury. "Grand Ra—"

"So what can we do about it?" Suzy interrupted.

The room fell silent again.

"The chips are made by some outfit in Utah," Eddie said after a moment. "Mental something."

"Mentaldyne," said Michelle.

"OK," said Suzy. "So we go find this Mentaldyne place and blow it up."

Everybody turned to look at Suzy.

"Weren't you just insisting a few days ago that you aren't a terrorist?" asked Mercury.

"Desperate times," said Suzy.

"Blow it up with what?" asked Eddie.

"Whatever," said Suzy. "Use your angel powers. Surely between the five of you, you can destroy a building."

"It won't matter," said Michelle. "It will slow down the production of the chips for a while, but it won't stop Tiamat. And she'll use the attack on Mentaldyne as a rationale for more security. I would."

"So we're screwed," Suzy said. "Tiamat's going to have absolute control over everyone in the United States, and there's nothing we can do about it."

The room fell silent again. If anyone could stop Tiamat, it was the six individuals sitting in this room, and none of them had any ideas.

# CHAPTER FORTY

*Washington, D.C.; August 2016*

Zion Johnson stood watching the news while he dressed for his flight. Zion Johnson was well aware that the idea of dressing for a flight was anachronistic; it was pathetically common these days for people to board flights wearing sweatpants or, God forbid, even pajamas. As with most signs of societal decay, Zion Johnson's reaction was to attempt to hold the line against barbarism by adhering to a strict personal code. So it was that Zion Johnson was tying a double Windsor knot in preparation for a three hour flight from Washington, D.C. to Grand Rapids, Michigan.

While he did so, the bubble-headed bleach-blond on the TV yammered on about what was happening in Grand Rapids. There had been some skirmishes between the National Guard troops and a few locals resisting the chip implantation. Whoever was currently in charge of the program had resorted to a heavy-handed policy of sending men in combat gear door-to-door to perform the implantations, and it was turning into a PR nightmare. Zion Johnson hoped he could get there in time to reverse the damage. He planned a much subtler, carrot-and-stick approach, setting up convenient implantation centers throughout the city, and linking certain benefits to chip implantation. For example, chipped citizens might get extra food rations or be allowed to travel throughout the city without having to show ID at checkpoints. Since the National Guard now controlled all traffic in and out of the city, the citizens were largely dependent on the government for food and other staples, and they'd long ago become acclimated to police checkpoints. It was the same strategy the government had used on public housing residents: get the people hooked on some government benefit—like being able to eat or move around—and then demand that the recipients prove their worthiness to receive the benefit. It worked every time.

And of course Zion Johnson planned to make a big show of all the officials running the program—including himself—getting chips implanted. So far the Washington, D.C. authorities and some local bigwigs had resisted implantation, the former on the basis that they were not permanent residents of Grand Rapids and the latter on the grounds that as government officials and pillars of the community, they were above reproach. But that was going to change. Zion Johnson was going to get chipped on national television at the press conference announcing his new position, followed by all of his underlings. Anyone who resisted would be sent back to Washington or fired—and then chipped anyway. So far the elites had gotten a free ride, but Zion Johnson was about to show the people of Grand Rapids that nobody was above being chipped. The program only worked if everyone was on board.

At least that's what Zion Johnson kept telling himself. Zion Johnson's entire life had been defined by following orders. He always did what was asked of him, even if it didn't necessarily jibe with his personal sense of right and wrong, in service to his country. Zion Johnson always followed orders. And that's what bothered him.

Zion Johnson didn't *need* to be chipped. He was like a dog who had never once barked in twenty-eight years being fitted for a muzzle. He should be given a medal for all the sacrifices he'd made for his country, and instead he was being put on a leash. Leashes were for the unwashed rabble, the pajama-wearing, Big Gulp-drinking, Walmart-shopping, tramp stamp-having masses. Not for Zion Johnson, who had given everything for his country.

And yet, why should it bother him? He'd already proved he'd do whatever the president asked of him, even if the president was being manipulated by strange beings from another dimension. He should be happy to be getting chipped. He'd no longer have to worry about overcoming his personal qualms or foibles to serve his country. Absolute obedience would be ensured. His mantra would no longer be necessary.

*Superior attitude, superior state of mind*, he thought. What would Mason Storm do?

Zion Johnson checked his watch. He had three minutes until he needed to leave for the airport. Three minutes in which he could do whatever he wanted.

Zion Johnson sat down at his computer and brought up his email. Sitting in his inbox was an encrypted file that someone in Tiamat's organization had sent him the night before. He clicked the Forward button, typed in an email address, and then hit Send. In a separate email he sent the decryption key. Then he shut down the computer, grabbed his suitcase, and walked out the door.

Zion Johnson had a job to do.

# CHAPTER FORTY-ONE

*Somewhere in Missouri; August 2016*

The five angels and one human hiding in a farmhouse in Missouri had spent most of the night arguing about how to stop Tiamat and, despite Eddie's best efforts to keep the discussion on track, engaging in bitter recriminations regarding who was to blame for their current predicament. Suzy and Michelle were the most vocal participants; Perp had little advice to give for once, Balderhaz had disappeared, and Eddie had his hands full keeping Michelle and Suzy from killing each other—or, more accurately, preventing Suzy from punching Michelle and Michelle from vaporizing Suzy with a snap of her fingers.

During a lull in the finger-pointing and backbiting, Eddie took a break to post an update to the BitterAngels.net site from his phone. He hadn't seen anything on the news about what had happened to Rosenfeld, and he didn't feel like he was in a position to break the story at present, so he simply posted a short note explaining that the BitterAngels.net staff were dealing with some "personal issues," and that they would resume updating the site as soon as possible. The conspiracy-minded frequenters of the site would undoubtedly jump to the conclusion that Rosenfeld had been "disappeared," which of course he had, and Eddie was totally OK with that.

The recriminations not yet having resumed in full-force (Suzy, being human, had fallen asleep around seven am, leaving Michelle without a sparring partner), Eddie then checked the

BitterAngels.com email address that was posted on the site for readers to use for sending in anonymous tips. Among the penis enlargement remedies, lucrative offers from Nigerian princes, and the usual dire and incomprehensible missives from the tinfoil hat crowd, there were two emails that caught his eye. The subject of the first was simply "Fish." The subject of the second was "Chips." Both came from an anonymous email account bearing the name *A Freeman.*

"Um, guys?" said Eddie, after decrypting the file and perusing its contents. "I think I might know how to stop Tiamat."

After Suzy was awoken and Balderhaz was found (he'd inadvertently trapped himself in the beet cellar), Eddie explained that he'd received a copy of the Mentaldyne specifications for the mind control program, with precise details on how the system worked. Balderhaz had been right: the chips were designed to directly interface with the nervous system, allowing a remote agent to control the thoughts and actions of potentially millions of people. Grand Rapids was only the first step; soon the whole world would be under Tiamat's control.

"So far," said Mercury, "I'm not seeing the good news."

"Ah, but here's the thing," said Eddie. "The mind control signals are transmitted via a complex array of radio signals, on several different bandwidths. It's a very delicate system requiring a transmitter specially designed for the purpose. They call it Myrmidon. Ultimately Mentaldyne plans to have a globe-spanning network of satellites for full coverage and redundancy, but at present there's only a single satellite, parked in geosynchronous orbit over North America."

"So," said Suzy groggily, "we take out that satellite and the whole program is toast."

"Well, yes," said Eddie. "But from this documentation, it's pretty clear that Mentaldyne is very aware of this weak point in their system. It says, and I quote, 'It is strongly recommended that BIO personnel be dispatched to protect the geosynchronous transmitter from unauthorized access.'"

"In other words," said Michelle, "it's going to be guarded by angels."

"Correct," said Eddie. "Also, taking out the satellite is only a temporary solution. They've got more satellites. They just need to get another one in orbit and they'll be back in business."

"Still waiting for the good news," said Mercury.

"OK," said Eddie. "Now we get to the really interesting part. You know how we couldn't figure out how Tiamat was circumventing the MEOW device? Well, it turns out she's got her demons implanted with chips as well."

"The same chips as they're putting in humans?" asked Suzy.

"Not exactly. They have an added feature, some kind of neural blocker that allows angels to safely remain within the range of the MEOW emissions. But here's the thing: the underlying chip is the same."

"So it has the mind control functionality?" asked Suzy, dubiously. "She implanted mind control chips in her own agents?"

"I told you," Mercury said. "She's a huge control freak."

"Well, in this case," said Eddie, "it could be her downfall. All we need to do is alter the programming of the satellite, and we can take control of every demon in her network. Including Tiamat herself, as a matter of fact. She must have a chip herself, if she's in Washington, D.C."

"OK," said Suzy. "So how do we do it?"

It ended up being a bit more complicated than Eddie made it out to be. For one thing, it would require breaking into the Mentaldyne headquarters to directly access the computer system that controlled the satellite. They would have to write a software patch to override the existing program to allow transfer of the mind control program to another location. The control software was thoroughly documented in the material *A Freeman* had sent, and Suzy was fairly certain that with a computer and a few days, she could write the patch.

The other complication was that the transmitter on the satellite was hard-wired to prevent exactly what they were trying to do: the chips implanted in Tiamat's demons use a different set of frequencies than the regular chips, and the transmitter was built to only allow transmissions on a pre-determined set of frequencies. Evidently Tiamat wanted to make sure the system was secure before risking losing control of her own agents. It was a smart move, and it made it almost impossible for anyone to take control of Tiamat's minions. Almost.

"Oh, I can build another transmitter," said Balderhaz offhandedly.

"Really?" asked Suzy.

"Sure," he said. "All I need is an old Timex watch, a wire hanger, six rolls of aluminum foil, an oil drum, a banana, a soldering iron, twenty feet of three-quarter-inch PVC pipe…"

"Hang on!" said Eddie, who was scrambling to find a pen and a sheet of paper.

"What's the banana for?" asked Suzy.

"For the monkey to eat," said Balderhaz.

"What monkey?" asked Suzy.

"Well, you didn't let me finish the list, did you?" said Balderhaz.

The other concern was that *A Freeman*, whoever it was, was setting them up. But there was general agreement that Michelle wouldn't risk so much simply to capture a few troublemakers, particularly now that her plan was so far along. In any case, they didn't have much choice: this was their only chance to stop Michelle.

Mercury and Perp spent most of the day rounding up supplies, starting with a laptop for Suzy and then moving on to Balderhaz's wide-ranging list of mundane and exotic ingredients. Mercury even found him a black-headed spider monkey, which was inexplicably floating a few inches from the ceiling of the living room shortly after Mercury delivered the poor simian.

True to his word, though, in three days' time Balderhaz produced a transmitter designed to transmit radio signals on the precise frequencies used by the chips implanted in Tiamat and her minions. At least that's what Balderhaz claimed it was. To everyone else, it looked like an oil drum topped by a giant umbrella wrapped in aluminum foil.

"Remember the hair dryer," said Perp to Mercury as they regarded the sad-looking contraption.

"Yeah," said Mercury. Sometimes it wasn't easy to remember that Balderhaz was a genius.

"What's that noise?" asked Perp. There was a loud banging going on somewhere nearby.

"Balderhaz is trapped in the beet cellar again," said Mercury.

Suzy finished the software patch a few hours later. Exhausted, she went to bed. The angels didn't need rest, but if she was going to hack into the Myrmidon control system, she needed to get some sleep.

Tomorrow night they would execute their two-pronged attack on Tiamat's authoritarian regime.

# CHAPTER FORTY-TWO

*Provo, Utah; August 2016*

Michelle crept along the shadow of the Mentaldyne building, with Eddie following about thirty feet behind, carrying a hair dryer. It hadn't been difficult to get through the first layer of Mentaldyne's security—just a matter of bending a chain link fence and then bending light to prevent the guards from spotting them. The next part, however, was going to be trickier. As expected, Tiamat had placed a Balderhaz Cube somewhere in the facility to forestall any attempts by rogue angels to use their supernatural powers to infiltrate the place. It was past midnight, but the parking lot was nearly full and occasionally someone would enter or exit the building. The facility was obviously working around the clock to meet the demand for the Myrmidon chips.

A door swung open a few yards ahead of Michelle, and she pressed herself against the wall to avoid being seen. A worker wearing an anti-static suit exited the door and began walking to the parking lot. Michelle, moving in complete silence, slipped behind the man and wedged her foot in the door before it swung shut. She peered through the opening, then stuck her head inside. After a moment, she pulled it back, motioned for Eddie to approach, and then slipped inside. Eddie, keeping his eye on the worker, who was now digging through his car's glove box for something, managed to grab the door before it closed, and slipped in after Michelle.

He found himself on a sort of factory floor, with dozens of workers in anti-static suits carrying out tasks at assembly line stations and various machines. Fortunately, they were so busy that for some time nobody seemed to notice the two intruders. Michelle continued along the wall to the left, acting for all the world like she belonged there. Occasionally a worker would look over at her and immediately look away, as if *he* were the one trespassing. Such was the power of Michelle's charisma: although she had the appearance of a thirteen-year-old black girl, she could generally go anywhere she wanted without being questioned. If Michelle had been in Alabama in 1940s, she might have ended segregation twenty years early through the sheer force of her will.

Eddie did his best to remain unnoticed in Michelle's charismatic wake. He felt completely out of place—although, to be fair, Eddie usually felt that way even when he wasn't skulking about a mind control chip factory. It didn't help that in this particular case he was inexplicably carrying a hair dryer.

Neither of them knew exactly where the control center for the transmitter was; the plan was simply to get inside and snoop around until they found it. It seemed like a terrible plan to Eddie, but he couldn't think of anything better, and in any case he had been overruled. So here he was, tailing Michelle through the Mentaldyne facility.

They must have been getting close, because suddenly Michelle was stopped by a burly foreman standing in her path. "This is a restricted area," he growled. "Where's your badge?"

"Where is my *badge*?" asked Michelle, with a tone of disgust. "Really? I count at least twenty ten-sixteen violations within thirty feet of here, and you're going to fixate on my *badge*?"

The man shrank back, suddenly unsure of himself. "Ten-sixteen violations?"

Michelle sighed as if to indicate her disbelief at having to deal with such unfathomable incompetence. "Inadequate lighting, insufficient ventilation, ozone levels off the charts..."

"Ozone levels?" asked the man.

Michelle breathed deeply through her nose. "Ozone! You don't smell that? My guess is that we're up around eight-eight, maybe eighty-nine pee-pee-em." She turned to look at Eddie. "What do you think?"

"Um, yes," said Eddie. "Eighty, like, at least eighty-eight. Maybe eight-nine pee-pee-ems." Then he sniffed for good measure.

"Even Eddie can smell it, and he lost sixty percent of his olfactory capability in the Halifax incident. You seriously don't smell that?"

The man sniffed nervously. "I don't... I'm not sure..."

Michelle produced something from her pocket. Eddie was pretty sure it was some kind of hair clip. She held it up to the man's nose. "Do you smell that?"

"Um," he said. "I think so?"

"What does it smell like?" Michelle asked.

"Um, vanilla?" the man ventured.

"Hell," said Michelle to Eddie, shoving the object back in her pocket. "Get Houston on the phone. Tell 'em it's Halifax all over again. We've got a Level Six with at least eighty percent olfactory loss." She turned back to the foreman. "Any seizures?" she asked. "Paralysis?"

He shook his head.

"Tell 'em the paralysis hasn't set in yet," she said to Eddie. She turned back to the foreman. "Do you have a cot? Someplace to lie down?"

"Um, yeah," said the man. "In the front office."

"All right," said Michelle. "Do you think you can get there on your own, or do you need Eddie to carry you?"

The man glanced at Eddie, whom he outweighed by at least a hundred pounds. "I can, um, get there on my own."

"OK," said Michelle. "We've got the TFZ team on standby. You go lie down, we'll be right behind you. And remember to keep breathing!"

The man nodded and shuffled away with a worried expression on his face.

Michelle continued into the "restricted area" as if nothing had happened. Eddie followed, feeling nearly overwhelmed with anxiety. He wished he could go lie down on a cot until the TFZ team got here.

At last they found a door with the label:

## MYRMIDON CONTROL AREA
## AUTHORIZED PERSONNEL ONLY

A bad feeling, over and above his near-crippling anxiety, gripped Eddie. Their little mission was going way too smoothly. He somehow couldn't believe that one easily cowed foreman was the only resistance they were going to meet.

Michelle turned the handle of the door and it opened. It was dark inside except for the glow of several dozen tiny LED lights. Michelle and Eddie slipped into the room and Michelle closed the door behind them. Eddie fumbled around until he found a light switch. A bank of fluorescent lights blinked on overhead, revealing a large room that was lined on three sides with computer workstations. Michelle took a seat in one of the dozen chairs and pulled a thumb drive from her pocket.

Eddie couldn't believe it. All she had to do was plug that thing into one of the computers and upload Suzy's patch, and they'd be done. Maybe he'd been worried for nothing. He pulled his cell phone from his pocket and tapped the screen, bringing up a text message. He typed:

we're in position. use gps to

But before he could finish the message, the door opened and six large men with assault rifles filed in. Michelle slipped the thumb drive into her pocket and stood up, backing away from the computers. Eddie had just enough time to hit Send before one of the men struck him in the temple with the butt of his rifle, knocking him to the floor. Eddie was vaguely aware of someone prying the hair dryer from his left hand and the cell phone from his right. His head throbbing, Eddie rolled onto his back in time to see a seventh man stroll into the room. This man was built like Bluto from the old Popeye cartoons. And he was smiling.

"Tiamat thought you might try breaking in here," said Gamaliel, closing the door behind him. "I'm a little disappointed that Mercury's not with you, but you two will do for now." He took the hair dryer from the man who had pried it from Eddie's hand. "And how considerate! You brought your secret weapon with you."

"You're making a mistake, Gamaliel!" shouted Michelle. "Tiamat is crazy. She's going to make this world into hell on earth. Come work for me. We'll overthrow Tiamat and—"

Gamaliel took two steps toward Michelle and punched her in the face, causing her to stumble backwards and crash into a monitor. She slunk to the floor, blood pouring from her nose.

"You have no idea how long I've been waiting to do that, you sanctimonious bitch." He turned to one of the men. "Tie them up. We'll lock them both in a closet until Possum Kingdom reopens."

# CHAPTER FORTY-THREE

*About a thousand miles above Earth; August 2016*

Mercury shot into space, pushing in front of him the absurd contraption that Balderhaz repeatedly assured him was a fully functioning mind control transmitter. The existing transmitter had to be removed and this one put in place in order for their scheme to turn the tables on Tiamat. Of course, the new transmitter would do no good if Suzy's software patch hadn't been uploaded to the Myrmidon server, but Mercury was blissfully unaware of the challenges facing Eddie and Michelle. Balderhaz had told him the installation was simple: he just had to rip the old one off the satellite, duct tape the new one in place, and connect the signal cable. A roll of duct tape was tucked inside the oil drum for the purpose.

Finding a satellite that was roughly the size of a minivan in the vast expanse of space hundreds of miles above Earth's atmosphere was tricky, even when you knew roughly where the satellite was. Mercury had managed to secure a GPS locator/altimeter, but it wasn't perfectly accurate and it didn't make it any easier to locate an object against the black canopy of space. He finally noticed the silvery outline of the satellite at the precise moment he spotted another object on the horizon. This second object was growing rapidly larger, and he quickly realized it wasn't an object but a person: someone was rocketing toward him at immense speed.

Mercury shot toward the satellite in the hopes that he could get there and secure the transmitter before the figure closed with him, but it soon became clear this wasn't going to happen. The figure was on a trajectory to intercept Mercury before he reached the satellite. Mercury put on a final burst of speed and then, just before the figure hit him, hurled the transmitter in the direction of the satellite. With a little luck, he'd be able to deal with the interloper and then catch up to the transmitter before it started falling.

Then the figure hit him like a freight train. Whoever it was, he'd been traveling several hundred miles an hour, and Mercury felt ribs snap as a shoulder impacted against his chest. He and the mystery man tumbled through space over the vast blue globe. Mercury could only hope that the attacker was in half as much pain as he was.

Mercury managed to wriggle out of the figure's grasp and, trying to ignore the pain in his ribs, pulled his knees up and then kicked hard against the man's chest. They had reached the apogee of their ascent and for a moment the two hung suspended in space, looking at each other. The man grinned at Mercury. He didn't seem to be in a lot of pain.

Izbazel.

If there was one demon that hated Mercury more than Gamaliel, it was Izbazel. And while Izbazel was no match for Mercury in a battle of wits, it was anyone's guess who would come out on top in a no-holds-barred exospheric donnybrook. Especially when Mercury already had half a dozen cracked ribs.

Getting his bearings, Mercury located the transmitter, which had nearly reached the apogee of its flight, still a hundred yards from the satellite. Within a few seconds, unless someone intervened, the transmitter would begin plummeting to the Earth below. Even at nearly a thousand miles above the surface, the grip of Earth's gravity was very strong.

Mercury wanted to say something clever to Izbazel, like, "Congratulations, you're not the dumbest person on Earth anymore," but his broken ribs—not to mention the near complete lack of atmosphere—made talking problematic. He contented himself with mouthing the word *asshole*, and then shot past Izbazel toward the transmitter.

He caught the contraption before it had fallen more than a couple hundred yards, and once again hurled it toward the satellite. He tried to overshoot a bit this time, to give himself a little more time to deal with Izbazel. Hopefully his aim in the quarter-mile oil drum toss wasn't any better than his aim with a ping pong ball, because if the transmitter hit the satellite at a hundred miles an hour, this whole plan was going to be moot.

Mercury was about to turn to face Izbazel when he noticed another figure rocketing toward him from the opposite direction. If he'd had any air in his lungs, and if he could move his chest without experiencing intense pain, he might have sighed. It figured that Tiamat wouldn't leave her satellite guarded by a single demon.

Allowing himself to fall toward the azure sphere below, Mercury concentrated for a moment on repairing his splintered ribs. Angels ordinarily heal at about a hundred times the rate of a human being anyway, but with some additional effort an angel can further speed the process by fusing broken bones and knitting together torn tissue. He'd almost completed the process when the second figure shot past a few hundred yards overhead. The second figure met Izbazel and the two of them stopped and changed direction to pursue Mercury.

He halted his descent and shot spaceward once again. This was going to be tricky. The transmitter had—fortunately—missed the satellite and was now falling once again. Mercury needed to zoom past the two demons fast enough that they couldn't catch him and then slow down to catch the transmitter without tearing it to pieces.

Barely slipping past the two demons, Mercury altered his course to intercept the transmitter. He caught it as gently as he could and once again hurled it toward the satellite. This was getting exhausting.

The transmitter had scarcely left Mercury's fingertips when both demons slammed into him simultaneously. This time Mercury couldn't wriggle away. Izbazel had his legs and the other one—whom he'd identified as Nisroc, possibly the only demon more dimwitted than Izbazel—had Mercury in a bear hug. The three angels focusing all their effort on the melee, they once again plummeted toward Earth. Mercury twisted, jerked, kicked and even bit, but the two demons wouldn't let go. Far above him he saw the transmitter once again arc past the satellite and begin to fall.

He tried to keep it in view, but Nisroc's hand clamped over his eyes. Meanwhile, Izbazel continued to hold his legs with one arm and pummel Mercury in the kidneys with his other. They fell for miles, with Mercury never ceasing to struggle. Finally he heard the faint sound of air whistling past his ears. As it grew gradually louder, the cold of space gave way to the burning sensation of reentry. Their rapid descent compressed the air beneath them, causing it to go from pleasantly warm to hellishly hot. Fortunately, since they were covering him so tightly, Nisroc and Izbazel took the brunt of it. He felt them twisting and turning to avoid being burned, but eventually they were either going to have to let go or exert some effort to keep from being incinerated alive.

Nisroc broke first, releasing his grip on Mercury's head and pushing himself away. But Mercury took advantage of Nisroc's shift to turn the tables on him, getting the demon in a headlock. A moment later Izbazel gave in, and as he tried to get away Mercury wrapped his legs around his neck, putting him in a scissor lock.

"What the hell are you doing?" Izbazel screamed. "We're all going to burn up!"

Mercury grinned as he felt the skin on his knuckled blister. "If I'm going down," he yelled, "you two dumbasses are coming with me!"

# CHAPTER FORTY-FOUR

*Provo, Utah; August 2016*

Gamaliel's men had just finished zip-tying Michelle and Eddie's hands behind their backs when Eddie's phone chirped. Gamaliel looked at the man holding the phone, who shrugged it and handed it to Gamaliel. "Text message," the man said.

Gamaliel frowned as he read the screen. "You," he growled at Eddie. "What does this mean?" He held the phone out to Eddie. It read:

ur covered ☺

Eddie smiled. "You're the one with the secret weapon," he said. "Why don't you tell me?"

Gamaliel glowered at Eddie and grabbed the hair dryer out of the man's hand. He pointed it at himself and pulled the trigger, blasting himself with hot air.

"What the hell?" said Gamaliel. "This is just a hair dryer."

"No shit," said Michelle, getting to her feet and wiping the blood from her lip with the back of her hand. Gamaliel noticed that somehow she'd gotten her hands loose. "Eddie, do you mind taking care of the goon squad?"

"Um?" said Eddie. "Oh, sure." Eddie waved his hand and the six men's guns were suddenly jerked out of their hands. The rifles hung in mid-air over their heads for a split-second, and then jerked backward, the butt of each gun striking its owner in the temple, as Eddie had been struck a moment earlier. The six men slumped to the ground simultaneously.

Meanwhile, Michelle had leaped six feet in the air, soaring toward Gamaliel as she tucked her arms and legs against her body. Gamaliel, who was still in shock that Eddie had somehow performed a miracle while inside the Balderhaz field, was taken by surprise. When Michelle was an arm's length from Gamaliel, she suddenly straightened, striking him full force in the mouth with the heel of her boot. Gamaliel's head jerked back and he stumbled backwards, falling to the floor and striking his head on the wall behind him. Michelle landed in a crouch.

"Eddie!" she snapped.

"Huh?" asked Eddie, who was still admiring his handiwork with the goon squad. He turned toward Michelle just in time to see her throw the thumb drive. He managed to catch it as Michelle renewed her offensive against Gamaliel. She leaped at him, trying to drive his head into the wall behind him, but Gamaliel had just enough presence of mind to slide out of the way. The butt of Michelle's palm slammed into the wall, crashing through the drywall. Gamaliel got slowly to his feet, spitting blood and broken teeth on the floor.

"Eddie!" Michelle yelled again, trying to extract her tiny fist from the wall. "The patch!"

Eddie nodded and went to one of the computers, plugging in the USB drive.

Gamaliel took a step forward, holding out his hand toward Eddie. Gamaliel wasn't stupid; he'd figured out that someone else nearby was using the anti-Balderhaz field gun to allow Michelle and Eddie to manipulate interplanar energy. But that meant Gamaliel could perform miracles as well. Wiping out data stored on magnetic media was the easiest thing in the world for an angel to do. A miniscule amount of interplanar energy could be converted into a powerful electromagnetic pulse, erasing every bit of data on every computer in the building. But Eddie was exerting as much effort as he could muster into not letting Gamaliel get ahold of any interplanar energy in the area. He couldn't hold Gamaliel off forever, but he could buy Michelle enough time for another attack.

Michelle had already gotten free from the wall and was moving toward Gamaliel when the latter suddenly crouched down and then shot directly upward, crashing through the ceiling. Through the hole, the night sky could be seen.

"Suzy!" cried Eddie.

"I'm on it," said Michelle. "Run the patch!" Michelle shot through the hole in the ceiling after Gamaliel.

Eddie found the patch file on the thumb drive, uploaded it to the Myrmidon server, and executed the file. A progress indicator crept across the screen as the software was updated. Behind him, several of the goons were stirring. Eddie tried to give them another knock, but he suddenly found himself unable to grab hold of any interplanar energy. Suzy must have moved out of range with the anti-Balderhaz field gun. The progress indicator was at thirty-seven percent. Eddie smiled nervously as three of the six men picked up their guns and got to their feet. They didn't look happy.

"OK, look, guys," said Eddie. "All I'm doing is patching the software. It's no big deal. It's like when that window pops up and asks you if you want to update Java."

The three men exchanged angry glances.

"I hate that fucking thing," said one of them.

The other two grunted in agreement, and Eddie realized he'd made a serious tactical error. Everybody hated Java updates.

The three men moved toward him. "Get out of the way," the first one said, "or—"

But at that moment Michelle and Gamaliel came crashing back through the ceiling, flattening the three men. Michelle was on Gamaliel's back, with her legs wrapped around his stomach and her arms around his neck. Gamaliel was growling and trying to pry her arms off.

Eddie glanced at the screen. The progress indicator was at fifty-eight percent. If he could keep Michelle and Gamaliel from smashing the computer in the next couple of minutes, their mission would be a success. Gamaliel got up, staggered back and forth for a few seconds, further trampling the barely conscious men he'd just landed on, and then barreled backwards into the bare wall behind him.

His goal had presumably been to dislodge Michelle, but he managed to hit the wall precisely between two studs, smashed through both layers of drywall, and disappeared from Eddie's view with Michelle presumably still firmly attached.

Meanwhile another of the goons had come around and Eddie ran over and pounced on him. Without the ability to perform miracles, Eddie didn't have much of a chance against a single unarmed man, to say nothing of six men with assault rifles. Fortunately this particular man was prone, dazed, and injured, which gave Eddie a fighting chance.

Eddie punched the man as hard as he could across the jaw, which had the dual effect of waking him up and pissing him off. The man gripped Eddie by the throat and threw him off as if Eddie were a light jacket. Eddie landed on top of another barely conscious man, who stirred and groaned. Eddie considered punching the man, thought better of it, and sprang after the other man, who had gotten to his feet and was heading toward the computer terminal. Eddie dove at the man, gripping him around the ankles. The man pulled one of his legs free and continued walking toward the terminal, dragging Eddie across the floor as he went.

He'd reached the terminal and was bending over the keyboard when Eddie heard a voice above him.

"Eddie!" the voice cried.

Eddie looked up to see Suzy peering through the hole in the ceiling at him. She was pointing a hair dryer at him.

Eddie smiled. The anti-Balderhaz field gun was a little too close for maximum effectiveness, but he only needed a very minor miracle at present. Eddie waved his hand and the man suddenly stood straight up, gasped, clutched his chest, and fell over backwards.

"Jesus Christ, Eddie!" yelled Suzy from above. "What did you do?"

"Stopped his heart," said Eddie, getting up to look at the monitor. As he watched, the indicator went from ninety-nine to one hundred percent. "Thank God," murmured Eddie.

Then the screen went black.

"Oh, shit," said Eddie.

"What?" asked Suzy. "What happened? Did it say the patch was successfully installed?"

"No!" cried Eddie. "It went to one hundred percent and then everything went black! I don't know what happened!"

"Did you touch something?" asked Suzy.

"No, I didn't do anything! It just went black for no reason! Is there some…"

A window popped up. It read:

## An update is available for Java. Would you like to update Java now?

"Holy fucking shit," groaned Eddie. He clicked **No** and the window disappeared. In its place another window appeared. It read:

## Myrmidon patch successfully installed.

"Never mind," said Eddie. "We're good. Mission accomplished."

"But you killed that guy!" yelled Suzy.

"Huh?" replied Eddie. "Oh, no. Hang on." He waved his hand and the man suddenly jerked awake and gasped for air. Eddie leaned over him. "You OK, buddy?" he said.

The man stared at Eddie with a look of terror on his face.

"He's fine," said Eddie. "Just had to restart his heart." He turned back to the man. "Stay out of trouble, OK? Don't do drugs."

Through the hole in the wall Eddie heard a distant crash. Evidently Michelle and Gamaliel were still going at it.

"Let's get out of here," said Suzy.

Eddie nodded. "Back up. Keep the gun pointed at me."

Suzy disappeared from view. Eddie floated through the hole in the ceiling and landed on the roof a few yards from her. "How do we get down?" he asked. Eddie had used the anti-Balderhaz field gun to allow Michelle to levitate Suzy onto the roof, and then tossed the gun to her. Getting down, though, posed some logistical problems now that they had lost a member of their team.

"What about Michelle?" said Eddie, as they made their way to the edge of the roof.

"Screw Michelle," replied Suzy. "I hope she and Gamaliel tear each other to pieces."

"Yeah," said Eddie, "but how do we get down?"

"It's not that far," said Suzy. "Just lower yourself over the edge and drop to the ground. Then I'll lower myself down and you can catch me."

Eddie stood at the edge of the roof and looked down. Some twelve feet down was pavement. He bit his lip. They could hear shouts coming from the hole in the roof.

"Fine," said Suzy. "I'll go first and you can float down, you big pussy."

Suzy climbed over the edge and hung for a moment before dropping to the ground. She got to her feet and Eddie tossed her the anti-Balderhaz field gun. She took several paces back and aimed the gun at Eddie, allowing him to float gracefully to the ground.

"All right," Suzy said. "Now let's get the hell out of here."

They scaled a chain-link fence and took off running across a vacant lot. Behind them they heard the shouts of pursuing men. But pursuit was futile, as Suzy and Eddie had left the Balderhaz field. Eddie scooped up Suzy in his arms and took flight, leaving the men cursing below. Gamaliel and Michelle were presumably still doing their best to kill each other.

Eddie, Suzy and Michelle had done their part. Now everything depended on Mercury getting the transmitter in place.

# CHAPTER FORTY-FIVE

*About a thousand miles above Earth; August 2016*

The transmitter once again shot past the satellite, reached its apogee, and then began tumbling back to Earth. Mercury, in the clutches of two demons, vanished into the great mass of blue and white below. The matter was now out of his hands.

Miraculously, as the makeshift contraption fell past the satellite, it slowed, came to a stop, and then reversed course. A small head peaked out from inside the drum, took a look around, and then disappeared back into the drum.

A moment later, the owner of the small head, a diminutive cherub named Perpertiel, climbed out of the drum and, with a roll of duct tape in one hand, fluttered toward the satellite, dragging the transmitter behind him. Strictly speaking the fluttering was unnecessary as there was no atmosphere to speak of, but then Perp didn't actually need the wings to fly in the first place. For Perp, it was all about style.

It wasn't particularly stylish to hide out inside an oil drum and nearly lose his lunch three different times, but that was evidently what was required of him. He was the only one who could fit inside the drum, and in any case he supposed that the indignity of his assignment was still preferable to being incinerated on reentry. He had to hand it to Mercury: when he got an idea in his head, he committed to it.

Perp levitated Balderhaz' transmitter while unscrewing the bolts that held the factory model in place. He let the old transmitter fall to Earth and moved the new one into place. A few yards of duct tape later, and he'd performed an installation that would have gotten the thumbs up from MacGyver himself. He plugged in the signal cable and that was that. Assuming that Suzy's patch had been loaded, they would now have complete control over Tiamat and her minions.

Perp let go of the satellite and fell toward Earth, his wings fluttering in the nonexistent breeze.

# CHAPTER FORTY-SIX

*Grand Rapids, Michigan; August 2016*

After a few initial missteps the chip implantation program was going remarkably well, and it was no coincidence that the turnaround coincided with the arrival of Zion Johnson. Zion Johnson had met with his staff an hour after landing in Grand Rapids to explain to them that they'd all be getting chipped on national television to demonstrate both the innocuousness of the chips and the fact that nobody was above the law. He'd only had to fire three of them, who objected on principle. They and their principles were now locked up in a makeshift holding cell, awaiting chip implantation. If it made them feel better to put up some momentary resistance, Zion Johnson wasn't going to begrudge them that.

Zion Johnson and his underlings were chipped at a press conference, as planned. After they had the chips implanted, a reporter asked them if they felt any different. They all laughed and said no. "What am I supposed to be feeling?" one of them asked, which struck Zion Johnson as funny.

Zion Johnson did feel different. Perhaps because he had always been so loyal, he was acutely aware of the tiniest seed of disloyalty inside of him. His patriotism was like the faith of an ascetic monk who flogged himself mercilessly for being unable to rid himself of the last vestiges of doubt. And now that doubt, that seed of disloyalty, was gone.

Some part of him missed it, missed the constant struggle, the need to recite his mantra in the face of adversity. Now his mantra was redundant. There were no longer any obstacles to perfect patriotism, perfect obedience, and so there was no need to struggle, to rally his will to overcome. *Superior attitude, superior state of mind* now held no more meaning to him than *six foot two, graying hair, size ten shoes*. His attitude and state of mind were always superior, and he was starting to forget why he'd ever needed a mantra in the first place. It seemed silly now. Why would anyone question authority? Zion Johnson wasn't going to tolerate anyone questioning his, and he wouldn't expect the president or Tiamat to tolerate it either. He'd initially had his doubts about Tiamat, but now he saw her as embodying all of his most cherished ideals. If she didn't always seem to be the most honorable, honest, or patriotic person, it was because her ways were beyond the understanding of a mere soldier like Zion Johnson. He would die for Tiamat if that's what she asked of him.

At present, Zion Johnson was overseeing the opening of the newest chip implantation center, in an abandoned Build-a-Bear store in a strip mall on the southeast side of the city. Smiling citizens were lined up out the door, and cameramen were documenting it all for the evening news. In actuality, most of the smiling citizens had already been chipped. They'd been asked by one of Zion Johnson's underlings to show up in a show of support for the chip implantation effort and, having been programmed to do whatever was asked of them by authority figures, they'd happily complied. Several of them had taken the day off work to wait in line, go into a back room when their names were called, exit out the back of the building, walk back around to the front, and do it all over again. They would happily do this for weeks on end if asked, but a few of them did have to be sent home after making themselves sick on the free juice and cookies.

Only about one in five of the "customers" was an actual implantation candidate, and half of those were homeless people who were only there for the free food. But that's how you had to start with these things. It was always easiest to control the disenfranchised. Once the distribution of food rations was linked to chip implantation, they'd start seeing more of the lower middle class showing up. And then, when people had gotten used to that, they'd start offering chip recipients special passes allowing unchecked travel throughout the city. The trick was to roll out these programs in an orderly and gradual way, to minimize the outrage. Of course, he could move faster in Grand Rapids than in a typical psy ops mission because with the chips, conversion was assured, instantaneous and irreversible. There would be no sunshine patriots or turncoats in Grand Rapids. Zion Johnson expected the entire city to be converted within a month. And then they'd move on to the next city. America would hit the tipping point within a year.

But as Zion Johnson stood by, admiring the efficiency of his operation and enjoying a chocolate chip cookie, he was suddenly struck by a pang of doubt. It was a small pang—tiny, even. The sort of pang that he wouldn't even have required even a single recitation of his mantra to exorcise. But it was such an unexpected sensation that he dropped his chocolate chip cookie on the floor and simply stood for a moment, regarding the kernel of doubt the way one might stop to observe a fragile faun that one has unexpectedly come across in the woods.

Then, as he stood there reflecting on his doubt, another feeling struck him: anger. He wasn't even sure at first what he was angry about, but the anger collided with the doubt like a breeze hitting a flame, and the doubt grew larger. The doubt fed the anger and the anger fed the doubt, and soon he was shaking in fury.

One of his underlings—a pudgy female Homeland Security intern—had apparently noticed the change in his demeanor and walked up next to him. "Sir?" she said. "Do you want me to get you another cookie?"

Zion Johnson turned to look at her, at first unable even to comprehend what she had said to him. Finally he murmured, "No. No cookie."

"Yes, sir," she said, and bent over to pick up the cookie he'd dropped.

"No cookies for anyone," said Zion Johnson quietly.

"Sir?" asked the intern.

"NO COOKIES FOR ANYONE!" Zion Johnson shouted. The people in line turned to stare at him. A few of them slipped their cookies into their pockets.

Zion Johnson drew his gun from its holster and held it over his head. "NO COOKIES FOR ANYONE!" he roared again, and fired five times into the ceiling.

The people in line screamed and scattered. A few of them may have come to the realization that they'd somehow been hoodwinked into coming to this place, but most of them just ran out of fear. Zion Johnson didn't care; he just wanted everybody gone.

"Sir!" yelled the intern. "What are you doing? What is wrong with you?"

Zion Johnson turned to look at the girl. What is wrong with *me*? He thought. No, what is wrong with *you*? She had been chipped two days earlier, with the rest of his staff. He looked into her eyes, trying to determine whether she was still under Tiamat's control. Is it just me? he thought. Am I the only one who is free? There was no way to tell. There was nothing in the girl's eyes but confusion and fear.

"Listen to me," he said to the girl. "This is wrong. This whole operation is wrong. Putting chips in people's heads to track them, it's wrong. It doesn't matter if we're doing it for good reasons. The whole point of being human is that you have the freedom to choose to do right or wrong without coercion. Can't you see that?"

The girl now looked even more frightened. She backed away from Zion Johnson.

The room had emptied out except for Zion Johnson, the girl, and a couple of equally frightened technicians. Zion Johnson had intentionally made the security presence virtually invisible to help with public relations. But invisible didn't mean nonexistent. Five national guardsmen suddenly burst into the room, brandishing their rifles.

"What the hell is going on here?" the sergeant in charge yelled. His eyes fell to Zion Johnson's gun.

"Stand down," ordered Zion Johnson. "We're shutting down this facility."

The sergeant's eyebrow went up. "On whose authority, sir?" he asked.

Now here's an interesting conundrum, thought Zion Johnson. He still wasn't sure if it was just his own chip that was malfunctioning or if the whole Myrmidon system was down. Was the sergeant questioning his order because the chip was telling him

Zion Johnson wasn't following Tiamat's orders? Or was he questioning it because he was actually thinking for himself? There was one way to find out.

"On *our* authority," Zion Johnson said. "Yours and mine. We're not doing this shit anymore. Implanting tracking chips in people's heads? Is that what you signed up for, Sergeant? Because it's not what I signed up for. I'm done." Slowly and deliberately, he held out the Desert Eagle, turned it around, and set it on the floor between him and the sergeant. The sergeant continued to watch him nervously. The men behind him were looking to him anxiously for some clue as to how they should handle this situation.

"Sir," said the sergeant, trying desperately to keep his voice from cracking, "I'm going to have to take you into custody while we sort this out."

Zion Johnson laughed. "Kid," he said, "I don't know how this is all going to turn out, but I can tell you one thing for sure: it's damn well not going to end up with me in your custody." He turned and began walking toward the door.

"Sir!" shouted the sergeant again. "Please stop!"

Zion Johnson sighed and turned to look at the man. He couldn't be more than twenty-five. He still had acne, for Christ's sake. "Look, kid," he said. "There's something I need to tell you. And I want you to know I'm not telling you this to be mean, OK? I'm telling you because you're a human being and you deserve to know. Eventually some really unbelievable stuff is going to come out about this whole program. And when it does, you're going to look back on this moment and try to make sense of it, maybe justify it, depending on what you do over the next few seconds. And when you do, you need to understand something: what you do right now, when I walk out that door, is all on you. Got it? There's nobody making you do this. You've got your orders, sure, but you also know what's right and wrong. And if you make the wrong choice, well, you're just going to have to deal with that. Whatever decision you make, you need to own it, OK? Don't make excuses. It's the only way forward."

The young man stared at Zion Johnson, more confused than ever. The intern, the technicians and the other guardsmen were all staring at him too. Zion Johnson couldn't help laughing. Were these people all under Tiamat's control, or were they just so unused to making their own decisions that they'd forgotten how? For a lot of people, mind control really was redundant.

As Zion Johnson turned to walk out the door, he was shot sixteen times in the back. He smiled as he fell to the ground.

*Superior attitude, superior state of mind.*

# CHAPTER FORTY-SEVEN

*Washington, D.C.; August 2016*

Tiamat was briefing President Prowse on the plans for the chip implantation program in Nashville when she was suddenly seized with the desire to stand up, walk to the center of the Oval Office, and make a startling confession.

"I'm a little teapot," she said, holding her left hand on her waist and raising her right in the air. "Short and stout. Here is my handle, and here is my spout."

With that, she walked out of the room, closing the door behind her.

After a moment, Danton Prowse picked up his phone. "I think we're going to cancel Nashville," he said.

# CHAPTER FORTY-EIGHT

*Somewhere in Missouri; August 2016*

"It's really that easy?" asked Suzy, looking over Balderhaz's shoulder. Balderhaz was sitting at the laptop, which was now directly connected to the Myrmidon server via the Internet. Suzy's patch had opened a port on the server to allow remote access by anyone with a particular access key—*MercuryR00lz*, in this case—and to disallow access from anywhere else, including the Myrmidon control room at Mentaldyne. Presumably somebody at Mentaldyne would eventually figure out what had happened and shut down the server until they could fix the security hole, but for now Balderhaz had complete control over Tiamat and her agents.

"Yep," said Balderhaz. "I just specify a target or range of targets—by age, race, geographical location, whatever—and implant an idea in their heads. In this particular case, I've suggested to Tiamat that she's a little teapot."

"That's it? You just told her she's a little teapot?" asked Suzy, amazed.

"I didn't tell her anything," said Balderhaz. "I put the idea in her head that she's a little teapot. The actions she takes in response to that idea are her own."

"So where is she going?" asked Eddie, who was looking over Balderhaz's other shoulder. They were watching the red dot representing Tiamat leave the White House and moving down Pennsylvania Avenue.

"I may also have suggested that she would like to take a nice dip in the Potomac," said Balderhaz.

"Good idea," said Suzy.

"All of Tiamat's other minions may be having the same idea in the very near future," said Balderhaz.

"...and then I wasn't sure I was going to have enough *duct tape*," said Perp, who was lying prone on the couch behind them. He hadn't stopped talking his ordeal with the transmitter since he'd gotten back, some twenty minutes earlier. In Perp's mind, he was clearly the hero of the day. They hadn't heard from Mercury yet; presumably he was still dealing with Izbazel and Nisroc.

Balderhaz was in the process of giving several dozen demons some ideas about synchronized swimming when the front door to the house opened. The assembled angels and human held their collective breath, hoping it was Mercury. It wasn't.

Michelle strode into the room, her clothing torn and her hair tousled, but otherwise looking no worse for wear. "So here you are," said Michelle to Suzy and Eddie. "I guess you misunderstood the part about us being a *team*."

"We had to get out of there," said Eddie nervously. "We figured you could deal with Gamaliel on your own..."

"Oh, I dealt with him," said Michelle. She gave a whistle, and they heard the back door open. A moment later Gamaliel walked into the room, looking even more tattered than Michelle.

"Um," Balderhaz said, looking up at the hulking figure of Gamaliel. "Isn't he one of the bad guys?"

"We came to an understanding," said Michelle. "With Tiamat out of power, Gamaliel is working for me now. And we're taking over Myrmidon. Balderhaz, please step away from the computer."

Balderhaz, who had been trying to locate Gamaliel's chip on the map, reluctantly stepped away.

"There are four of us, and only two of you," said Suzy.

Michelle laughed. "I'm the general of Heaven's army," she said. "And Gamaliel is the best fighter of all Tiamat's minions. I think we can handle three cherubic twerps and a human female. Face it, sweetie, you've been played. I'm back in power, and now I've got Tiamat and her minions under my control as well."

"See, this is your problem, Michelle," said a voice behind her. "You only think in terms of power and control."

Michelle spun around to see Mercury standing in the corner. It was impossible to say when he'd arrived or how long he'd been there.

"What are you blabbering about, Mercury?" snapped Michelle. "You've taken control of Myrmidon. And now I've taken it away from you."

"We took control of Myrmidon temporarily," said Mercury. "Tell her, Suzy."

"He's right," said Suzy. "The patch is designed to self-destruct six hours after it's activated. And that window is almost up. In twenty minutes, it will erase the Myrmidon software completely. Everyone will be free. Even Tiamat and her minions. They'll be very damp, but they'll be free."

"Then I'll just have Mentaldyne reload the original software," said Michelle.

"That *would* work," said Suzy, "except for an additional feature that Balderhaz and I put in the patch."

"Which is what?" demanded Michelle.

"A high-energy burst on all receiving frequencies," said Balderhaz. "Before Myrmidon self-destructs, it'll short out all the chips. So even if you take over Myrmidon, you'll have no puppets to play with."

"Then I'll shut it down," said Michelle. "Gamaliel, call Mentaldyne and have them shut everything down!"

"Won't work," said Suzy. "The burst instruction has already been sent to the satellite. The satellite is programmed to send the burst when Myrmidon shuts down. Whether it shuts down because of the self-destruct or because you pull the plug, it's all the same to the satellite. The burst will go out, and the chips will stop working."

"You could try to get to the satellite before that happens," said Balderhaz. "You've got eighteen minutes to travel a thousand miles, so chop-chop!"

Michelle stood with her fists clenched, fuming. Gamaliel's expression was that of someone who had, for the umpteenth time, picked the wrong team in the big game.

"Like I was saying, Michelle," Mercury continued, "your problem is that you think everybody is just as power-mad as you are. That's fine when you're up against Tiamat or Lucifer, but you're out of your league when you're faced with three hundred million people who are free to make their own decisions. You've got no legions and no place to stand for leverage. Your minions have deserted you, and the reins that you're clutching at so desperately don't connect to anything. Hell, even Gamaliel has lost interest in being your waterboy, and he never met a tyrant whose boots he wasn't prepared to lick."

Gamaliel had indeed deserted her. The door of the farmhouse slammed behind him.

"Fine," said Michelle. "You've won for now. But you overestimate these people. When they find out the truth about Myrmidon and the Brimstone bomb, they'll be more terrified than ever, and I'll be right there to reassure them that everything will be alright if they just keep quiet and do what they're told. If this whole experience has demonstrated anything, it's that most people are sheep. I don't need computer chips to control them, I just need a little fear."

"Maybe," said Mercury. "But there will always be a few people who won't bow down to you, Michelle, and I'll take one of those people over a thousand of your sheep. And I don't know if you've noticed, but there aren't any sheep in this room, so I suggest you go looking elsewhere for your flock."

Michelle glared at Mercury. "This isn't over," she said, and turned to leave.

"It never is," said Mercury.

"So that's it," said Eddie, after Michelle had left. "We won."

Michelle stormed out of the room.

"For now," said Mercury. "But there's one more thing I need to do."

# CHAPTER FORTY-NINE

*Camp David, Maryland; August 2016*

After Tiamat's bizarre performance and the sudden disappearance of several other key advisors—the ones who hadn't run off screaming a few days earlier—it was decided that President Prowse should take a few days away from the White House while the Secret Service tried to determine what the hell had happened and how the hell to keep it from happening again. So he was alone in a quiet office at Camp David when he received a third angelic visitor.

"Oh, no," he said when the supposedly locked door opened without warning. "No more. I quit."

A tall man with angular features and ridiculous silver hair strode in. "You can't quit now," the man said. "I promised Judy you'd be at her birthday party next week. You don't want to disappoint Judy, do you?"

"Who in the hell is Judy?" Prowse demanded.

"Wow," said the man. "I am *not* going to tell her you said that. So, how's the job treating you these days?"

"The job?" asked Prowse. "How would I know? I haven't been in charge of anything for months. First it was Michelle, and then that horrible Tiamat person, telling me exactly what I can and can't do. I can only assume you're next in line? Another 'reorganization'?"

"Mmm," said the man. "Something like that. My name's Mercury. I'm here to advise you."

"Yeah, that's what Michelle said. And Tiamat. And if I didn't take their 'advice,' they'd find someone to replace me."

"Well, I'm not going to replace you," said Mercury. "And frankly I don't have the patience to hang out with you and give you advice on trade deals with Guatemala or extradition treaties with Bulgaria. Bulgaria. That's a real place, right? Bulgaria?"

Danton Prowse nodded. "I think so, yes."

"Anyway, like I said, I don't have the patience for that crap. And I don't have any grand schemes for scaring the shit out of people with bombs or shoving computer chips in their skulls. But I do have an agenda that I need you to follow. And if you don't, I'm going to make things as unpleasant as I can for you."

"I knew it," said Prowse bitterly. "So what's the agenda?"

Mercury pulled a sheet of paper from his pocket, unfolded it and began reading.

"First," he began. "I want to talk a little about a woman's right to choose. I strongly support a woman's right to choose. It should go without saying that I also support a man's right to choose. To my way of thinking, they should take turns. For example..." He trailed off. "Hey, this is my manifesto! I thought I left this in the woods!"

Prowse looked aghast at him. "*That's* your agenda?"

"Oh, goodness no," said Mercury. "This is my manifesto. Here's the agenda." He pulled another sheet from his pocket and handed it to Danton Prowse.

Prowse frowned, unfolding the paper. It began:

We the People of the United States, in Order to form a more perfect Union, establish Justice, insure domestic Tranquility, provide for the common defence, promote the general Welfare, and secure the Blessings of Liberty to ourselves and our Posterity, do ordain and establish this Constitution for the United States of America.

"This is the Constitution," said Danton Prowse.

"Damn straight," said Mercury. "And like I said, you're going to follow it or I'm going to make things very unpleasant for you."

"Who made you the judge of whether I'm following the Constitution?" snapped Prowse. "What makes you think you understand it better than I do?"

Mercury laughed. "I'm no judge," he said. "I'm just a guy keeping you honest. I'm not going to interfere with you doing your job. But if you start sticking computer chips in people's skulls, then there's a very good chance people are going to find out about a certain illegal bomb-making program that you were intimately involved with. Understood?"

Danton Prowse nodded. "So you're really going to let me run the country?"

Mercury shrugged. "Frankly," he said, "I don't particularly like you. A president with any balls would have told Michelle to take a walk rather than be her lapdog. But the people of this country elected you, so what do I know? Grow a spine, do your job, and you have nothing to worry about from me." He turned to leave.

"What, that's it?" asked Prowse. "You throw a copy of the Constitution on my desk and then leave, just like that?"

Mercury grinned. "A better man than you taught me an important lesson," he said.

"Which is what?" said Prowse.

"Know when to leave the stage," Mercury said, and walked out the door.

# POSTLUDE

*Philadelphia; August 1796*

Mercury walked quietly up the steps to the second floor of the four story house, made his way down the hall and knocked on the door.

"Come in, Mercury," said a man's voice from inside.

Mercury opened the door and walked inside, shaking his head. "How do you do that?" he asked.

Inside the room a tall, lean man sat hunched over an old oak desk, his massive, gnarled hands gripping a sheaf of papers in front of him. He looked up as Mercury walked in. "I know your walk," said the man. "I know the gait of every man who works for me. I could identify every one of my officers as they walked up from behind me, even at Valley Forge, where the snow was three feet thick. Makes it difficult to sneak up on me."

"Next time I'll levitate," said Mercury. "We'll see if you can hear *that*." He added, after a moment, "Mr. President."

"What brings you here, Mercury?" asked Washington. "I frankly never expected to see you again. I thought you angels had sworn off politics."

"Technically that restriction only applies to the District of Columbia," replied Mercury. "I assume that Philadelphia is still swarming with demons."

"Not that I've noticed," said Washington.

"Really?" asked Mercury. "So you haven't seen any of the demons I described to you? Lucifer, Tiamat, Gamaliel?"

Washington shook his head.

"Huh," said Mercury. "I guess they figure they'd be wasting their time with you."

Washington sighed. "With me, yes. Even so, I must remain vigilant. My trust was betrayed once, and I cannot let that happen again."

Mercury nodded. Washington had never really gotten over Benedict Arnold's betrayal. It was the one wound from the Revolution that had never healed.

"I'm sorry about that, Mr. President. If I had..."

"It's not your fault, Mercury," said Washington. "I should have seen that Benedict was motivated more by his ego than love for his country. He felt that he had become a pawn in a struggle he didn't understand, and that was more than he could take."

Mercury nodded. "Sir," he said after a moment. "If you don't mind me asking, what about you?"

"What do you mean?" asked Washington.

"I mean, it must have been quite a shock when you found out about us. About the angels and demons, that is. Don't you sometimes feel like a puppet of forces beyond your understanding?"

Washington shook his head. "The hand of Providence guides us all, men and angels alike," he said. "I do what I can with what I've been given. To wish for more than that is foolishness. And in any case, we've somehow managed to keep both angels and demons out of the District of Columbia. The Capitol Building is nearly finished, as is the new presidential residence, which they are calling the White House. The next president will live there, inside the protective field we've put in place."

"*You* put it in place," said Mercury. "You laid the cornerstone. And the whole thing was your idea."

"But you convinced your superiors of the wisdom of the idea, Mercury. This wouldn't have happened without you. Imagine! The first government in the history of the world completely free from the meddling of angels and demons. Just human beings, free to govern themselves as they see fit. What a wonderful thing that is!"

Mercury nodded, trying to share the president's enthusiasm. "You said the next president will live in the White House. Does that mean you're not running again?"

Washington nodded. "I'm getting old," he said. "I've guided this country as well as I know how, but now it's time for someone else to take the reins. Hamilton, maybe. Or Adams."

"With respect, sir," Mercury said, "do you think that's wise? You're still a relatively young man. The situation with Britain is tense, and war is brewing in France. Meanwhile there's the Indian problem, not to mention the rebellion in—"

"There's always going to be some crisis, some conflict," said Washington. "If I don't leave at the end of my second term, I'll be tempted to stay forever. And then where will this country be? We'd have thrown off the yoke of one King George only to be enslaved by another. No, Mercury, sometimes the wisest thing you can do is to quit while you're ahead."

"But what if the country isn't ready?" asked Mercury. "What if the presidency falls into the hands of a power-hungry tyrant or a weakling who fails to protect it from its enemies? What if you've done all this work for nothing?"

"That was always a possibility," said Washington. "But as I say, we're all under the hand of Providence. Will the republic last, or will it crumble, rotted from the inside by petty partisanship or crushed by foreign enemies? I do not know. But the one sure way I know to stifle this new experiment in human governance is to insist that it be kept completely under control. The more tightly I grip the reins, the easier it will be for some future tyrant to exert his will. No, the solution is not for me to hold on as tightly as I can; it's to trust the people of this country with their own destiny."

"And you think the people can be trusted not to fall for some silver-tongued demagogue who promises them security in exchange for their freedom?"

Washington stood and walked to the window, where he could see shopkeepers and tradesmen passing on the street below.

"We'll see, Mercury," he said. "We'll see."

Made in the USA
Coppell, TX
23 July 2021